Tuesday

beyond

Lust

Tuesday beyond Lust

A BIZARRE HOMOEROTIC ROMANCE

SLAVE THE THRALL
(NORMAN McCLELLAND)

TUESDAY BEYOND LUST
A BIZARRE HOMOEROTIC ROMANCE

iUniverse books may be ordered through booksellers or by contacting:

iUniverse
1663 Liberty Drive
Bloomington, IN 47403
www.iuniverse.com
1-800-Authors (1-800-288-4677)

Because of the dynamic nature of the Internet, any web addresses or links contained in this book may have changed since publication and may no longer be valid. The views expressed in this work are solely those of the author and do not necessarily reflect the views of the publisher, and the publisher hereby disclaims any responsibility for them.

Any people depicted in stock imagery provided by Thinkstock are models, and such images are being used for illustrative purposes only.
Certain stock imagery © Thinkstock.

ISBN: 978-1-5320-2040-7 (sc)
ISBN: 978-1-5320-2039-1 (e)

Library of Congress Control Number: 2017904854

Print information available on the last page.

iUniverse rev. date: 04/29/2017

Introduction

It has been the experience of this author that human sexuality is far more complex than some would like to accept. People are labeled heterosexual, homosexual, or bisexual, but in fact what we all are is just sexual. Most people will be one of these throughout life. However, sometimes we are thrown into situations that call for us to abandon any rigid borders and experience our sexuality from another perspective. This story attempts to express that lack of rigidity.

An author's note has been included at the end of the book to explain in greater detail the various sexual terms and concepts referenced in this story that may be unfamiliar to some readers.

> To be in love is lunacy.
> It strips man of reason.
> First, it will make a fool of him
> And then a prisoner.
> No man of wisdom, self-respect
> Should lend himself to this.
> But love is a harsh deity
> Whose strength few can resist.
> It ravishes the strongest minds
> And rapes the greatest wills.
> Therefore, when I succumb to it,
> Forgive and pity me,
> For I choose not this captive state.
> Love drove me to this fate.

Chapter 1

∽℘⌒

July 11 would come to be remembered as the Tuesday beyond lust, and I was mad at myself for not asking more about his goddamn wife. That was all I could think about while driving home. I couldn't be sure whether Jonathan was a closet case or one of the rare straight men who was confident enough in his own sexual identity not to be threatened by being friendly to a gay man. Either way, there was no real future in hanging out with him. With teaching and trying to write a book, have time for some gay socializing, and get laid once in a while, I had little time left. So no matter how much he was my type—a bear that could easily maximize my member—why would I be interested in developing a platonic relationship with him?

By that night I didn't know if I was more upset with myself or Jonathan, whether he was straight or gay. I knew I was in a self-made maddening mood, and I thought to do something about it. But as soon as my hand went for my hard-on, an image of bears, and then of one specific bear, arose. A solo jolly jerk-off to that image was hardly a way of getting him out of my mind. Still, I was now as horny as hell because of him, so I needed some relief. Or was it escape? Well, at least partial escape, for even if I tried to deny wanting him, I couldn't deny wanting what was in his pants.

> A man who loves another man
> Is the less common way,
> But if it is mutual,
> Who should think it wrong or say?

A Tuesday night wasn't the best time to go to a bar in hopes of getting some trick and treat, and I had only two close choices. There was the Stag, a truly sleazy leather bar that, if not busy earlier, at least got a later crowd that had failed to make out elsewhere. In the main room of the Stag, little more than intense kissing and nipple play went on, but there was a back room, known as the Cafeteria, for stand-up sucking and fucking. If I couldn't find satisfaction there, then it was the Jack of Diamonds bathhouse only two blocks away. I had only been to the latter twice, and that was several years ago. The first time was with just one guy who wanted nothing more than stand-up vanilla sex.

> He was a hot, horny bloke
> Who wanted to give me a poke.
> When he pulled down his pants
> And you gave it a glance,
> What he stroked was clearly no joke.

By the time I had dropped my pants, he had put on a condom. He turned me around, bent me over a little, did his thing, pulled up his pants, and walked away. We said not a word to each other.

The second time, after I had sucked off two guys, I was approached by a man who had a poor command of English. In fact, I wondered just how long he had been having sex with men since he asked if I wanted a "windy work." I asked him what a windy work was, and before I had a chance to say anything more, he cleared up the mystery.

> A creative synonym
> Also alliterative.
> Call it windy, call it blow,
> Call it work or job.
> Don't worry about its name—
> The act is always the same.

I had no real attraction to either guy, which helped sour me on the Jack of Diamonds. So this night I was hoping that the Stag would supply some relief, especially since my so-called membership at the Jack had long expired and I didn't want to waste money on a new one just for a quick blow or fuck. Besides, the fucking at the Jack was a particularly touchy issue since, while condoms were readily available, some of the Jack's clientele were reluctant to use them, and no stranger was going to get into my homo hole without one. The persuasive perversity of barebacking had taken the lives of too many of my friends.

> Bathhouse: a sanitary euphemism
> For multiple opportunities
> To stick a dick in above or below,
> Cleansed from crude craving for a day or so.

Some vanilla friends have asked me if leather bars are as dangerous as they've sometimes heard. I tell them that the only time I've been faced with a threatening situation was when I picked up someone in a vanilla dance bar. The guy was taller and heavier than I—my preference—and hot. We went to my place, and no sooner were we in bed than he was holding me down telling me he wanted to fuck me. Normally that was nice, but realizing how thick his fuck pole was, I tried to explain that it wouldn't fit into me. He told me that was my problem.

We hadn't negotiated this kind of scene. In fact, we hadn't negotiated any scene in particular. Since it wasn't a pickup at a leather bar, I hadn't considered negotiation necessary—clearly my mistake. Nonetheless, I kept my cool and explained to him the disadvantages to rape. "You will have to hold me down with one hand while using the other hand to force yourself into me, which leaves you with nothing to stop me from screaming, which would cause the neighbors to call the police. However, I'm not going to even raise my voice. Instead, as you are raping me, I will claw your eyes out."

The guy's response showed how seriously he took my threat. "In that case, I'd better leave."

I'm a certified slut, so once the threat of rape was over and I knew I had won control of the situation, I said, "I picked you up because I thought you were hot, and now that we have established the parameters, I'm still interested. And besides, I don't want my time at the bar to have been wasted, so we can still take care of each other."

After taking a moment to think, he said, "Okay."

> When faced with an unwelcome surprise,
> It pays to keep a cool mind.
> Negotiate for a better deal,
> Something that has more appeal.

Maybe nothing potentially threatening has ever happened to me at bars like the Stag because, whether topping or bottoming, I've always made the dos and don'ts clear during negotiations, and with that, I've never had any troubling surprises.

Before heading out to the Stag on the Tuesday beyond lust, I put on my cock ring, jockstrap, Levi's, T-shirt, boots, and leather jacket, and to the locked dog chain around my neck I added an unlocked leather slave collar. Wearing two collars may appear to be overdoing it, but each had its own meaning. The locked one represented my root master, the man who first collared me and whose authority I revert to if I do not have a local master. The unlocked one implied that I had no such local one. The dog chain comes off rarely, typically just if I am going through some security machine; otherwise it's an almost permanent fixture on me. In particular, I never fail to wear it to a bar, since it attracts attention and more often than not serves as a conversation, if not negotiation, opener.

> Sad is any masterless slave.
> He lives his day and worse each night
> Without an owner's guiding light.

I got to the Stag about eleven and found a parking space only a half block away, which, as expected, didn't bode well for a good crowd. But if worse came to worst, there was the bathhouse.

Entering into the Stag's semidarkness, I walked up to the bar and ordered my usual bottle of beer. I really don't drink the stuff. In fact, I don't drink alcohol period unless forced to, as my first master would do. As a reminder that I was under his authority and did as he wished, he would take a mouthful of beer, force my mouth open, and drain the beer into it as I swallowed. I have had people tell me that is disgusting, but I remind them that it is no less so than someone shoving his tongue into another person's mouth. Another master decided that this was too much work, and so he would periodically put a bottle up to my mouth, not allowing me to touch the bottle, and make me take a swig that way. In this present situation of being without a master, by buying at least one bottle, even if I only pretended to drink, I was supporting the bar and playing the game.

I found a spot near the back and began cruising. I tried to scan around the walls of the Stag as best as I could without being too obvious. I had learned a long time ago that being obvious implied being desperate, so while my eyes moved from side to side, my head stayed more or less straight forward.

As in most gay bars, the light was only bright enough to see the outlines of people on the far side, but that was just as well considering some of the activity that went on here that could get one arrested by the vice squad.

There couldn't have been more than ten guys in the bar, and at first, none of them appealed to me, if for no other reason than none of them had any more leather on them than their belts. While it was only Friday and Saturday nights that the bar got the real leather crowd, I was hoping for at least something that looked more than vanilla, because I was in a wild mood.

Raw display of hunter's pride,
Black leather to this mind.

5

Wild want its origin,
Transformed in modern times.
Savage rite of union,
This night to be its goal.
To come forth empowered
In body and in soul.

After maybe twenty minutes a guy came up to me with a "good evening."

"Good evening."

"I like the leather." The fact that he was not in leather might have been enough to tell me that he probably didn't own anything in leather, other than the fashionably vanilla, but this comment confirmed that assumption, because no real leather man would say, "I like the leather."

"What's your name?"

"Coy."

This is my leather name, and I generally prefer to give it rather than Dan in these bar situations, not for secrecy, but to feel more sexualized. It is actually short for Coydog, which is a hybrid of a half-wild coyote and a domesticated dog.

With a locked canine collar
Placed well around my neck,
Just like some bitch wild slut
Positioned on all fours,
I will take it in the ass.
In this, I won't whine.
I'll regard it as just fine.

Only when I think that there may be future encounters with a guy will I give him my legal name, and even before this guy offered his name, I suspected that he would at best be a one-night stand.

"I'm Bob."

"Nice to meet you, Bob."

"So what are you into?" The fact that he got right down to business impressed me. After all, none of us were there because we liked small talk.

"As you can see from the collar and belt buckle"—which said slave—"I'm a slave and so into serving. Would you like me to be more specific?"

Since he had not yet convinced me he could be more than a vanilla top, I wasn't prepared to use *boy* for myself or *sir* for him yet.

"So you're looking for a master?"

"For tonight I'm looking for less than that. Nonetheless, I'm still under the rules of a former master and thus only allowed to engage in activity he would sanction."

Bob hesitated for a split second before saying, "I see." This hesitation suggested that I had surprised him by my slave admission, which further confirmed a vanilla orientation. But it also indicated that he was either curious about the slave thing or thought that to withdraw too suddenly might show him to be a wimp.

"It sounds like you had a heavy master."

"He was heavy enough to toughen me to like what he wanted to do with me without any complaints on my part."

If I was sure that I had surprised this guy before with the word *slave*, I was even more certain that I had really overpowered him with all these kinky details. It seemed time to lessen the blow.

"Perhaps I've given you more information than you wanted, but often when I say I'm a slave, people think I'm looking to be abused, but I'm not."

"Right."

I could tell that at this point the guy was ready to be mercifully released, so I said, "If you have no more questions?"

"Uh, no, none. Thank you."

"You're welcome."

With that, he turned and moved off to hopefully find less exotic company. I was about to call it a night and head for the door when I spotted another guy staring at me intensely. He at least was half my type, slightly taller and heavier, although completely clean-shaven. I've picked up and been picked up by less, and I was desperate to put my pecker into a mouth or ass or have one in mine. As a beggar I couldn't be much of a chooser, so I signaled interest, and the guy started toward me. After having frightened the other guy away, I decided to cool the slave thing this time.

As he passed the bar, he stopped, put his empty beer bottle on the counter, and ordered another, all the time watching me watch him from the corner of his eye. He got his beer and walked over to me. He introduced himself, but I haven't the foggiest memory of what his name was. In fact, I don't even think I was paying enough attention to his introduction to have ever heard it. All I was interested in was getting to the negotiations. If the guy had been wearing leather or had been bearish, the negotiations would have included who was going to be the top and who the bottom, but this guy was not dressed to top. So my leather automatically meant top if this guy wanted me. Actually, topping was not really what I wanted that night, but it was better than a bathhouse or going home to mere mono manipulation.

> While preferring to be a slave,
> I can a free man be.
> So when it comes to getting laid,
> The choice is up to me.

With this guy, there were only two items to negotiate: if we were going to do it in the bar, in which case he was going to blow me, or if this was a going-home event, his place or mine, which meant he was going to get the rumpy-pumpy.

I was a little concerned that the guy might have had more than two beers, but he didn't seem drunk, so maybe he had not been in the bar long before I spotted him. I make it a policy not to go anyplace with someone who's had too much to drink, especially if he's a drunken top.

I was determined that if this guy started in on getting-to-know-you bar small talk, such as "Do you come here often? Is this your regular bar? I haven't seen you here before," I would put a stop to it right away. The second inquiry I don't mind, but the first I do. That's because it suggests that I'm both a slut and a drunk. The slut part I accept. After all, anyone who has been in as many orgies as I have is a slut. In fact, in one case, I was fucked by three different men, one after the other. So slut—yes. But drunk—no. Even the slightest implication that I might be a boozer infuriated me.

> Some called this gay man a whore,
> For getting fucked until sore.
> But the label is unjust,
> For I ask you please to trust
> No one has paid me to score.

Since the vanilla-dressed, beer-guzzling guy was still facing me, I couldn't see if one of his back pockets was hankie coded for anything other than what I wanted. I decided that without being too rudely aggressive I would be far blunter than usual, certainly blunter than if the guy were a leather man, bear, or both.

He said, "Hi." The informality of "Hi" more or less guaranteed vanilla in comparison to "Good evening."

"Good evening." My first words to establish dominance.

"I like the collar."

I thought, *Oh, God, he thinks that it's a fashion statement and that I'm into no more than that.*

"I like to get sucked, and I like to fuck, safely, condom," I said to make sure he understood that I had decided who did what to whom.

"Yes, sir" was his immediate response.

That settled it. He knew who was in charge, which meant that I didn't need to politely ask him to do anything. All I had to do was give an order. I told him where I lived and asked where his place was. He said that it was about a ten-minute drive, which was closer than my place, so I opted for his. My first order was "If you want to finish your beer, do so, and let's get out of here."

We got to his place, and no sooner was I inside and the lights went on than I knew exactly why he had to be the bottom. The walls were covered with framed posters of movie actresses, most of whom had by then been mentioned in some obituary column. I swear the furniture must have been right out of *Gone with the Wind*, even down to the green velvet curtains. He quickly excused himself to take a pee, which gave me more time than I wanted to look around the place. When he came back, I decided I should also try to pee. Otherwise I might have to do so in the middle of the sex. Even his bathroom had the same kind of pictures on the walls, except, in contrast to the pictures of major stars in the living room, all the ones here were of lesser actresses. I thought, *Living room with queens, bathroom with princess. A royal court.*

By the time I left the john, my playmate for the night had the bed already turned down and was standing at the foot of it completely undressed. He definitely was in a hurry to get things going. That room thankfully was movie queen–free. If it hadn't been, I wouldn't have been able to function. Cock on the walls turns me on, not cunt. Maybe I wasn't the only trick that had such a problem, which could be why the court had not migrated here. It was then that I realized this queen's place was not where I wanted to be, and he definitely was not the man I wanted to be with. He was just the opposite of Jonathan—more hairless Venus than hairy Mars. Mars! How appropriate. That god's assigned day is Tuesday, the Jonathan day.

I was disgusted with this place, I was disgusted with this guy, but most of all I was disgusted with myself. This was no ordinary disgust but one born of a sense of hopelessness. It reminded me of what my sex life had become—one-night stands and those two short-term, failed relationships—and that was probably how it was going to be for some time in the future.

I live in a floating world
Where love passes like clouds:
One moment storms of passion,
Then a long, loveless drought.

Disgust and self-pity should have been enough to make me apologize and get the hell out of there, but I didn't. Maybe it was the fact that the guy was already aroused and starting to unbuckle me. At first, I just stood there and let him finish zipping down my pants and pushing them down around my ankles. Seeing the jockstrap clearly excited him, as he dropped to his knees and pushed his whole face into it before pulling my dick out. I was still flaccid, but then Mr. Vanilla's tongue and lips went to work. As I became aware of my developing erection, I found myself in a head space I had not experienced before. I'm prone to radical mood swings, but this guy was swinging me toward a feeling of meanness, and meanness with a hard-on is a bad combination. All the rules of treating the other person with some respect disappear.

Most of the time when I'm with a trick that I'm topping, I get him to remove my boots and pants, only to have him put my boots back on.

As far as one's authority
Few items can match the boot.
As the master puts each one on,
The slave should be on his knees.
This is a power attribute
To his rule as absolute.

This time, however, with the exception of my pants around my ankles, I planned to remain clothed. This was the standard game in which the naked bottom is made to feel totally subordinate, if not vulnerable, to the clothed, "armored" top.

After a couple of minutes of sucking me, he started pressing his forefinger against my hole, which might have suggested that this bottom boy wanted to finger fuck me or more, but that thought was soon dispelled by the question, "Sir! Would you like me to rim you?"

Normally, before leaving home I wash my asshole off with soap and/or beer (a mild disinfectant), as my default master insisted I do, but I hadn't this night. Moreover, if I am going to rim someone else, I insist on washing him off, but this was more complicated. To give into this request and first clean off would mean pulling my pants up and going back to the boy's princess bathroom, which I wasn't willing to do. Unless he asked otherwise, what he was going to be offered was an unwholesome hole for his toilet paper tongue. Also, I far prefer to get rimmed while on my back, but I still didn't want to give in to taking my pants off all the way. Without a word I turned around, bent over, and placed my hands on the edge of the bed, and he immediately went into oral-anal action.

As good as that felt, I thought I could get better, and since I still was clothed from the waist up, I decided to give in to being pantless. I stopped him and turned around.

"Boy! Lick the boots and then take them off."

"Yes, sir!"

He did. I pulled my feet out of the pants and the jockstrap, slipped back into the boots, and got onto the bed, faceup.

> He asked if he could lick my hole,
> Which always sends me into heat,
> So over my face went my feet
> With my hand playing with my meat.

Now I've been done by any number of really ruttish rimmers, but this guy could best them all. He made every possible effort to spread my cheeks to the limit to get his tongue as far into where the sun never shines as I thought anyone could, and it was ecstasy. Tragically, ecstasy must always come to an end, and eventually he stopped, probably from a tired tongue, and transferred his action to his hand. Unfortunately, this transference pushed me once again into an unhappy head space. I didn't want what might be just a joyless jack-off. I pulled the guy up, turned him around, pushed him facedown, and began to beat his ass. I had been into many spanking scenes before, both as a giver and getter, but even the ones with a heavy top had had a playful quality to them. This one did not. I only stopped when my hand was as red as the guy's butt and the slapping was hurting me. I was surprised that the guy had not made some attempt to ask me to stop. All he had needed to do was tell me I was getting too rough, and it would have given me the perfect excuse to let him go, make some face-saving remark like "I thought you understood that the leather meant that I was into power play," then dress and leave. But he just took it without a word.

I noticed that he had some condoms and lube on the nightstand that either lived there permanently or had been put there before he went to the bar. Still feeling mean, I shouted, "Stay!" grabbed a condom, tore it open with my teeth, rolled it on, lubed it, and yelled, "On your back."

There was still no protest from him. On the contrary, he showed his willingness to be fucked by going into the helium-heels position.

"Take hold of the collar."

As a bottom in that position, I appreciate it when the top grabs my collar and I feel his hand pulling and pushing against my neck in sync with what he is doing in my asshole, so I do the same when I top.

I entered this boy-princess with absolutely no rectal resistance, which told me he was familiar with larger erections than mine. For some unexplainable reason this made me feel weirdly wicked, and as a result I don't think I have ever butt banged anyone with as much force as I was doing it then.

The crackling sound made by my leather jacket only intensified my desire to really give it to this guy. The expression on his face told me that my sadistic actions were sending him into sub space, a state of mind I was familiar with from when I was in his position, and as I explosively climaxed, he squeezed his rectal muscles tightly to suggest he really wanted to keep me in there.

As my hard-on went down, I more or less lost interest in the guy, but I assumed that he probably wanted to climax. Therefore, without a word, my mouth went down on him until he was at the point of no return, and I finished him off with a masterly masturbation. Standing up, I realized the condom was hanging off my dick. I took it off and looked around for a place to dump it only to have the guy take it from me with a smile on his face, jump off the bed, and head for the bathroom. I was exhausted, not so much physically as emotionally. I just sat down on the edge of the bed, not sure what to do next.

I didn't need to decide. He came back, took my jacket off without resistance, pulled off my shirt and boots, picked up my pants, and carefully put everything on a chair with the boots underneath. I didn't even make the slightest effort to resist as he took my hand, had me get up, led me to the edge of the bed, and had me lay my head on the pillow while he covered me up. I remember nothing after that until I woke up the next morning having to pee so badly that I ran for the bathroom.

Chapter 2

The royal-court bathroom brought the memory of last night back in all its desperate details, and the first thing I thought was that I was damn glad I had peed before the sex. If I hadn't, I'm sure right after pulling out of his asshole I would have sprayed all over him and fallen asleep on a stinky, wet mattress. Even if I had been a dedicated fan of water sports, I wouldn't have wanted to sleep on it. I finished peeing in the royal court and went back to the bedroom only to see that my host was not in bed.

I heard noises in what sounded like the kitchen. I got dressed and entered the kitchen with every intention of apologizing to him for my manic behavior, but to my bewilderment he was in an obvious happy mood. With what I thought was a nauseatingly cheery voice after the circumstances of last night, he said, "Good morning, sir. I hope you slept well."

"Yes, thank you, I did."

"Last night was great. You were so wonderfully rough on me. I really like that in a man."

"Well, thank you."

There was no doubt that I had been his dream for last night. I could have dealt with that and lost at least some of the sense of guilt I felt over my behavior, but did he have to use the word *great*?

"Would you like some breakfast, sir?"

"Thank you, but I never eat breakfast."

"Oh, that's how you keep so nice and slim. I like slim but rough men."

I almost expected him to propose marriage, there and then. Indeed, he obviously had wife-like qualities. Damn! Why did I have to think of the word *wife*? I suppose it was because it went hand in hand with *great*. *Out of here, out of here, out of here* became my inner mantra.

"Oh! Look at the time," I said. "It's later than I thought, and I have a number of things I need to do. But thank you for last night."

"Can I give you my number, sir?"

"Sure," I said with as polite a smile as I could manage.

I was going to accept his number despite knowing I would never call him. We all do that, knowing perfectly well that the chances of getting a call are pretty lousy.

> When passions are on fire,
> We rarely are quite sane.
> So don't trust the promises
> That love or lust may make.
> Tomorrow too we hope for,
> But with the morning sun
> Reason has returned to us,
> Regrets of said and done.

He wrote his number out, and as he handed it to me, he gave me a hug and a kiss, which I felt obligated to return. I then headed for the door much slower than I would really have liked to. He stood in the doorway and watched me walk down the street toward my car. While any meanness on my part had certainly been slept off, disgust was still wide awake. This was not last night's disgust at him anymore. It was now only disgust at myself.

How could I have actually treated another person the way I had treated him? It didn't matter that it all had turned out well. It didn't justify what I had felt and allowed myself to do. He may have been a voluntary victim, but that didn't make it okay to be a victimizer. Still worse, I now remembered that just before I'd decided to "rape" him, I had tried to justify it to myself by stereotyping him as just some queen who deserved a good hard fuck.

Who in the hell was I to so belittle another person like that and then use that as an excuse for an act of violence? Had I forgotten those times that I had been walking down Sunset and some half-drunk straight bastard had screamed out something meant to be humiliating? "Hi, sweetie, you want to be my queen for tonight?" If I ignored guys like that, the response was usually something like "Fucking faggot." Since when had I become the paragon of a butch butt? My hole was as open to a fuck as much as that of even the Nelliest of queers.

> If you meet a horny queen
> And your mood is to demean,
> It is wrong to think rough play,
> So instead just walk away.

I have no delusions about myself. I know that I can be demonic at times and get into mean scenes, especially the face-slapping kinds, but only after negotiations do I have the right to do so, and meanness had never been part of the negotiations with this guy.

> I think I should respect each trick
> To keep my sex from being sick.
> So what was negotiated
> Ought not to be violated.
> But that is so hard on my dick.

I got home, and since I still had lube in my crotch hair, I took a shower. Then I fixed myself some breakfast, which I do eat, and tried to work on my book, but the image of Jonathan kept popping into my mind. But why? Considering my master-slave proclivity rather than a daddy-boy one, I wondered why I could possibly be obsessed with Jonathan. Yes, he was a bear, but he was certainly not a master bear type, and I doubted whether he was inclined to be a slave bear type, since both are fairly obvious to someone as attuned to master-slave types as experience had made me. In other words, he would never be able to fulfill what the slave in me needed, so it was once again time to push him out of my mind.

There is a master of my dreams,
For the slave in my soul.
For both of us to be fulfilled
Each one must know his place.
The slave should never say, "I want,"
Instead, "I need/would like."
The master decides what you get
For both to be in role.
The slave must discipline himself
In thought, in speech, in act.
If he should fail in one of these,
Just punishment deserved.
The slave says, "To you, I submit,"
Meaning it as no lie.
Then to that prideful incarnate
Who must the master be,
The devil's kiss will the slave give
While on his humble knees.
Only then the pleasure of pain
Should be the slave's reward.
Otherwise, there is no deep trust,
Only a shallow game.
For the true master and true slave
A slap can signal love,
But only if without deceit
We each other complete.

What could any of that possibly do with Jonathan—a straight, closeted gay or a big bisexual bear who, on the Kinsey scale, was a mystery? But whatever, the last thing I needed in my life now was a double dude—an ordinary-appearing and -acting guy who lived a double life as either an active bisexual or closeted gay who was also in a relationship with a woman, especially with a wife. He simply would not work for me, or rather for my dominate-submissive side and the power parts I played in that.

No! The only thing that will work for me—I stopped in mid-thought. What or who was going to work for me? None of my relationships had turned out to work for me. Or should I say none of the gay ones. Maybe, just maybe, that was what made Jonathan so obsessively attractive to me. He was a mystery. But mysteries can be dangerous, especially when there is a wife involved.

> A relationship that differs
> From all the ones before
> But this one is a fantasy
> That is downright offshore.

How the hell did I get into the Jonathan head space in the first place? Maybe if I stopped trying to push that out of my mind and instead went back to our meeting I could see where I'd gone wrong and be free of him. He had attended yesterday's set of workshops for writers sponsored by the community college at which I teach. At the late-afternoon social event that concluded the workshops a small group of us guys were standing around when what's-his-name decided to tell a faggot joke. Everyone laughed at it except me.

"Didn't you get it?" what's-his-name asked me.

That's when I made everyone uncomfortable. "Yes, I got it, but being a gay man, I don't find faggot jokes especially funny." With that I excused myself.

As a faggot some would say
My fate is to burn in hell,
But I reply, "I burn now
In a lascivious life."

I went outside on the patio feeling isolated, alienated, and demeaned. After a few minutes I heard, "Excuse me, Professor Campbell." I turned around, and there was Jonathan. "I would like to apologize for laughing at that joke. It wasn't really even funny."

I felt that such an apology was both courageous and gracious. The average man would have simply brushed off any embarrassment he had felt as being of no consequence, perhaps even thinking, *Well, he's gay, so he has to expect things like this.* But the sheer decency and even compassion in Jonathan's apology didn't seem to indicate that. I now felt less like a put-down faggot or an irate gay man and instead a little bit more like someone who had as much right to dignity as anyone else.

"Thank you," I said, "but actually it was funny. Still I don't laugh at jokes about Jews, black people, or other minorities."

He then formally introduced himself. "By the way, I'm Jonathan Miller. I was in your morning poetry-writing class."

"Yes, of course."

This guy was more than your average trouser-tenant treat. He was a bearded hunk, and naturally I'd spotted him when he'd walked into my classroom, and for a moment I'd forgotten about all the others in the room.

"Since I went right on to the next workshop, I didn't have time to tell you how much I enjoyed your class. I've always been interested in poetry. I don't have much of a talent for writing it, though, so I confine my interest to just reading it. But I really liked your idea that poetry is something everybody can write if they have an interest in it and if they're not worried about meeting some official standard of excellence. I especially enjoyed your discussion of senryu, those short three-line haiku-like poems that tend to have comic themes. In fact, I wrote one."

He reached into his pocket and pulled out a piece of paper, unfolded it, and read,

> "Life is delicious
> But so complicated
> Compared to chocolate."

I laughed and said, "You see, you can write poetry."

"Thank you. That's very kind of you."

"Not kind at all, Mr. Miller. I meant it when I said anyone can write poetry. All you need is to allow what is inside of you to speak. Sometimes the simplest poems written from genuine feelings can be more meaningful than some that get awards for their technical virtuosity."

I wasn't sure how much of myself I should reveal to this man. He already knew I was gay, so what did I have to lose if, in explaining what I was talking about, I used a counter-erotic example. So I said to him, "For example,

> "My poetry comes from my head
> But also my genitals.
> All of it comes from a full life
> Of longing, love, and laughter."

"That … that was beautiful," he said with a broad smile.

I was just getting ready to inquire into what other workshops he had gone to that day when he interrupted me.

"Could you excuse me for a minute? I need to use the restroom, and I'll be right back."

"Certainly."

As I watched him go back inside, I was reminded that the moment a gay man mentions anything about genitals to a straight man, the latter finds a diplomatic excuse to flee. And "I have to take a pee" is the most convenient of excuses. In fact, it's the one even gay men use in the bar when we are trying politely to say, "Sorry, but not interested in you."

> Pity the poor straight men
> Who think we are a threat.
> Is their sense of manhood
> As vulnerable as this?
> Or is it due to their fear
> They might like something queer?

I didn't expect Jonathan the hunk to return, and I wanted nothing more than to leave the event, but as part of the workshop hosting committee I was expected to stay to the end; therefore, it was to my surprise and delight when he did reappear.

"Now, Professor Campbell, where were we?"

"Well, first of all, my name is Dan, and I was wondering what other workshops you attended."

"I'm a freelance journalist, so the other two I attended were more journalistic in orientation. In fact, except for your class, the main reason I signed up for workshops was to write an article on the college's outreach program and to make new contacts for possible future articles."

I knew very little about the ins and outs of freelance journalism, so all I could say was a very trite. "That must be very interesting work. Have you been doing it for long?"

"I've been doing it most of my career life, and it can be interesting, but sometimes it can be very routine," he said. "How long have you taught here?"

"Eight years."

"And do you teach classes other than those on poetry?"

"Yes. Most of my classes are on standard college writing."

"Are you teaching this summer?"

"No. I took this summer off to work on my book."

"You're writing a book?"

"Yes."

"If I'm not being too nosy, may I ask what it's about?"

When a person starts a question with anything like "If I'm not being too nosy," you more or less have to provide the requested information because the only alternative is to imply that the person is being too nosy. So unless I wanted to be insulting, I had no choice.

"The title is *New England Transcendentalism and Poetry*. It's about the influence of the New England transcendentalist movement on late nineteenth-century American poetry."

"That sounds most interesting. I know that the movement was associated with names like Emerson and Thoreau but not much more."

I appreciated that he knew at least that much but was also starting to appreciate more than that, especially what was below his belt.

> My mind is such a painful paradox,
> A battleground of conflicting needs—
> Seeking the transcendental above
> Where there is no more an I to die
> yet also wallowing in the mud and guts
> Of the grossest self-indulging lusts.

"New England," he said, "I thought I detected an accent from that part of the country."

"Yes. I was raised there."

"And your family, do they still live there?"

"My mother and her people do."

"Not your father?"

I was starting to feel he was asking too many personal questions, but I was not about to say that to him. "My father died when I was an infant."

"I'm sorry. I shouldn't be asking such personal questions."

> The moment one begins to mention death
> The conversation changes direction,
> With no reminder of our common doom.

"As for your book—"

He was interrupted by someone coming out to the patio to tell us that they were cleaning up and closing down the area. It was then we both realized that most of the other people had already left. As we began to leave, he said, "There's a new exhibit at the county museum of nineteenth-century American folk art. Have you seen it?"

"No. I didn't know about it, but I'm sure I'll go see it now that I do."

"My wife and I saw it and found it most enjoyable."

There was that disappointing word *wife*, which made me look at his hand to confirm that there was a ring on it. If up to that point his attention to me was a surprise, imagine my near shock at what came next.

"However, I'd be interested in seeing it again. Perhaps we could go together."

Despite the light camaraderie between us, I still could not believe he could be serious about doing something together. I figured that it was only his polite way of saying thank-you for the conversation and good-bye, without being insensitively abrupt. So I had no reason to feel I might regret my answer.

"Yes, that would be very nice."

My surprise then really increased.

"Great. Why don't you give me your phone number, and we can arrange for the day and time?"

Now I wondered if my gaydar had been malfunctioning and if he was not really straight but a closet case. Yes, he'd mentioned a wife, but everyone knows how many gay men try to conceal their homosexuality in heterosexual relationships.

> There are men who hide away
> Trying to deny they're gay.

> In a closet with a wife
> They spend most of their life
> Till they stray for a man to lay.

Well, if Jonathan was a closet case, I wanted nothing to do with him. But if he was straight and really was interested in a one-time get-together at a museum, the only thing I had to lose was a few hours of working on my book. I handed him my card with my number on it. Taking it, he offered his other hand to shake, and the moment I felt my hand in his I experienced a chill down my spine. We said good-bye and departed in separate directions.

By the time I got home, I had gone over a list of just how much Jonathan was my ideal physical type. I judged he was four to five inches taller than I, so about six or six one. He had just enough girth, without being overweight, to be abdominally sensual, and then there was his short, neatly trimmed beard, slightly darker than mine. His hair was about standard length in contrast to my crew cut, and added to this he had beautiful blue-gray eyes. He was all-over handsome, not in a rugged sense, but in a cute way, a teddy bear. Finally, his teeth were clearly well taken care of, with no signs of smoking stains.

> A hairy face is a hot man's trait.
> It attracts me as a beast to bait.
> It is what I wish for in a mate
> Since a pussy I cannot fellate.

None of this reminiscing on bears was doing anything to drive out of my mind my self-inflicting infatuation with Jonathan, the daddy-type bear. Still, I couldn't seem to help myself. I've been turned on by bears or at the very least by bearded men ever since my first sexual encounter with one—an encounter that left such a lasting imprint on me I decided to grow a beard if only as a cub.

25

I met Roger, the bear, in my last undergraduate year while cruising in the local park. He was wearing shorts and a tank top that displayed his ample fur. We played for a short time the eye games of look at, look away, and look at once more to make sure there was a mutual interest. I approached him, but he was the first to say hi. We made small talk about how nice it was in the park that day and then introduced ourselves.

Roger had a lover, who at that time was at work. He asked if I would be interested in getting together with the two of them and top his lover while Roger topped me. This was something new to me, and all I really wanted was a bear-cub fling with just Roger.

> I love the feel of heavy flesh
> Pressing down upon me.
> How sweet his weight upon my back,
> Still better face-to-face.
> Here our two lives together merge
> To fill our common urge.
> It may be for just one night,
> But for me that is all right.

Nonetheless, the proposition sounded interesting enough, so once I was assured that a three-way was acceptable to the lover, Jay, I agreed to try it. We arranged for the three-way, and I must say it was exciting.

> Making love one-on-one
> Is mostly the best way,
> But do not fear a third
> Before your hair turns gray.

I only did this once with Roger and Jay since I missed the personal attention that a one-on-one offers. I had a number of other opportunities for three-ways, but of those I accepted (some sounded too bizarre even for me), each was just a one-night stand.

One of the too-bizarre propositions that I turned down happened in a bar in San Diego. I saw this young, very butch guy, with a military haircut, staring at me. I nodded in interest, and he walked over. After a quick introduction, the guy came to the point: he and his other half were looking for someone for a three-way. No sooner had I asked the whereabouts of his partner than he signaled the partner to come over. The notable age difference between the two made me immediately think a daddy-boy relationship. After some more chitchat, the younger one got around to explaining what they were into, and I was glad that I had not yet committed myself to anything.

One was an elder queen
Into a favorite scene.
In bra, girdle, and stockings
His young partner looked shocking
When you realized he was a marine.

Chapter 3

The heavy-handed night with Mr. I Like It Rough had given me enough sexual relief that I was able to submerge myself in working on my book for the next two days. This was work I had been frustratingly trying to finish for the past five months, and by Friday morning I had more or less forgotten about Jonathan, or at least the likelihood of his calling. Instead, I was starting to think about whether to go out that night or wait until even-busier Saturday. At about two thirty that afternoon the phone rang. I picked it up and said hello, and then I nearly dropped it.

"Hi, Dan! It's Jonathan Miller."

I composed myself to what little degree was possible. "Uh, uh, hell-hello" was the best I could articulate.

He reminded me about the museum, then proceeded to list the entire schedule for it and tell me the days that he was available to go, which included the upcoming Sunday, July 16. With some hesitation, he asked if that was too soon.

"Uh, uh, n-no."

"How about one o'clock?" he asked.

"That's fine."

"How do you want to do this?" he asked next. "Do you want to meet at the museum, or do you want me to pick you up?"

We had never exchanged addresses, so we could be thirty miles away for all either of us knew, and he was asking about picking me up. I later realized that my area code must have assured him that I lived within a reasonable distance. Nonetheless, getting picked up was something I only associated with someone I had slept with at least once.

"I'll meet you there," I said.

"I'll see you there then."

The fact that he said "I'll" rather than "We'll" implied that only he was going to be showing up, not the wife. But to make sure, I asked, "Your wife doesn't want to see the exhibition again?"

"No, not really."

I didn't know whether that was a relief or not. I had no interest in meeting his hausfrau, but at the same time, it might have helped to settle the question as to whether he was more closeted gay than straight. The former would never have brought her along for the fun, while the latter might have done so as protection. Once again there was that little question of whether most straight men still believe that gay men are predators seeking to seduce, if not convert, hets to queerdom. This thinking suddenly bothered me since it was unfairly stereotyping all straight men, which was a form of unjustified prejudice. Besides, Jonathan had already shown that, assuming he was more or less straight, he was not uncomfortable around gays, or at least not this one. On the other hand, maybe I was dealing with a fag stag—a straight man who liked to hang around with gay men for nonsexual reasons.

I was about to say out of politeness that I was sorry his wife was not coming, but I was not really feeling polite about this situation, so I simply said, "Okay."

"Great, I'll see you there. Good-bye."

"Good-bye."

The fact that I had agreed to this get-together meant that any further efforts to work on the book and any thought of waiting until Saturday night to go out disappeared. It would be tonight that I would go hunting for man meat in my mouth, my mouth on some man meat, some rear revelry, or any combination of the three.

To be or not to be
The bottom or the top
Is an endless question
When you want your rocks off.
Sometimes to show one way
Means you get not to play.

Although the Stag was closer to home, I didn't want to return there so soon. Besides, I might run into Mr. I Like It Rough again, so I decided on the Texas Inc., which was a Western-themed bar. It consisted of one very large room with a bar on one side and a sizable dance floor in the middle.

Opposite the bar was the entrance to a much-smaller back room with extremely dim lighting. Most of the guys that went to the Texas were there just to dance and, if possible, to pick up someone from the dance floor to go home with. It was only a small group that ever took advantage of the other room, and then mostly much later at night when their blood alcohol levels had risen. The action there was a lot of tongue sharing, a fair amount of crotch groping, and only an occasional blowing. I had yet to see anyone take it up the ass there, although maybe I had never been there at the right time. The relative tameness in that room was probably because most of the men were getting their energy off on the dance floor. I had personally spent as much time in the back room as on the dance floor.

I put on my cowboy chaps, cowboy boots, hat, neckerchief, and so on, and headed out.

The bar was crowded, and I had to wait a couple of minutes to get the bartender's attention to order my beer. While I was standing there, this guy came up to the bar, turned to me, and in a clearly mocking way asked, "So, cowboy, you got your horse tied up outside?"

I turned to him and said, "I can ride, and I've ridden both horses and jackasses—a lot more of both than you have, I'm sure. I suspect you're the latter of the two." With that, I got my drink and walked away.

No more than five minutes later the jackass came up to me and said, "I'm sorry. That was rude."

I wasn't sure whether to accept his apology or not, so I said, "The only way I'll accept your apology is if you give it to me on your knees, boy."

"You're joking."

I just turned my face away from him. He walked away, but a few minutes later he was back. He looked around at the others in the bar as if to see how much humiliation he was prepared to publicly accept, turned back to me, and started to shake a little, which told me he was ready. As he took one more look around, I gently rested my beer bottle on his shoulder and, getting no resistance, pressed down. It took him a minute or so to respond with a nervous and rather clumsy kneeling.

I bent over and whispered to him, "Are you ready for me to take you home, where I'll rough up that rude rear of yours until you beg me to stop? Then I'll fuck out whatever impoliteness is still in your bruised butt, boy. If not, you're dismissed."

His silence told me he both wanted it and was afraid. But after less than a minute, he gave me a timid "Yes, sir!"

The whole scene was a real turn-on, perhaps because I was going to dominate someone who I was sure was new to the scene. Not only was his rude remark a clue to that, but he also seemed totally oblivious to the fact that I was signaling bottom.

"Take my beer and put it on the bar. I'm going to take a pee and will meet you at the door." Besides really needing to pee, I figured this would give Mr. Rude Jackass an opportunity to chicken out, which I half expected him to do. But when I came out of the bathroom, he was waiting at the door.

He followed me in his car to my place. As soon as the door was shut, I told him to strip, and as he did, I just stood there glaring to make him feel vulnerable. Once he was completely naked, I ordered him to follow be into my extra bedroom, which, besides serving as my extensive library, contains the closet where I keep my toys for big boys. I ordered him to open the closet, and when he did, I wasn't sure whether his expression was one of surprise, excitement, anxiety, or fear.

"I did say you were going to get a spanking, didn't I?"

"Yes, sir!"

Ignoring the assorted floggers, handcuffs, shackles, digging-into-the-neck slave-training collars, hoods, blindfolds, and assorted torture kits, I pointed to the leather and wooden paddles and said, "Once my hand gets sore from whacking your bare butt, I'll use one of those. Your choice."

I like the smell and feel of wood well enough on trees and furniture, but the smell and feel of leather is something else entirely. It gives me an instant hard-on. I was glad he picked the leather one for that reason as well as because the wooden one would have been too much for a possible first-timer.

To be platitudinous, he took everything like a man, and after his rump was brightly reddened to my satisfaction, it was time to ride him.

He watched silently as I took off my shirt, boots, chaps, Levi's, and jockstrap, only to put the chaps and boots back on. I got the condom, a latex glove, and lube and said, "On your belly, jackass." He obeyed. I rode and then gave him permission to take care of himself.

As I got off the bed, he followed, and I said, "I think the most appropriate way to thank me for my disciplinary kindness would be for you to lick these boots." He got on his knees and thanked me accordingly with his tongue.

A cowboy is for you to ride
Or you to be ridden by.
Either way, one should lick some boots
After a cock one salutes.

32

The escapist riding relief of Friday night was followed by a more or less calm Saturday of working on my book. Sunday morning I awoke to real stress over the Jonathan issue, and before long I convinced myself that the only proper thing to do was call him back and make some excuse to cancel the whole thing. Yes, maybe I would hurt his feelings, but in the long run, it would be better for both of us. I had decided he was obviously a closet case, and I didn't need such an entanglement. I had already been through two doomed-from-the-start relationships, despite the high hopes I'd had at the beginning of each. The first had had lots of love in it, but the sex had left much to be desired, while the second had had very satisfying sex but questionable love.

> When first you meet him, he's a great delight,
> And you start hoping that he's Mr. Right.
> But then too soon all the flaws appear,
> And you find him to be no longer dear,
> Which in a short time sends you into flight.

After those disappointments, I was looking for someone who could satisfy both my needs, and a married closet case wasn't going to qualify. I became angry. *How dare he—with a wife—try to drag me into his presumably unsatisfactory sexual situation!* I already had the phone in my hand when I realized that I had given him my number but had never asked for his damn number. Okay, so I just wouldn't show up. But that's not me. I agreed I would be there, and I'd fulfill my promise. However, I figured that I'd be polite but distant, and to keep that distance I would keep in mind the thought *The wife, the wife, the wife.*

I arrived at the museum about fifteen minutes early, only to see that he was already there. Walking toward him, I became intensely focused on the way he was dressed. At the college workshops both of us had been in standard business attire, but here he was in a T-shirt and Levi's pants and jacket. He was definitely more slovenly hot, an erotic enchantment, and I was glad that I had come in a similar outfit. I kept on reminding myself of the damn wife, but despite having no intention of doing so originally, I greeted him with an overly friendly handshake and smile, which he reciprocated. We went side by side through the museum, and every once in a while I would look up to the side of his face and couldn't help thinking,

> *To whisper love into your ears*
> *Is but a prelude to the lust*
> *Of my tongue taking its delight,*
> *Ending with a sensual bite.*

Beyond that the tour of the museum was a near blank to me. I know I talked and presumably offered some acceptable response to the displays, because afterward he commented on the intensity of my interest in everything. I must have been totally on automatic pilot, because the only things I could remember were the way his belly fell just enough over his belt to be appetizing and the way his butt filled up his Levi's enough that the seam went right into his crack—beautiful buttocks. He was definitely an aphrodisiac.

The wife, the wife, the wife was replaced by *If right now he was in some gay bar, I might be on my knees licking that belly and moving my tongue downward.* Of course, while thinking all of this, I was doing all I could to control myself from slightly shaking, which I couldn't have been too successful at, since he asked if I was cold and wanted to borrow his jacket. I wanted to say yes, in the hope of having him put it on me and feeling his arms touching my shoulders. Instead, I regained control of myself enough to politely say, "Thank you, but I'm fine." What he didn't know was that any temperature problem I was having was due to anything but cold.

When we finished viewing, he commented on how "great" it was, a word he seemed to like to use a lot. At first, I thought he was referring just to the display, but then with some exuberance, he said it was really nice to be able to do something like this with someone who enjoyed it as much as he did. He didn't have a clue that it wasn't the activity that I had enjoyed as much as it was allowing my fantasies about him to run wild.

Then, as he was suggesting that we should do something like this again, he caught himself and added, "That's if you would like to."

To my later regret I found myself saying, "Yes."

"Okay, I'll give you a call," he said with a huge, adorable smile on his face. He leaned forward, grabbed my hand, and shook it as he said good-bye. This time, instead of a chill down my spine, I went hard.

> His hand grasping mine,
> Little did he know
> It was like a hope
> For a manly grope.

Why did I say yes? But what was I supposed to say? No? Maybe I should have tried to somehow explain that while I liked him, I had a life that didn't really include a straight man, especially a straight vanilla man. But that would have brought up too many issues that I didn't want to mention to a more or less stranger, especially one who I suspected would not understand. How would that explanation have gone?

"Jonathan, I'm into the leather set."

"Leather set?"

"Yes. You know, the dominant and submissive, the master and the slave, and S-M play."

Perhaps I could have described to him my slaving experiences with my various masters. That would certainly have ended everything.

> A slave, a slave, is one who works
> To please more than himself.
> Obedience and punishment
> Are what he must accept.
> His master he must satisfy
> In body and in mind.

To do less he regards a sin
With damnation to win.

I suppose that before he'd gotten the wrong idea about me being a slave, I would have had to explain that I meant voluntary slavery.

No force compels me outside of myself
To accept the role of another's slave.
No outer master but the one within
Can command me to become what I crave.

In other words, genuine slavery does not start when one agrees to serve under a master. It starts well before that, sometimes years before that. Slavery begins when the slave within the person awakens, and once that happens—whether the inner slave ever seeks or finds an outer master to make him an outer slave—that slave can never return to what he was before that awakening.

How awfully sad is masterless slave,
To be without love, to be without pain.
So pray for the one who will dominate
With kindness and cruelty to mate.

Master Hal, my first master, was the one who introduced me to more than book-slave protocol. His real name was Harold, but he hated that name, which automatically created a problem for me or any other slave he had, because slave protocol does not allow a slave to call his master by a nickname, since that implies equality and automatically weakens both their roles. The inappropriateness of this was more or less ameliorated by making absolutely sure that I always preceded *Hal* with *Master*, and in public, where that might not have been looked upon favorably, I referred to him as "Halsir." In other words, we agreed that I would slur *Hal* and *sir* together, which brought no unwelcomed attention to us.

In what way is a name used
That makes a slave untrue?
To refer to his master
Without formality.
Andrew, Denis, George, or John
Without adding a *sir*;
Mark, Rex, Tyson, or Walter
Without a *Master* first.
Such signs of disrespect
Are intolerable.
Be aware of when or where
The right name he to bare.

There was only the briefest formal contract between Master Hal and me because we could only get together on weekends. Nonetheless, I learned all the basics from him and regarded him as my master, and he regarded me as his slave once he had ritually baptized me in front of witnesses, two persons of his choice and two of mine. The ritual requires the master, in front of the witnesses so they can verify it, to formally piss on the naked slave, like a wolf marking his territory or, in this case, his property.

I was no urine yearner,
But faced with this right sir,
I accepted ownership
Through a glad golden glow.

Master Hal was not a particularly tolerant teacher in that I learned each lesson only after I had made, or rather had been allowed to make, an unintentional mistake and was punished for it. This may not sound like an especially lucky learning process, and I suppose some people would consider it an abusive situation, but those people simply do not understand the dynamics of the master-slave relationship. As far as I am concerned, an abusive relationship is one in which anger is the main motivation for punishment. I have done my best not to allow a master to touch me in real anger unless I'm absolutely sure I was super wrong.

Pseudo-anger is often a part of master-slave role-playing, as when the master threatens to punish the slave if the latter does something that displeases the former. But the experienced slave knows exactly what is happening and plays along. This can even involve the slave knowing that the master wants the slave to do wrong purposefully so the slave can "suffer" the appropriate consequences. For example, Master Hal knew that before sex I liked getting my face slapped followed by a spanking or belting of my bare ass as fetish foreplay, and so he would always grab me by the throat and tell me what he was going to do to me if I didn't obey, at which point I would, in forewarned defiance, spit in his face. This absolute insult to any master then elicited just enough slaps to both sides of my face to leave a temporary mark.

> There could be no question
> That pleasure came from it,
> The slaps upon each cheek.
> That I would clearly seek.

Master Hal was a great disciplinarian, and I had no problem with his philosophy.

> A slave should be beaten
> For his role once a week.
> To show him less caring
> Is cruelty, indeed.
> A slave should be beaten
> For his role once a week,
> Or he will soon believe
> That he is close to free.
> A slave should be beaten

For his role once a week.
How else can a genuine slave
Of a kind master speak?

Since our master-slave relationship was only a weekend situation, Master Hal had no delusions about me not seeking some midweek satisfaction with someone else. But that didn't mean he was prepared to relinquish full control over me. If I met someone who wished to trick with me, I was obligated to let that person know that I was under the overall authority of a master by stating the exact limitations of having sex with me. This specifically meant that I had to recite to them the following:

This slave is permitted to take only his master's cock cream in his mouth and to allow only his master's unsheathed shaft up his asshole. A condom for both sucking and fucking is otherwise required. If rimming is demanded, this slave must first wash off the asshole to be tongued. If this slave is to be bitten, as on the back of the neck or butt, the biter's teeth may not break the skin. If pissed on, this slave can be so baptized by others only while naked and only below the neck since only his master can shoot recycled beer into this slave's mouth or on his clothes. Moreover, any pissing must come before any flogging, not after, and any flogging must be done with this slave's toys, not any other's. Also, if this slave is to be slapped in the face, grabbed by the throat, pushed around, or otherwise strongly manhandled, these actions cannot be performed in any way that would damage his body. Even this slave's master in his most forceful punishment never does anything this slave would regard as abusive, and no one else may abuse this slave. Finally, if this slave is to be handcuffed, it must be done only in the front since only his master or a familiar dom may cuff him behind. Also, either this slave's cuffs must be used, or this slave needs to see the key to any other cuffs.

While Master Hal hoped this would frighten off some prospective tricks, it actually turned other tricks on, especially those who had never tricked with a slave before and found it exciting.

My relationship with Master Hal only lasted about a year because, while he was out as a gay man, he was an extremely closeted master who refused to allow me to go out with him wearing even a simple locked chain dog collar. My desire to be more publicly open as a slave eventually caused us to go our separate ways. Soon after that he found someone who didn't mind being a closet slave. The major thing I regret I didn't do for Master Hal or ultimately for myself was to get the *S* brand, for slave, on my right shoulder.

> Red-hot metal against one's flesh,
> An *S* to symbolize true self,
> A scar that shouts you would be owned
> More than might any mere tattoo.
> For some, this might seem an extreme,
> But for a slave it's no taboo.

I had a more formalized slaving experience with Master Abe. I signed up with him for a nine-week trial master-slave relationship. It was a detailed contract that specified what a slave was as far as he and I were concerned, the slave's responsibilities and the master's responsibilities, extrasexual activities, activities that would be unacceptable to the slave, the punishments that the slave might be subject to, the conditions under which either the master or slave could rightly terminate the contract, financial issues, and respect for the slave's spiritual practice. The contract went into effect only after the slave-owing ritual, which, as in Master Hal's case, required four witnesses.

To drench, to drench, yes, first to drench—
The need to be a slave to quench.
To those who smell, it clearly means
To be owned by the master's stench.

After the sixth week, I knew I was not going to renew the contract, because of the master's limited version of a social life. It turned out that social life for Master Abe was built around inviting between one and three guests over each Saturday evening for sex play, or more specifically for me to be a group sex toy. Now, while this slave slut was tolerant of the sex with multiple partners, as either a bottom or top, as the only form of social life, it was less than satisfying.

There was a master as black as pitch
Who owned a white slave for his pet bitch.
The slave was ordered over to bend
So as to be exposed to a friend.
But from bottom to top one could switch.

Although I didn't sign up again as Master Abe's slave, I also didn't entirely abandon him. Being a slut but now a free entity, I sometimes joined him and his friends on Saturday nights for a few months until he acquired a new slave.

My next contract was with Master Peter, and it was very different from that of Master Abe's. There was some of the standard stuff of every contract, but this new one fully acknowledged that I was as much of a slut as Master Peter was and that it would be ridiculous to even pretend that either of us could be expected to be monogamous.

Monogamy is thought of as romantic,
Two hearts that beat for each and for no more.
But if some stranger's body is attractive,
Pure faithfulness could simply be a bore.

The rule was that if either of us was away from the other for more than three days, we each had a right to trick out. However, if we did so, we were contractually obligated to tell the other, after which the slave was to be punished. Yes, as the slave, I was punished not only for my permitted infidelity but also for Master Peter's infidelity! Master Peter's motto was "When we cheat, then you I must beat." After all, he was the master, hence the one who had the inherent right to trick out; a slave had no such inherent right. Nonetheless, for a slave to be punished for a master's wrongdoings seems unfair, but as every master and slave know, the situation is far more complicated.

> A slave is prone to punishment
> But is so by his free will.
> Therefore, what might seem an abuse
> May be a ruse to seduce.

The degree of punishment for this cherished cheating was clearly stated in the contract. For just getting sucked off there was no penalty. The least penalty was if either gave a blow job to someone else, the next was if either fucked someone else, the third was if either sucked off and fucked someone, and the fourth or worst penalty was getting fucked by someone else. The punishment usually consisted of some version of authority sex, where the slave either milks himself or is milked by the master to de-eroticize the slave. Then sexual demands would be made on the less sexually interested slave at a level 1, 2, 3, or 4, which could include a nonerotic flogging. In other words, it was sex mainly to establish the master's slightly sadistic authority over the slave.

Although Master Peter gave me outside sexual freedom, as in the case of Master Hal, there were restricting strings attached. If I was playing around, I could only do it without exposing more of my flesh than was absolutely necessary for the sexual act. If I was getting a blow job, I was to unzip and pull out my dick only to the degree I might when peeing and was never to unbuckle my pants or push them down. If I was getting fucked, I could unzip, unbuckle, and push the back of my pants down to expose my bare butt, but no more than the minimum I would need to if I were sitting on a toilet. Furthermore, the guy behind me was not allowed to touch my dick. It was front work or back work, never both. Also, in either case, my feet had to remain on the ground. Naturally, this limited my tricking-out possibilities to little more than standing-up quickies, usually in a back room or restroom with a lockable door. These restrictions were Master Peter's way of limiting the amount of access another person had to my body and reminding me that I was still his property and could only be fully naked when serving him. He was permitting me candy while making it almost impossible to eat.

> The games that masters will play
> To control what they would own.
> Some are quite ingenious
> To frustrate the slave alone.

I thought that with Master Peter I had found the right owner, since he claimed I was the best slave he had ever had.

> The slave who is obedient
> Should be considered good.
> But the one also obeisant
> Should be judged as the best.
> To discover a slave like this
> Is every master's quest.

However, even if I was the best he had had, that apparently was not sufficient. As far as I was concerned, our relationship was working fine until he wanted to add a third person into it. It wasn't that I objected to a third party, but the addition was, without a doubt, a boy toy who was never going to be a real submissive. This was proven by the fact that the boy resented taking orders from me as the senior sub. In fact, he made it absolutely clear that he regarded a slave as lower than a free boy toy. I repeatedly asked for Master Peter's backup on this matter, but what I got was only lip service since the boy refused to be punished. Naturally, this made me wonder whether Master Peter shared that evaluation of me as well. Finally, I rebelled.

> Sometimes a slave must rebel
> To keep his sanity.
> This should be permissible
> If he accepts its cost.
> What cost, what cost, or what price?
> Punishment to entice.

After a three-way shouting match, Master Peter took off his belt and shouted at me to drop my pants and get down on all fours. This time, it wasn't just that I resented his taking the boy's side, but he was now demanding that I be punished in front of the boy toy. A slave can be punished in front of another master or another slave but not in front of a boy toy. Proper protocol required that the master either order the boy out of the room or that the boy ask and receive permission to be excused. Clearly, neither was going to happen, and my anger would not allow me to demand it. If Master Peter was going to violate protocol like that, I was going to use it as ammunition for what I knew I would soon do. I just stood there defiantly staring at Master Peter, but then he yelled, "Slave!" and, still blazing with hostility, I did as I was expected to do. I dropped my pants, got on all fours, and received more than I would have been expected to tolerate if this were an erotic scene. As I took my punishment, I reconnected with my sense of slavehood, and a state of submissive calmness came over me.

To obey, to obey
Is the duty of every slave.
Such has been, such has been
Since the first master in the cave.
Such will be, such will be
Until the last goes to the grave.

Master Peter dropped the issue, but I could not. I was not prepared to simply walk out on the contract and allow Master Peter—or, worse, the boy toy—to defame me as a quitter. Instead, for the next two weeks I became passive-aggressive, doing things or not doing things that required punishment until Master Peter finally realized I was going to tire him out with this. He asked what I wanted, and I told him I was not willing to cope with the current situation anymore and requested that either the boy leave or that our contract be dissolved. Master Peter made the choice. The boy toy stayed, and I was given my freedom. That, however, was not the end of it. Without a slave to discipline, Master Peter began to treat the boy toy as a boy slave, and that never works out. He thus found himself without a slave or a toy.

I have to admit that part of the problem was mine. First, I was envious that the boy toy was satisfying Master Peter's romantic interests while I was being denied them. Second, while the boy toy may have thought of himself as superior to a slave, I felt that since he was willing to commit far more effort (discipline) to the relationship than any boy toy needed to, I was superior to him.

Master Peter asked me to return, but it was too late. He had not given me the slave respect I was due, and I could never trust him on this issue again.

Every slave is due respect
As honored property.
He should not be thought as less
Because he wills to serve.

A master should feel enriched
By he who licks his feet.
To disrespect is abuse
Of one's authority.
Esteem, esteem, what you own,
Or have no property.

Chapter 4

For the next two days I tried my best to forget Jonathan, and by Wednesday morning I had succeeded. But then early that afternoon he called again. After reiterating what a nice time he'd had on Sunday, he told me that there was something he had wanted to tell me both at the workshops event and after our museum visit but that he had been somewhat embarrassed to do so and that it had been playing on his mind. He said that he had great admiration for people who didn't let themselves be put down and that he was really impressed by the "great" way I had stood up for myself. I thanked him for the compliment, and as I did, I once again thought of Kinsey. Where was he on the scale of straight to gay? A straight or even just predominantly straight man saying he admired a gay man seemed to me to indicate significantly less than 100 percent heterosexuality. But why should I be concerned about percentages? A compliment is a compliment, and I had no business trying to analyze it. Jonathan then got around to the rest of the reason for his call. "Would you like to go to a movie about the Civil War?"

The words *Gone with the Wind* instantly came to mind, and I shuddered. Then I stupidly asked, "The American Civil War?"

"Yes, the American Civil War."

I tried to cover my blunder as best I could. "There are so many civil wars going on in the world today that you never know."

I could tell by his answer that he clearly submitted to my political sophistication.

"Right."

Here was one plus for gay, one minus for possible straight.

Part of me wanted to find some excuse to say no, but the winning part said yes; however, I did then get up the nerve to ask the crucial question. "What about your wife? Isn't she into movies?"

His answer came without a moment's delay. "She only likes romances and comedies."

We arranged a day and time, Sunday, July 23, for the 1:30 matinee. As before he wanted to know if we should meet at the theater or if I wanted him to pick me up. I realized that I didn't know where he lived, so I asked him where he was coming from and where the theater was. He said he was coming from Marina del Rey, and this gave me the perfect excuse to meet him at the theater, as it was approximately equal distance between the two of us.

"Great, I'll see you there." He did love that word.

That he and his wife lived in such an affluent area suggested to me he must be doing well financially, which surprised me since I didn't think journalism would be a particularly well-paying profession. He must be very good at his work.

As soon as I hung up the phone, I was again questioning my sanity. Why was I going to a movie I might or might not be interested in with a married man whom I had no business being interested in? Well, it was too late to change my mind, since once again I had forgotten to get his number. Forgotten? Was that what it was? Or maybe I simply didn't wish to call him only to have *her* answer the phone. What would I have said?

> I think your man is beautiful.
> He's like a bearish beast.
> When it comes to hunger,
> I'd like on him to feast.

Then it hit me that this was one of the more absurd times in my life. What kind of weird fate would punish me by holding in front of me a sexually desirable man who had a possible interest in me but who was presumably straight, not to mention married, and so doubly off-limits?

> What sin have I committed
> That I should earn this curse?
> The fact that I do not breed
> And instead waste my seed?
> If another cause it be,
> Let some dream remind me.

The next few days were, in fact, miserable. I wanted to stop thinking about him, but I couldn't. I turned to my writing to try to distract me, but that didn't work. I thought several times of jerking off in the hopes of getting him out of my head, but as soon I started, I found myself fantasizing about him, so I stopped. I even had trouble eating. It was like I was hungry, but whatever I prepared, even my favorite food, seemed totally unsatisfying. I tried going out to eat, and that was no better.

By Friday night my ambivalent feelings about Jonathan were driving me crazy, and I just wanted the escape of the man-meat kind. I thought once more about the Texas and the Stag, but since I had just been to the first and would probably go to the second the next night, neither would work. This left me with the San Fernando Valley.

I considered going to the local stand-up sex club Stul. The last time I had been there I had gotten a blow job from a guy who was gorgeous but definitely a nonbutch. Shortly before he had gotten to me, I'd seen him working his talents on another guy, and as I'd left the place, a third had already been benefiting from him. As promising as Stul might be this night, I was hoping for something a little more personal than anything available there. Besides, Stul was open until the early hours of the morning, so if I didn't make out elsewhere, I could always end up there. My next thought was the Wolf Den, which was about as close to a leather bar in that part of town as any and was near enough to Stul if I had to resort to it.

Wanting to get relief any way I could, I figured that although my flogger, Brute Bliss, was on my right side, signaling sub, I could switch sides if approached by a bottom, as I had done every other time I'd been to this bar. To my surprise the Den had an unusually large crowd, which I attributed to the really hot weather we were having. People just wanted out of their homes.

Two different guys cruised me in the first ten minutes, but despite having decided I would be less picky this night, I knew neither would work out. The first one was signaling leather top but was dressed like a slob, and a dominant who doesn't have enough pride in himself to dress the part is a turnoff to me. Even if I go out as a sub, I try to dress like a self-disciplined one.

The second guy, as far as I could tell, wasn't signaling either top or bottom, which was okay, but he was holding up the wall as if to say, *I am too weak or too tired to stand up by myself.* Sometimes in a crowded bar, one gets involuntarily forced against a wall, but this wasn't the case here. Although he was obviously with some friends, he kept turning to look at me every once in a while, and I knew that if I merely nodded at him, he would disengage with his friends and join me. However, it was obvious that he was dominating the conversation with his friends, giving them little time to talk, and sex and a run-on mouth do not work for me.

After an hour or so I was about to give up and head for Stul when I noticed another guy staring at me. He was quite good-looking, although much younger than I. The way he had locked his gaze on me especially caught my interest. Also, despite the warmth outside, he wore not only a leather jacket but also leather gloves, as well as a flogger on his left hip. While the flogger on the left was the most obvious signal of a dom, the gloves certainly reinforced that.

To make sure his interest was genuine, I nodded at him, and he nodded back. The question then was who would approach whom. The standard rule is that the dom either moves to the sub or points to the sub and to his side or front, indicating that the submissive has been summoned. I waited, but when he made no move, I walked about half the distance between us and stopped. I figured if he wanted me, he would do his part. If he didn't, I was out of there.

The guy again nodded to me and then turned his head to signal that I was to continue my approach and stand beside him. As soon as I was close enough for him to hear me over the rest of the bar noise, I initiated what by then I was hoping was going to be a pickup.

"Good evening."

"Good evening."

While neither of us made any break in our deadly serious on-the-hunt faces, he moved around in front of me, put his fist right against my chest, and began rubbing his knuckles over my tits and down my belly.

Wanting to follow suit, I showed him my fist and asked, "May I, sir?"

"Yes."

Then with his body, he pushed, or rather pinned, me against the wall. I was now more or less constrained while he was free to check me out. Since I'm generally not interested in a guy who will not kiss, I ran the tip of my tongue over my lips, and he picked up on the signal. Putting his hand on the back of my neck, he forced his tongue past my lips into my mouth, and I offered him my tongue. He then grabbed hold of my belt buckle to further force our bodies together, and I felt his knee go between my legs, not so much to push his crotch against mine, but to force my legs and feet apart in a manner that said, *You stand the way I want you to stand.*

I was not used to a much-younger man—I judged him to be in his late twenties—being as sexually aggressive as he was. I have found that younger tricks expect me to be the more aggressive one. However, far from being put off by such aggression, I found him exciting. He then initiated a decidedly dom-sub dialogue.

"You like that, man?"

"Yes, sir!"

"What else do you like?"

To make sure that he understood that I was willing to be a sub, I initiated the next commitment. Although in age I was his senior, such age differences have no meaning in the dom-sub scene. The dom is *sir*; the sub is *boy*.

"Sir! In this boy's case it is less a matter of like than of need."

"So what does this boy need?"

"To submit and service a sir!"

"And how do you do that, boy?"

"By having my mouth, tongue, dick, and asshole put at the disposal of the sir." The words "put at the disposal" were an obvious message that I was prepared to offer him total submission. The fact that this young sir didn't hesitate for a moment upon hearing this told me he was familiar and comfortable with that kind of deference. I could have added that I like discipline, but I didn't have to, since he started to handle Brute Bliss.

"You sound like an obedient and well-disciplined boy. I like that."

"Thank you, sir. I try my best."

He unhooked the flogger from my belt and said, "Nice. How long have you had it?"

"Several years, sir."

He ran the thongs over my chest and then pushed the handle against my lips, obviously expecting me to open my mouth and hold it between my teeth. I did as expected of me.

Taking it out, he then pushed the handle up under my jaw and said, "I suspect you need to feel some pain, boy."

"If that would be sir's pleasure."

"It would."

"Thank you, sir!"

"I think it's time to leave, boy."

"Yes, sir! But if I may say something?"

"Certainly."

"I'm always into safe—condoms, no drugs. Sir!"

Safe usually implies condoms, but I thought in this situation I better make doubly sure, because a lot of the younger crowd, unfortunately, has decided that, despite AIDS, barebacking is okay because of the new drugs that keep HIV positives alive now.

Passion is a servant
Of ever dreamless sleep.
It takes but one mistake
And death by some disease.
So beware, play with care,
For love and life to please.

"Mind if I do some grass?"

"Not as long as I don't have to do so, sir. After all, a submissive should always have a clear head to do proper service, sir."

He smiled as he said, "Right."

I wasn't being entirely honest with my answer. I did mind, but this guy was really hot and presumably offering to flog me, which I really wanted, so I was willing to compromise on the grass, but nothing stronger.

"Fine with me. You ready to go?"

"Yes, sir! But could I use the restroom first?"

"Sure."

Although I really did need to pee, that was not the main reason I wanted away from him for a couple of minutes. It was to call one of my silent-alarm partners (SAP). There is always a danger in going home with a stranger, even one picked up in a vanilla bar. Considering some of the games we leather folk play, it is always recommended that you notify a friend, presumably one into the scene, about where and with whom you are going for such play. Since I didn't know this young sir's name, much less where we were going, I could hardly be too informative to my SAP, but at least I could tell him that I was leaving the Wolf Den at this time and could describe the guy I was leaving with. Furthermore, I told him that if I got more information, I would leave it as a phone message. In any case, I would call the following morning to let him know I was all right.

I peed and returned to the sir.

"Ready?"

"Yes, sir."

He put his hand behind my back to gently push me toward and out the door—a true dom action.

"Where's your car?"

Pointing to the left, I said, "About two blocks that way, sir."

"That makes it easy. Mine is one block down. I'll drive you to yours; then you can follow me."

As we walked to his car, I was careful to watch his posture. It was straight up, face forward, almost military, another good sign of a dom. His car suggested that he, for all his youth, was more than a dom; he was a master type. The car was washed, and even the inside showed that he was into tidy self-discipline.

I followed him for about twenty-five minutes. He stopped near an obviously convenient parking place, and I parked. I had been paying attention to the street signs as I drove, so before getting out of my car, I left an updated SAP call with my street location.

I got into his car, and moments later he pulled into his driveway.

I thought to ask him his name, but then I remembered that some overserious dom or master types think that volunteering their name too early in the situation lessens their mystery power over the sub. He also hadn't asked for my name yet, so I decided to refrain from asking for his for now.

Once we got into his house, he turned on the lights with a dimmer so that the room was only partially lit, and I automatically assumed the proper submissive position with my hands behind my back, at which point he ordered, "On your knees and lick these boots."

As I did so, he ran the throngs of his flogger over my back.

Aggressive talk is a turn-on
When backed by a masterly hand.
He tells me how I will submit
To his every dominant wish.
But when it comes to the real thing,
Better is it if it should sting.

"That's enough. Stay on your knees, hands behind you, and don't move from here."

"Yes, sir!"

He disappeared into the darkness of either a hallway or another room.

By the order given me, this young sir showed that he really knew the proper dominant-master technique, because should the dominant have a legitimate reason for leaving the room, some symbol of his authority should always remain behind. In this case, it was requiring me to be in a kneeling position until he returned. To have simply left me to my own devices would have given me a sense of freedom that would have automatically weakened the power relationship.

In less than a minute Young Sir returned holding handcuffs. I hadn't seen any sign of handcuffs on his person in the bar, so I'd made no mention of any resistance to wearing them. The fact is I like being handcuffed, but only with someone that I know well enough to feel safe with.

Still, I had been in situations like this before and with one exception had been able to do some on-the-spot negotiations. In only one case the top had been unwilling to compromise, so I'd stopped the scene and just left.

"Sir, I apologize to you for not asking about handcuffs in the bar—my fault—and I would accept some discipline for my oversight, but being handcuffed behind my back by someone I don't know is a serious problem for me. Would cuffing my hands in front be acceptable to you, sir?"

Front-cuffed hands, while still a touchy issue, would leave me a lot freer to defend myself than back-cuffed ones would if the scene went wrong.

He thought about it for a moment and said, "Yes."

Sign of a good submissive—try not to make the dominant feel foolish or like he is giving up some control to the sub, especially by acknowledging that the dom has the right to discipline the sub once he's agreed to the sub's request. This impresses all but the most insecure dom. Sign of a good dominant—pretend that the sub's request is not out of order and don't show offense at the request. Then accept the sub's willingness to be disciplined, especially since you know the sub wants it or wouldn't have mentioned it.

> It may be called discipline,
> But to it I consent.
> What some think is pure torment
> With it I am content.
> From hell-bent to heaven-sent
> So I far from lament.

Young Sir held the cuffs in front of me, and I offered my wrists to him. Locking the cuffs, he ordered me to stand up and remove my boots, socks, and pants. Trying to get those items off while handcuffed was not easy, and I had to back up to the wall. The fact that he had decided to let me keep the jacket on gave me some extra sense of security. As I was undressing, he stood there silently, intensely watching. *Yes! He is a watcher type of dom.*

Once I was fully naked below the waist, Young Sir ordered me to move away from the wall. Then he circled around me three times without once touching me. Having scrutinized me sufficiently, he ran the fingers of his left hand down my chest and stomach but didn't touch my semierection as I expected he would do. Instead, he went around behind me and ran those fingers down my spine, stopping at my crack.

"Put your hands on your knees and bend over."

I did as I was told, and what I more or less knew was coming came.

"Did you like the feel of sir's slap, boy?"

"Yes, sir!"

"You're going to get more of that soon, very soon, boy."

"Yes, sir!"

I wanted to say, "I hope so, sir!" but that would have ruined his sense of being fully in charge. Saying something like that would work in vanilla but not in leather.

"Follow me, boy."

He led me right past a room with no lights on to a second room that was only dimly lit, but I could still see that it was a fully equipped play room with toys everywhere. Besides the leather-padded play table, the most conspicuous item was a Saint Andrew's cross. Leaving me there to take in the scene, he moved to a small table with a box on it, opened it, pulled out a joint, and lit it.

Holding that between his teeth, he picked up a leather dog collar and buckled it around my neck just above my own dog chain.

"Boy, lean over the end of the table." As I obeyed, he picked up a leather paddle and said, "You did say I could punish you for your resistance to the cuffs behind you?"

"Yes, sir."

Now technically, according to one line of thought, items used to punish a slave should not be the same as those used in erotic play. However, in this case, since I'd accepted his slapping my butt, Young Sir was probably well aware that I would accept this as an erotic discipline, which was true.

With the paddle, he hit one cheek then the other, and each time he did I responded according to sub protocol with "Sorry, sir!"

This went on for ten to twelve strikes. When I knew I'd had enough, my "Sorry, sir!" reached a shouting level, and he knew what that meant.

"Turn around and back on your knees, boy."

He unzipped and pushed my face into his bulge, making it clear that he wanted my mouth to rub against his open fly.

"You know what I want you to do with those hands, don't you, boy?"

Saying, "Yes, sir!" I reached my still-cuffed hands inside to feel a jockstrap, which I began mouthing. Since he still had his belt on, it was difficult for me to reach inside and get free what was already hard from the constraining strap.

"Sir! Do I have permission to loosen your belt and unbutton your pants?"

"Sure."

Doing so would allow me to withdraw his now-full hard-on from the strap. He was a little less than average hung, which meant that he was going to be easy to take if he planned on butt banging me, which I hoped he was. I knew he expected me to go down on him, and I thought about requesting a condom. After all, I had mentioned them at the bar, although I had not specified that one would be needed for oral as well as anal, as I often do. However, I was so turned on by him at this point that I decided to ignore caution, and I went down on him.

"Get up."

Rebuckling his pants but leaving his zipper zucchini out, he grabbed the chain of the cuffs and asked, "Ever been pissed on, boy?"

"I've been the privileged urinal of several men, sir! I only ask that it not be on my face or on my jacket, sir!"

"Not a problem."

He led me into the bathroom and ordered, "Stand in the tub." His earlier stiffness had subsided enough to allow him to piss easily.

Getting into the tub, I realized that this was my first piss play since my last master, although without formal witnesses it was not a declaration of more than a one-night ownership.

"You ready for this, whelp?"

Before I had a chance to further consent, he started pissing all over my man member.

Some think it is a perverse act
To be well avoided.
But others see with different eyes,
Viewing it as a prize.
It comes out of the same male hole
That gives birth to his cum,
So how could one think to be prim
As it shoots out on him?

Young Sir then surprised me by kneeling and rubbing his face over my wet crotch, then sucking it, which clearly demonstrated his pleasure at the whole scene. This was no mere ritual ownership scene; Young Sir was obviously into full water sports. By this time I must have been intensely aroused, because he then insisted on pressing his piss-smelling face into mine with his piss-tasting tongue into my mouth. Not being into true water sports, under less erotic conditions I would have found this intolerable. In past piss play highly concentrated uric acid or the end results of whatever the man had eaten had made any attempt to get the piss close to my nose unacceptable. But in Young Sir's case, not only was the smell of his piss mild enough, the guy's aura of dominance was also turning out to be even hotter than it had been in the bar. Satisfied with this piss play, he turned on the tub water, handed me a washcloth, and then, when I was clean enough, handed me a towel. He then wiped off his own face, and without a further word, he motioned for me to get out of the bathroom and follow him back into the playroom/dungeon.

"You know what's next, don't you, boy?"

"The cross, sir?"

He had already pulled out a key to the cuffs, which he unlocked, and with his left hand on my back he slowly pushed me to the cross.

At this point he pulled my jacket off, then my shirt, which left me completely naked. He took off his gloves, jacket, and shirt but then put the gloves back on. He got ready to attach wrist restraints, but I said, "I can stay put without those, sir!" He undoubtedly understood that if I was not willing to be cuffed behind my back, I was not going to be willing to be trapped like this. He simply nodded.

It is not that I have never let myself be put on a cross with both wrist and ankle restraints. To the contrary, I like it, but only with a player I know and have learned to trust. The only exception to this is when I publicly bottomed on the cross, but that was with a dozen or more people around whom I could appeal to for help if the top was overdoing it.

As I spread-eagled, I said, "Please, sir, not the small of my back!"

"Not a problem."

Anyone who had been properly trained in the flogging scene knew that you didn't hit the small of the back, because that could damage the kidneys. The shoulders and buttock were more or less safe targets.

"Let me know when you've had enough, boy."

"Will do, sir!"

He started slowly and gradually sped up. I had not been flogged in months, and so this was a sorely needed sensation. After too short a while he stopped, came up to me, and asked, "How are you doing?"

"I'm fine, sir! And by the way, I'm not a butterfly."

He must have gotten the message, because, as he started up again, the lashing became more intense.

> Leather thongs assaulting
> Both my back and butt.
> Liberating lightness,
> A heavenly high.

I finally cried out, "Thank you, sir! Thank you, sir! Thank you, sir!"

He stopped. "You can take a lot."

"I hope enough to please you, sir!"

He answered me but not with words. Instead,

Like a sidewinder snake
His wet tongue meandered
Cautiously up my spine,
The crevice to the neck,
There to bite so to hear
My delicious squealing,
An act to discover
The pleasure that is pain.

He released me and said, "Now lick by boots again."

After a minute or two on my knees with my tongue on his boots, he said, "Get up and on the table, boy."

"Back or belly, sir?"

"Your back if it isn't too sore."

As I went supine, Young Sir took off his gloves, boots, and pants, then brought out the cuffs again, which I was quite happy about. I really like being fucked with cuffs on, and I assumed such ass play was coming next. But what came next made me regret I was in them. My nightmare: tit—or, even worse, possibly scrotum—clamps.

"Sir, please, I have supersensitive tits."

He looked at me intensely for a moment, then pulled up my shirt. He lightly and then more intensely squeezed my nipples with his fingers until he reached my pain threshold. The gritting of my teeth plus the near-crying expression on my face told him all.

"Wimp, boy."

"Yes, sir! Wimp. But a really sorry one if he has disappointed you, sir! A really sorry one."

A sub trying to renegotiate a scene while in restraints of any kind takes talent.

"I'm sorry, sir! But if you had played with my tits in the bar, you would have known just what a wimp I am, and you wouldn't have wasted your time and effort on such a worthless wimp."

Reminding him gently that it was his fault for not finding this out beforehand while at the same time allowing him to save face by deprecating oneself is usually a good sub's strategy. Nonetheless, no matter how indirectly and politely I had said no to him, I waited to see if such disobedient rebellion would be followed by deserved punishment. He put the clamps aside and climbed up on the table. He slapped my face with his pecker a number of times, and the earliest sign of his liquid of life touched my lips.

He grabbed my jaw, forcing my mouth open, and proceeded to drool saliva from his mouth into mine. Considering what he could have done, this was a more-than-acceptable humiliation for a sub that had dared to challenge the dom. To finish my discipline he raised up my butt and gave me a few hits with the paddle, which again I thanked him for.

> Discipline need not be cruelty
> If serving to state who is in charge.
> Also, it repairs any chasm
> That is caused by disobedience.
> So discipline may be the asked for,
> Dom and sub brought together once more.

The next thing I knew he had his hand under the leather pillow my head was resting on, and he pulled out a condom and tube of lube. He rolled the condom on and bottom buttered up my butt with his fingers, which I appreciated because, even though he was thin enough for me to take without anal foreplay, it was always more pleasant to my ass to receive such play. He pulled my legs up onto his shoulders and said, "Is the wimp ready, or is he going to cry about this?"

"Yes, sir!"

As he was fucking me, I saw, for the first time, a smile on his face. I smiled back, and it was clear now that we were dropping some of the dom-sub roles and just enjoying a good top-bottom interaction. When he shot, I was sure his groan was loud enough to be heard in the neighboring house, but if this was anything like my gay-dominated apartment building, most residents were probably used to hearing climaxing neighbors.

Usually, at this stage of play, I would have started to jerk off, although not before asking permission. However, as soon as he withdrew, he went down on me, and he was definitely good at it. He kept his mouth muscles so tight around my dick that it felt like he was sucking the jolly jism right out of me, and it was fantastic. However, once I exploded in his mouth, he insisted on again pushing his still piss-smelling and piss-tasting face and mouth into mine, which by then was far less tolerable than earlier when I was still sufficiently aroused to find some eroticism in it, but I did my best not to gag.

He soon took off the cuffs and handed me my shirt and jacket. Obviously, there was going to be no sleeping over tonight. I went into the living room for my pants and boots, and as I dressed, I hoped that Young Sir might offer his name and perhaps even his number or ask for mine, but he didn't. At first I was sorry, but then I remembered the tit clamps and thought it was just as well. Nonetheless, with minor exceptions it had been an incredibly hot scene.

Night of a sadist's love,
The masochist in heat.
Two animals at play,
The owner and the owned.
Spread-eagled on a cross,
To tame by pain of whip.
Released to revere him
Humbly on one's knees.
The master satisfied,
The slave is gratified.

Escapist sex gave me some relief for Saturday, but Sunday morning I woke up and realized why I had the eating problem. What I was really hungry for was Jonathan's hard-on in either orifice he might choose to stick it. There I went from my vow to not let him affect me sexually to something unabashedly unchaste.

Why not pray that his penis
will penetrate my portal
To be a playful partner?

By the time I had showered, forced myself to eat a respectable breakfast, and read the newspaper, it was time to leave for the theater. I drove to it in what I figured was close to a manic-depressive state. Sure enough, he was already there.

He was dressed more or less the same as at the museum. He greeted me this time not with merely a broader smile and a handshake but with a strong, manly pat on my shoulders, and within a minute or two, I became acutely aware that I had a noticeable bulge. If he was straight, he wouldn't notice, since straight men don't go about instinctively looking at other men's crotches. If he was gay, I assumed he would be far from intimidated by it. As for anyone else noticing it, at this point, I couldn't have cared less.

He already had the tickets, so I pulled out my wallet to pay for mine.

"No, it's on me."

"Are you sure?"

"Yes."

"Thank you very much."

As I said those last words, my heart was beating so fast that I was sure if I took the effort to say anything more, I might need cardiac resuscitation. Being among the first into the theater, we had our choice of seats, and he insisted on me deciding. I generally prefer the seats on the aisle and toward the back because then if I need to pee, I can get out and back quickly. I told him that and then practically melted at the smile and laugh he gave me, which were followed with what was obviously his trademark: "That's great." I wondered if there was anything in the world that was not "great" to this man.

I slipped off my jacket, and he said, "You have tattoos."

I realized that I had not removed my jacket during our tour of the museum, so this was the first chance he had of seeing them.

"Are they just on your arms?"

"No. Chest, back, legs, and butt."

The uninitiated who asks
About another person's tattoos
Expects to hear arms, chest, back, legs, butt.
Yet if you should add cock, you would shock.

No sooner had the movie started than I became acutely aware of not being sure what to do with my damn left arm. Every time I went to rest it on the armrest, his arm was there, which I knew would merely encourage me to get stiff once again. However, keeping my hand in my lap did the same thing. I think the only other time I had found myself in this predicament was when I was nineteen. A guy from college had invited me to a movie, and I hadn't been absolutely sure he was gay. It had turned out he was, and after the movie, we'd ended up having wild sex. But then, he hadn't had a wife.

The arm problem, of course, was resolved only with the end of the movie, and because of that problem I had not paid a lot of attention to much of what was going on screenwise. So when Jonathan asked me what I thought of the movie, I was unsure of what to say. I knew that it ended with the main character happily alive and in the loving arms of his sweetheart and that there was a lot of carnage in it. But beyond that, all that I could really tell him was the part that was the most offensive to me. At different points in the film people on both sides evoked God in support of their cause. I found that sickening. So I simply told Jonathan that I thought the movie as a whole was good but that I had problems with that God part.

"Yes, I see what you mean. I missed the full absurdity of that. Thanks for pointing that out to me."

It's actually not that I'm totally opposed to a belief in God. I'm just completely turned off to the biblical kind of belief. Instead, for a long time I've thought of myself as a dedicated pantheist in the sense that God is everything in nature and everything in nature is God.

I see God in my lover's eyes,
In rainbows and moonlight.
I hear him in my lover's voice,
In thunder and songbirds.
I smell him in my lover's sweat,
In flowers and moist earth.
I taste him in my lover's lips,
In good food and grief's tears.
I feel him in my lover's arms,
In warm days and cool nights.
I know God through my senses,
As pleasure and as pain.
God is no ascetic spirit;
He is the love of life.

Jonathan asked me if I'd like to go for coffee. I told him that after the popcorn and Cokes he'd insisted on buying both of us, I was too full for anything more. I hoped that would bring closure to the afternoon, and then we could go our separate ways.

"Oh, sure."

He said that with such a decidedly sad intonation that I couldn't help but wish I had not put a damper on his coffee idea. So I quickly sought to repair the damage.

"But that doesn't mean we can't go and get you a cup."

"Great! There's a café right down the street."

So off we went.

We got seated in a booth, and he ordered coffee and pie, while I ordered just pie and only because I was taking up a seat. Movie talk went on until our order arrived. He finished the pie quickly and then dropped the bomb that metaphorically blew me to the other side of the café.

"My wife, Ruth, and I"—this was the first time he had actually named her—"would like to invite you to dinner."

I must have momentarily stared at him as if he had just announced, in a totally believable way, that the world was coming to end. Then I asked what must have been an obviously suspect question.

"She knows about me?"

"I've told her all about you—how we met, how you so beautifully stood up for yourself, my embarrassment at laughing at that stupid joke, how you were kind enough to accept my apology, and about the really great book you are writing and what a great time we had at the museum."

Maybe to get out of this I could reverse my "I don't eat breakfast" to "I don't eat dinner," but then he might suggest lunch. What was I supposed to say? This guy didn't seem to have a clue as to what I was going through. That alone screamed straight. Moreover, not even the dumbest closet case would tell his wife he was hanging around with an openly gay man. But was the wife, this Ruth, as naive as her husband? Was she trying to check out my possible corrupting influence?

This turn of events left me speechless long enough for him to question my verbal paralysis.

"Is everything okay?"

I came to my senses, or did I? "Fine."

"So what about dinner?"

"I'm a vegetarian."

"Oh, I don't think that's a problem. Ruth can cook anything."

My options were limited: yes, no, maybe sometime in the far future.

He didn't wait for any of those. "Would tomorrow evening be too soon?"

That he was suggesting it that soon practically gave me a case of lockjaw, and I thought to make some excuse. Perhaps I was scheduled for major surgery tomorrow. But then I realized that unless I totally brushed him off, he was just going to come up with another day. If I had to face purgatory for the want of my pecker, then at least I might as well get it over with as soon as possible. "That's fine."

"Great."

That word almost made me want to grab him and yell, *Stop! Stop! No more with the greats! It's not great. It's a disaster.*

The waitress came by wanting to know if we were ready for the check. I was, but it was clear Jonathan wasn't. He ordered another piece of pie. He then proceeded to tell me about his marriage. He started by saying that the two of them had recently sold their house and moved to a condominium because they had been offered a really good price for it and no longer needed as much space, since their daughter, Esther, had gotten married immediately after she'd finished college. Here was a new revelation—a daughter.

Jonathan explained that he and Ruth had not yet made any real friends in the new place and so would be delighted to have company over for dinner. At first, I thought that I wasn't really interested in his marital life, but then I figured if I had to do this dinner, I better find out as much as I could about it. Foreknowledge can offer protection.

> Once a wife takes care of procreation,
> Perhaps less need for her approbation.
> So less interest in such affection
> Suggests he seek male connection
> That will save him from mere masturbation.

I asked him how old his daughter was, and he said twenty-three. He then said that he would have preferred it if she had waited a little longer before marrying, because he didn't want her to end up with any of the problems that he and Ruth had gone through when they'd married immediately after college. Both of them had been working full-time jobs while trying to get their master's degrees, but Ruth had gotten pregnant a year later and had had to first quit school and then work. Ruth's pregnancy had not gone well, and although Esther had been born perfectly healthy, the doctor had said that it was not likely that Ruth could have more children.

Nonetheless, Ruth had gotten pregnant again about two years later, but in her last trimester there had been serious problems. Their son, Daniel, had been prematurely born dead. I could tell from Jonathan's voice and change of expression that even now he was still experiencing grief over his son's death, and for the first time it was my heart and not my hard-on I wanted to offer him. I reached over the table and put my hand on his.

"I'm sorry."

"Thank you."

He made absolutely no attempt to pull his hand away, but I was feeling uncomfortable with it there, I guess because I had previously figured that there would be a sexual significance to the first time I might put my hands on him in any way, and this was not the time for anything like that. His second order of pie arrived, and now it was I who didn't want the conversation to end, so I ordered another piece of pie. Jonathan offered me his piece of apple pie, but I said that I would rather have blueberry.

Jonathan said the stress of working full-time and trying to go to school part-time for the first three months of her pregnancy had probably contributed to Ruth's problems with Esther's birth and ultimately the death of their son. That was one reason he was opposed to his daughter getting married so soon after college, since both she and her husband, Frank, also had to work full-time to make ends meet. To my question of what Frank did for a living, Jonathan said he was a medical intern and that as such he was required to still go to school.

I asked why they had let their daughter go the same route they had gone, considering what they had gone through. He explained that with the death of their son, Ruth had tried to be the very best possible mother she could for her daughter, which had included taking a teaching position at the private Jewish elementary school that Esther had eventually attended, a job Ruth still held. *Jewish*, I thought. *Yes, Jonathan, Ruth, Esther, and Daniel are all Old Testament names. In front of me is kosher candy.* Jonathan went on to say that as a result of Ruth's overmothering, their daughter was so spoiled that by her teens she had been barely tolerable to live with. Overmothering was also the reason Esther was far closer to her mother than her father. It turned out that almost all the arguments he and Ruth had were over the spoiling of their daughter.

I couldn't help saying that I thought he and Ruth must love each other very much for their marriage to have survived so long despite whatever differences they had over Esther's upbringing. He said that ever since they'd met in their first year of college, he had never wanted any woman other than Ruth and he was sure she felt the same about him. Jonathan further volunteered that they had gone through a lot together in the past twenty-five years and that he would be devastated if he should lose her. I couldn't help thinking that the most I had been able to sustain a relationship had been a month short of two years. After that breakup I'd fantasized becoming a celibate.

> Sex is just pure agony,
> Torture to the touch.
> It's a vicious joke that's played
> By my foolish mind.
> So from it, I will refrain,
> Just a saint to remain.
> This I'll do, at least until
> I need the pain again.

My pie had arrived, and Jonathan had not eaten his second piece, so the conversation broke up while we both stuffed down the pie. It was clear that we couldn't continue to order more pie, and besides, we had spent enough time in the café; it was time to leave. I insisted on paying the bill, and we left. He asked me where I'd parked my car and then refused to accept that he didn't need to walk me to it. When we got there, he offered his hand, which I took, but then I took the chance of asking him if he would be offended if I gave him a hug. His smile said certainly not, and he met my hug with one of his own. I didn't want to let go, but I also didn't want him to feel obligated to hold on, so with a thank-you I released him, and again he smiled.

"Thank you," he said as he backed away. "See you tomorrow evening."

I had to thank whatever wits I still had about me, because he was already some yards from me when I called out to get the address and the time. He slapped his forehead in the way we all do when we realize how dumb we are to forget something like that. He came back, pulled out his wallet, and retrieved a business card that had his home phone number on it, and on the back he wrote his address and the time.

"Do you know your way around the Marina?"

"More or less. I had a friend who used to live there."

"Great! Then we'll see you tomorrow." He gave me another hug, and as he headed for his car, I stood at mine watching him, especially his tight ass, walk away, leaving me with a rise in my Levi's.

As I was driving home, I did some math in my head. He'd said that his daughter was twenty-three; that he had married right out of college, which would have made him about twenty-two; and that his wife had become pregnant about a year later—all of that added up to him being about forty-seven. He'd also said that two years after his daughter's birth Ruth had gotten pregnant with their son. This would have made the son about twenty if he had lived. Here was a man who no longer had a child to be responsible for, who had recently let go of his family home, who was at that age for a midlife crisis, and who still mourned his dead son to some degree.

Was that what all this attention toward me was about, finding a surrogate son? I am a thirty-three-year-old man, not a twenty-year-old. My beard! Would his son have had a beard like him, a beard like mine? If this was the situation, what was I to do now? It wasn't that I was not attracted to daddy types, but the things I wanted to do with this daddy were not what a real daddy and son were supposed to do with each other.

For the first time since meeting Jonathan, I perceived him as other than a sex object, and that made me cry a little. Was it because I was ashamed of earlier having turned him into that? Or was it because I sensed there was an emptiness inside of him that I didn't think I could fill, as much as I might like to. But then I took some comfort in the fact that he loved and had the love of Ruth, who could compensate for his sadness.

By the time I got home I was again regretting getting further involved in Jonathan's life, this time through meeting his wife. All he knew about me was what he could see on the surface. Gay he may have had no problem with, but my sadomasochistic side he would find less inviting. How would he have reacted if I had told him about being part of a punishment club or my mummy trip?

Chapter 5

We called the punishment club Dungeon de Sade. It had been founded by four of us, and it met once a month. It always had ten to fifteen men participating as either sadistic tops or masochistic bottoms, although some of us would change roles during the night. Each month one of the participants was charged with thinking up a villainous theme, such as animal play, gladiators, prisoners, vampires, Inquisitional rebellion, and especially mummification.

> Some call it a sick passion,
> But I, healthy release.
> Some name it repressed hatred,
> But I, a sharing love.
> Some declare it is from hell,
> But I to heaven go.
> No matter that some condemn;
> I alone the real truth know.

Dungeon de Sade, unfortunately, only functioned for a little over a year because the site we were using was sold and we couldn't find a suitable replacement that would be friendly to our activity. Yes, our activity. I doubt that Jonathan would be too friendly to it either.

To those not in the know
Judgment can be quick,
Condemned as a pervert
Or as simply sick.

While the club introduced me to the mummy scene, this was expanded upon in private by a pair of experts, Neil and Alan, who took me to a whole new level of leather play. This was mummification sans sex; in short, cocooning. As in regular mummification play, my naked body was bandaged in plastic wrap and duct tape but this time covering even my dick so that only my nostrils and mouth were exposed.

Neil warned me that the extreme sensory deprivation could cause me to enter completely into an inner mindscape. At its safest this meant indulging in inner fantasies, but it could also lead to a less safe hallucinatory meeting with my personal inner gods and demons. Neil was right. As my sweat built up, it became a kind of atavistic amniotic fluid, which in the restraint environment of the cocoon made me regress to a kind of life in the womb. In fact, I started to imagine a maternal heartbeat, which I found out afterward was caused by Neil playing a drumming CD. Without question, he had turned me into a hallucinating adult fetus.

Neil also warned me that I might panic as some do, but I didn't, because of the trust I had in Neil and Alan, who had promised that they would uncocoon me at the slightest sign of distress. I soon lost any sense of time as I began to meet both the gruesome and captivating creatures in my mind. The result was both a frightening and yet thrilling experience.

There is a means which you can use
To enter your own mind.
It is a process while alive
That makes of you a tomb.
You are cocooned in bandages

Like some Egyptian corpse.
But soon life's heat, as well as sweat,
Returns you to the womb.
Yet be forewarned of fear that's real,
For ghouls may nest within.
These all peace of mind can steal,
Which can cause deadly gloom.
The price for insight is risky,
But some think not too much,
For this inner sanctum is
Where your gods you may touch.

◆◆◆◆◆◆

When Monday morning arrived, I couldn't stop thinking of Jonathan. I wanted to see him again. I made the excuse to myself that this was only in the hopes that he was not as melancholy as I believed he had been when I'd left him last. However, I still wasn't happy about meeting Ruth.

Since I knew only the little that Jonathan had specifically told me about himself, I decided to see if I could locate some professional information about him on the Internet. I put his name into several search engines and came up with quite a few articles he had written. It was clear that he was not only a good writer but a sought after one.

Five o'clock came, and there was the issue of what to wear for dinner. I thought perhaps elegant casual. But once I was dressed, I decided it didn't look right. I was dressed as if I were someone Ruth already knew and was comfortable with. It would have been fine if Jonathan and I were having dinner alone, but we weren't. Besides, a too-relaxed look might show a kind of threatening confidence in myself with regard to Ruth. I decided on a more formal look, a blue-gray business suit, white shirt, and dark blue tie. I figured better overdressed and nonthreatening than underdressed and threatening.

Following Jonathan's instructions, I found his condominium complex and a nearby parking space. The complex had a security gate, so I had to look up Miller in the directory and dial the number. It was Jonathan who answered. He buzzed me in and told me to wait in the lobby, saying he would be right down. Perhaps it was my imagination, but the buzzer on the gate sounded to me like the buzzing of one of the chainsaws in horror movies like *The Texas Chainsaw Massacre.* I was hoping that this was not a foretaste of what was to come.

Jonathan arrived in the lobby dressed in elegant-casual attire. Smiling, he grabbed my hand and shook it vigorously. He commented on how good I looked and made the standard polite inquiries about having any trouble finding the place, traffic, and how my day was going. He then said that the maze of hallways could be confusing to a first-timer, and I immediately had the thought that I wasn't intending to ever be a second-timer.

He ushered me into their unit, and from the stairs on the left side of the living room wall I could tell it was a duplex. The living room was large. There was a separate dining area with a large table and chairs. The kitchen was out of sight, but I presumed it was of a suitable size to match the rest of the area. The size of the area downstairs suggested that there were either two large bedrooms or one large and two small bedrooms upstairs.

Ruth then appeared from the kitchen with a polite smile, offering her hand to me while Jonathan introduced us to each other. Ruth was also dressed in elegant casual—black silk pants and a sleeveless black tunic-like top. She invited me to sit down on the couch while she sat on a large upholstered armchair across from me. Jonathan asked if I wanted anything to drink, and I answered no. I didn't want him leaving me alone with her. Besides, I really had to pee, so I asked if I could use the restroom.

All that Jonathan needed to do was to point to the door of the guest bathroom under the staircase. Instead, he walked me to it and opened the door for me. I felt like saying, *Thank you, Daddy*, but I didn't. I was so nervous that I forgot to pick up the lower lid and peed on it. I wiped it off, flushed the toilet, and returned to my assigned seat. Jonathan, thank Moses, was also sitting on the couch but with enough space between us to offer no logical protest from Ruth, who then explained that dinner would be ready soon.

As silly as it sounds, I was glad that there was a coffee table between Ruth and me because I thought that if she suddenly launched an attack, the table would slow her down long enough for me to reach the front door. But in that maze of hallways, which she knew and I didn't, I could get trapped at a dead end. I hoped she didn't think that my downcast eyes meant shyness, because they didn't. I was focusing on the length of her fingernails as potential weapons.

Ruth got up and suggested that Jonathan should show me the rest of the place while she checked on the dinner. He naturally replied with a "Great." We went upstairs, and my second guess was right, one large bedroom and two smaller ones. The first one he showed me was clearly the master bedroom, and although it had obviously been decorated to a woman's taste, it was not overly feminine. Ruth definitely had not taken lessons from Mr. I Like It Rough.

The second bedroom had been turned into a workroom for Jonathan: two computers, bookshelves with lots of books on them, and papers everywhere. The third room had been carefully set up as a unisex guest bedroom with nothing either too feminine or too masculine about it. There was a medium-size bathroom nestled between the two smaller bedrooms that Jonathan barely let me see.

Instead, he was intent on taking me through their bedroom to the master bathroom, where he suggested that we both wash our hands for dinner at the his-and-her sinks. After handing me a bar of soap, he pulled up his sleeves to wash. I tried to clean away my erotic feelings for him by focusing on the soap, but it didn't work.

My poetry's erotic;
It loves handcuffs and rope.
To some it's pornographic,
My mind in need of soap.

77

I had learned all about Jewish ritualized cleanliness some four years ago, while I was a goy visiting one of the local gay synagogues. I hadn't gone for religious reasons but because there had seemed to be a greater concentration of bearded men there than any place other than at a bear night sponsored by the Bear's Club. I had made out fairly well in the synagogue, but after a few months I'd stopped, maybe out of a sense of being disrespectful, not to Yahweh, but to the people there who had a right to have their faith in God respected, even if that faith did include Leviticus 18:22 and 20:13 and the teaching that a man who has intercourse with a man as with a woman should be put to death. The fact was I had never had intercourse with a man as with a woman but only as a man with a man.

> I am an incubus,
> Philander is my name.
> Unlike most of my kin
> No woman need fear me.
> I'm lover of but men
> And seek just them to bed.
> As sweet dream or nightmare
> I'm Satan sodomy.
> I insert and receive
> My horn and hole for these.
> If you need my service,
> Just chant my sacred hymn:
> "Hail, my dear Philander,
> Merciful incubus.
> Give me a sodomite
> To satisfy my night."

Cleanliness aside, Jonathan and Ruth were obviously not Orthodox, not in the way either of them dressed, and I even doubted whether they were Conservatives. This left nothing else but Reformed as far as I knew. After our purification ritual, we went back downstairs, and dinner was on the table. Thankfully we didn't start with a prayer, and I didn't see anything on the table that looked like two sets of dishes, kosher style. I was given the seat at the end of the table with Jonathan on one side of me and Ruth on the other, opposite him.

At first, I didn't like this arrangement, since I was still paranoid enough to feel it gave her direct access to me, and there were knives on the table. After a few minutes, I changed my mind, as a different seating might have forced me into constant direct eye contact with her, which had been the case in the living room.

Ruth opened the table conversation. "So Jonathan tells me you're a teacher and are writing a book."

"Yes."

"That must keep you fairly busy."

I really would have liked to answer her with something like *Not busy enough that I wouldn't have time to play with your husband's suck-and-fuck pole.* But I have been sufficiently socialized to the niceties of polite society that instead I answered more appropriately. "Between my job and my writing I'm kept pretty busy."

Jonathan began asking about the book, and as I gave him details, he never took his eyes off me. I kept watching Ruth's reaction from the corner of my eye, especially the way her gaze went back and forth between Jonathan and me, as if she was carefully trying to evaluate Jonathan's interest in me and vice versa.

I thought that I might have captured her husband's attention more than enough as far as she was concerned, so I deliberately turned away from him and politely smiled at her. That gave her the opening she needed.

"What about your family? I understand your mother lives in the East?"

This subject is almost always one that women are more interested in than men.

"Yes. She lives in Boston."

"Do you have any brothers or sisters?"

"No, I am an only child."

Since she'd mentioned only my mother and not my father, I assumed Jonathan had told her he was dead. Most people don't feel that they have the right to grill you about deaths in your family the first time they meet you, so she focused on my mother.

"Your mother must miss not having you live closer to her."

This was also not an unanticipated question, since most mothers do prefer to have their children close by and presumably Ruth would prefer to have Esther closer than San Francisco. But I wondered if her question didn't entail something more, like *Why don't you go back to your mother and leave my husband alone?*

> Perhaps a testy wife
> Who with a verbal knife
> Would cut me from his life.

I was hoping my answer would get us off the subject of family. "My mother lives very near to her sister, so she doesn't miss me as much as she might if she lived elsewhere."

My hope was dashed.

"Yes, but a sister is not the same as having your own child nearby."

Clearly, Ruth's motherly approach was not to be easily avoided. At that point, I figured that maybe the only way to get out of this topic was to make her feel slightly embarrassed by her curiosity.

"My mother misses me, and sometimes I miss her, but we didn't have the best of relationships as I was growing up. I suppose trying to cope with raising a child by herself contributed to her alcohol problem. She has stopped drinking now, partly because of support from her sister and partly because I threatened never to talk to or visit her again if she didn't find help."

"Yes, of course," a now slightly self-conscious Ruth said, ending her nosiness.

Unfortunately, the husband was like the wife in wanting to know personal details and not being particularly embarrassed to ask them. But then I remembered how open Jonathan had been with me, a relative stranger, in talking about Ruth's pregnancy problems and the death of their son. Nonetheless, I would have preferred that he ask me the next question in private and not in front of his wife.

"I know a lot of parents can be unsupportive when they discover that their child is gay. How was it with your mother?"

I appreciated the way he phrased the question with the word *unsupportive* rather than something like *a problem with*. The first put any onus on the parents, while the second could apply to either parents or child.

"I came out toward the end of my first year in college. When I told my mother, she said that she had suspected it for years since I had no interest in sports and was very bookish."

> I remember that very queer day
> That I saw men in a different way.
> I had known how to fuck
> But then learned how to suck,
> And since then I have known I was gay.

This personal revelation seemed to make Ruth a little bit more at ease with me, but it was hard to be sure. Anyhow, what I didn't say to Ruth was that there are some sports I have a deep interest in.

> I have no interest in footballs
> And even less in baseballs,
> But because of this do not think
> I do not play games with balls.

Dinner was fine: vegetarian lasagna, carrots, wine. Once we had finished eating, Ruth suggested that we retire to the living room for dessert and coffee. Jonathan and I sat in the same places as before, only this time he was closer. Ruth brought out a tray with a coffeepot, cups, cream and sugar, and three pieces of blueberry pie, which had probably been bought just earlier in the day. As we finished the pie, Jonathan picked up the conversation.

"I've discussed this with Ruth, and I'd like to see if you'd be interested in helping me. In all the years that I've been writing journal articles, I have never written one about the gay community, how that community has had to fight for its civil rights and what that has entailed. I got the idea to do something like this after seeing how you stood up for yourself."

I was dumbfounded. This was what all his attention to me was about? I was to be a useful informant for an article on the faggot community. I suddenly remembered that Jonathan had stated he was attending the workshops to make new contacts for possible future articles. I wanted to tell him he was nothing but a prick tease, and I would have if Ruth hadn't been there.

Instead, I offered the excuse that I had to use as much of the summer as possible to work on my book and would have almost no time to be of much help. He said that he would need only a few hours to talk and be shown around some of the major places gay people socialize, such as the Gay and Lesbian Center and some gay churches that he had heard about. He wanted to get a feel for the variety in the gay community.

> Tall men, short men, fat men, thin
> Are a great delight as my faggot kin.
> Oral, anal, hand jobs too—
> The Bible says each is a sin,
> But that's God's loss and my win.

I told him that I didn't really attend either of those places (with regard to the center that was a lie) and would be useless if he wanted an introduction to them. I said that even though I didn't drink, I socialized with most of my friends in a couple of bars on weekend evenings. It was my bad luck that this didn't discourage him.

"Well, that's a start. If you could take me with you and explain to those friends what I'm doing, they might be willing to be interviewed at their convenience."

I wanted to get out of there so badly that I agreed.

"Great" was the miserable word I heard, followed by "Which is better—Friday or Saturday night?"

Not thinking too well, I automatically blurted out Saturday. He wanted to know if we could start this coming Saturday, July 29, to which I gave a desperate "Yes." I made a big thing about looking at my watch and announced that I had better get home because I had lots of things I needed to do the next day. The two of them got up and escorted me to the door. I reluctantly shook both their hands and resented Jonathan putting his other hand on my shoulder.

Jonathan guided me once more through the hall to the lobby and then had the audacity to ask if he could give me a hug. I remained silent, but he took that as a yes. I put my hands around him and pretended to hug him, feeling more like giving him a good punch, and on release, I walked away as quickly as possible while also trying not to look as desperate as I was.

Reason caught up with me but only for a moment. I asked myself why I was getting so emotional about this whole deal, and then the truth slapped reason right in the face. In the past couple of weeks a simple lust for Jonathan had turned to love. I felt not only intellectually used but emotionally abused. I felt wounded. And now the beauty of love had turned to its ugly opposite, and I wanted to wound back.

How easily love can turn to hatred
When what was beautiful has been betrayed.
And though revenge may be God's right alone,
Few people wait for that doubtful promise.
And so it will be with a careful plan
That I will punish that bear of a man.

I headed for home as fast as I could, almost fast enough to get a ticket if a cop had been around. Once I got about halfway, I pulled into a parking space and totally lost it in tears. I was thankful that it was dark and neither passing pedestrians nor car passengers could see me too closely. Within fifteen to twenty minutes I began to compose myself and form a plot.

He wanted to use me to enter the gay world; I would be pleased to do so. I would show him a side of the gay community and my participation on that side that he hadn't the foggiest idea about. I would take his so-called admiration for me and shove it down his betraying throat so he could choke on it. I would do this in two stages—first with the Texas Inc. and second with the Stag. When I finished with him, he would know the real me, and if he wanted to write an article on that, then he could do so.

Daytime is dry color
In contrast to the night.
The warm boring sunshine
Gives way to moonlight's thirst.
No more need to suppress
Our violent urges.
Just act like a beast,
Compulsive want to mate.
Desire to be cruel
To partner and to self.
Abandon everything
To some exquisite pain,
While holding back nothing
For carnal loss of self.
Lick the sweat, tongue the cum,
To all else, act as dumb.

Chapter 6

Monday ... What happened then? I tried staying in bed as long as I could the next morning, tried writing, tried reading, tried listening to music, but all of these were useless as a calming diversion.

Thankfully by Tuesday, I had calmed down enough to get back to some work on the book. However, Jonathan was still there in the back of my mind, but not as what I might once have thought of him.

> To make men into gods is not enough,
> For such flesh is far beyond the divine.
> It is of love that so transcends all else
> As to be the beginning and the end.
> It is true this very elevation
> Comes with the price of sad mortality,
> But is this not far better than no death
> In some realm where lust has been abolished?
> To speak of lips, tongue, nipples, and armpits,
> Of cock and balls, buttocks and an asshole—
> How real are these compared to some sky ghost
> Who is imagined as a neutered male?
> Show me a being with a pair of arms
> That can embrace this body night or day
> And into my ear whisper of pleasures
> Reaching such a level as to be pain.
> This and only this to me is heaven
> Even if it also must be my hell.

Trying to work on my book and plotting my revenge on Jonathan at the same time was exhausting, and by Thursday I decided I needed some relief, both emotional and physical, especially the latter. That meant handling some hard candy other than my own. I thought I would check out the Texas in preparation for Jonathan's introduction to that part of the gay ghetto on Saturday night.

I was in the bar for less than thirty minutes when a guy showed interest in me. He was a good ten years older than I, and although the harness he was wearing signaled top, intuition told me he was a bottom.

This was soon confirmed as he approached me with a "Good evening, sir!"

The fact that he said, "sir" despite the fact that I was in a bottom harness told me that he was unfamiliar with the harness code and decided that I wouldn't even touch him if he pushed for being a top, so I simply said, "Good evening."

His smile told me that I could make him dump any pretense at topping. Vanilla tops have more freedom to smile than leather ones do, and if he had been a real leather top, he would not have smiled before he had gained dominance over me.

I decided to push the issue, asking, "What's your interest tonight, boy?"

"I like bondage, sir!"

I was right—bottom, 100 percent. Still, the fact that he'd come right out and said what he was interested in impressed me. Some guys are afraid to admit that they're looking for something other than the usual sucking and fucking or at least something in addition to that. In those cases, they either take forever to tell you their wants, or worse, they surprise you with them once home.

Elaborately tying someone up is not one of my preferences. Also, since such play should always have a third party present, for an emergency reason, I was reluctant to go any further with this guy. However, there was his smile, which was kind of adorable and made me not want to disappoint him or make him feel rejected. I decided to negotiate.

"That's fine, but what about sucking and fucking?"

"Yes. Of course, sir."

"My place all right?"

"Absolutely, sir!"

He followed me in his car, and luckily there was a parking space about a block away. I waited while he took it. He grabbed a duffel bag out of his truck, and as he got into the passenger side of my car, I could hear the sound of chain clanging from the bag. I hadn't inquired exactly what kind of bondage he was into; I had just assumed ropes—my mistake.

No sooner had the guy walked in the door than he dumped his bag on the floor and began to take off his shoes.

"What are you doing?" I asked.

Naturally, he seemed surprised by the obvious until I made things unconditionally clear. "You come into the space of a top and think you have the right to dump your stuff on his floor and begin to undress before you're given permission?"

"Sorry, sir!"

"What kind of guys are you used to playing with, boy?"

He obviously didn't know how to answer that question, and I had definitely put him into a state of stress. My role as top—no, dom—was cemented.

"You put the shoe back on, pick up your stuff, and stand there until I tell you otherwise, or you get your rude bottom out of here."

He obeyed.

> One must establish right away
> Who is the one to obey.
> In vanilla there is leeway
> But not in the game I play.

"Now, boy, you may put down the bag." He did, this time not as a dump but carefully, as if any sound might offend me.

When I'm playing the dom, I usually like to determine when and how much the bottom, or in his case the sub, should strip. I started out simply, saying, "The shoes, and don't just toss them on my floor. Arrange them neatly together. Then the pants."

He obeyed. As soon as he pulled his pants down, I had to do everything in my power not to laugh hysterically—white-and-purple paisley boxers.

Pants off, he waited.

"Now the shorts."

He was wearing a cock ring, a metal one.

"Now we have a problem, boy. A serious problem."

"Sir?"

"What do you think that thing you're wearing *over the shirt* is, *boy?*"

He looked down and said, in a clearly intimidated voice, "A harness."

"*I know that, boy,* but what *kind* of harness?"

His look at me showed he had no idea what I was asking about. It was time to educate this Texas pickup. I decided to label him Texas Trash.

"You're standing here, boy, half-naked like a bottom before someone you came home with as your top, and yet you are wearing a *top harness.* To add insult to injury, you are wearing it *over* your shirt instead of right next to your skin. Take it off."

I had him so nervous now that he had trouble unbuckling the damn thing, and I had to take over.

"Now the shirt."

He obeyed.

"Follow me, boy."

"My bag, sir!"

"You don't need that yet."

I suspect he thought I was leading him into the bedroom, so when it turned out to be the bathroom, he just stared at me as if to say, *Why here?*

"Get in the tub."

"Why, sir?"

"You don't ask a top that. You just do it, boy."

"Yes, sir!"

I unzipped, pulled out my dick, and sprayed him from his pecs to his pecker. He didn't protest, and I asked him, "How did that feel?"

"Warm."

> Golden stream of body heat,
> Water falling on his meat.
> Divine humiliation this,
> To be covered with my piss.

I turned on the shower and let him clean off. Then I handed him a towel, led him back to the living room, and said, "Now, let's see what's in your bag." He bent down, unzipped it, and pushed it all the way open for me to see. I looked in and said, "Take everything out."

Out came enough chain to go around him at least four times plus clothespins, alligator clips, heavy and thin rope, candles and a lighter, weights, and—thank heaven—a bolt cutter. This guy at least had the good sense to have this last item on hand for an emergency. Without a word I pointed to the only wooden chair in my living room (a rocker), and he headed right to it.

I took off my jacket and asked if he wanted anything to drink, saying I only had nonalcoholic beverages. He wanted nothing, at least nothing to drink. He was most assuredly in a hurry to get started, so I picked up and fondled the chain, trying my best to tease him. From the way his tongue caressed his lips, I knew I was succeeding. I said, "Don't move from there, and I don't want to hear a word out of your mouth unless it is to answer a question." To intensify the tease I held the chain just out of his reach. His lust to be touched by it grew to near desperation. Still I refused to give into his clear craving to commune with the chain, bringing him to tears of frustration. Such is the way of salacious sadism.

"Please, sir! The chains."

I didn't like the way he'd indicated his desire and told him so. "It's not 'Please, sir! The chains.' It's 'Sir! If it would please you to chain me, I would be honored.'"

"Sorry, sir!"

I waited. It took him nearly a minute to realize that I expected him to repeat my words or something damn close to them. Finally, he said, "Sir! If it would please you, I would be happy to be chained." Clearly, he had gotten only half the message right in that his "I would be happy" was all about him, while "I would be honored" was about me as the top.

I decided not to push this communication issue any further, and in a tone that demonstrated my dissatisfaction, I said, "That's a little better." I draped part of the chain over him, and his mouth opened to release what must have been a long-held breath. This was the first inkling that he was coming alive with sexual pleasure. As I completed three circles of chains around his body and the back of the chair, I realized there was nothing to secure one part of the chain to the other. Perhaps he expected me just to circle the chain around and leave it at that. To make sure I asked, "Lock, key?"

"Oh! Yes, sir! They must still be in the bag. Sorry."

Letting the chain just drop into his lap, I went over, reached into the bag, and found the lock and key in a plastic sandwich bag. There was two or so feet of loose chain left, so I wound it loosely around his neck, collar style, and locked it. His smile showed his appreciation.

Place a chain around his neck;
Secure with a strong lock.
Then speak of love's slavery
And how he might serve my cock.

I almost asked him if he didn't find the coldness of the chains on his otherwise warm body uncomfortable, as I would have in his situation. I hate the cold and would have screamed had the cold chains been on my body. However, the expression of delight on his face as soon as the chain had touched him told me we lived in different mental temperatures.

Cold chains encircling him
Like some caressing python:
Erotic captivity.

Texas Trash was now securely immobilized, and I wondered if he realized how vulnerable this made him to anything that I might have in my dutifully depraved sadomasochistic mind. But this boy's toys on my floor told me that he didn't want me to leave him sitting there like a sculptured artwork, so I had to think fast. If he had not been attached to the chain, my first inclination would have been to shove my cream stick into his mouth and make him suck me for a while, but cold steel near my member does nothing for me.

We had not exchanged names before or since leaving the Texas Inc. I thought such an exchange now might be detrimental to the nature of this scene, so I said, "Boy! I don't know your name, and I don't care what it is. As long as you're here, you will be Texas Trash. Understand?"

"Yes, sir!"

"So, Trash, what kind of play do you think would please me now?"

"Sir," he said with a slight whine in his voice, "have you ever done things to cock and balls?"

Displeased by the possible suggestion that I might be an amateur, I said in an angry voice, "I'm a gay man. Everything I do is with cock and balls."

"Sorry, sir! I didn't mean to offend."

Of course, despite my deliberate outburst, I knew that his question was not about my general sexual experience but was a cautious inquiry into whether I had ever done cock-and-ball torture. With a disgusted look on my face I took inventory from the items on the floor: clothespins, alligator clips, heavy and thin rope, candles and a lighter, and weights.

I figured it was rather foolish of this boy not to have mentioned his cock-and-ball interest in the bar. If I had been an amateur at such play, he could have ended up coming out of this with a damaged dick and bruised balls. For his failure to mention it I figured I had the right to teach him a lesson he wouldn't forget. I looked again at the objects he had brought and realized he was expecting a lot of effort on my part to satisfy him. Not only had I not bargained for the chains, I hadn't for this either. I suddenly lost interest in all the work it would take to do a really good torture scene. The problem was how to get out of giving him what he wanted without just telling him I wasn't in the mood anymore.

An idea came to me. I went into the kitchen and brought out a small carving board, a lightweight hammer, and three thin nails. I spread them out on the floor for Trash to see.

"What are those for?"

"Patience."

> Beware the brutal bottom
> As a terrifying top—
> The getter as the giver
> Of raw pleasure and raw pain.

I then went to the bathroom and brought back a bottle of alcohol. To my surprise the guy at first said nothing. I think he was in a mild state of shock. He just looked at everything with that horrified expression and finally asked, "Sir, what are those for?"

"Boy, you told me you were into c-and-b torture, didn't you?"

"Yes, but ..."

"What do you mean, yes, but? It's 'Yes, but, sir!'"

"Yes, but, sir! But what are those for?" The high pitch of his voice implied he was getting scared.

"Well, boy, I thought that if you were really into c-and-b torture, I would sterilize one or more of these nails and secure your scrotum to this board. Wouldn't you like that?"

"No! I mean no, sir! I mean that's not what I meant."

The poor boy was clearly becoming incoherent with fear at the thought of what I was offering him, and since (a) I wasn't really into terror-torture play and (b) I didn't want him to have a heart attack, I decided to show benevolence.

"Boy, I know there are tops who will play with all those items you brought with you, but for me those are not for serious players. If you're not up to what I have to offer, you had better rethink what you're asking for."

> There are many diverse ways
> To torture the cock and balls,
> But nothing will be better
> If fear makes him a sweater.

"Right, sir! I think I've had enough."

"Are you sure?"

"Yes, sir!"

"Does that mean you want out of the chain?"

"Yes, sir!"

"Okay."

I unlocked the chain and made him wiggle out of it. Without even asking permission, he dressed and packed up his toys, though he didn't touch the harness. Perhaps he thought that would have made me mad. Still, it was his property, and although I was pretty sure he would not mistakenly wear it again, I asked, "What about this?"

"I don't need it, sir."

I smiled and said, "Good boy."

"Good-bye, sir!"

I opened the door with only my harness and boots on and said, "Boy, protocol requires that you should lick my boots before leaving."

While holding on to his toy bag as if it might suddenly be taken from him, he got down on all fours and worshipped my leather-covered feet with his tongue.

"Thank you. You're dismissed."

With a "Thank you, sir!" he left.

> Sir's boots are to be licked, either first or last.
> The first says, "I submit to a master's wish."
> The second says, "Thank you for your discipline."
> Clearly, the best slave displays double duties.

This Texas Trash incident might be something I could tell Jonathan about once I'd taken him to the Texas Inc. to see if it caused him to squirm. Whether I did so or not, one thing I was sure of was that when I took him to the Texas Inc., not to mention to the Stag, everyone would be too busy with their own agendas to give a damn about giving interviews to some straight guy who wanted to play urban anthropologist in a queer bar. After all, no matter how pro-gay Jonathan might be, he would arouse some suspicion. Trust does not come easily to those oppressed by straights.

> Oh! He wants to study us,
> Perhaps like a platypus.
> Are we such an oddity
> For such curiosity?
> His own business he should mind
> By staying with his own kind.

Chapter 7

Friday afternoon Jonathan called to finalize Saturday's meeting. Since parking was always a problem, I suggested we take only one car, and he agreed to meet me at my place at nine thirty. I gave him my address and directions. I told him that we were going to go to a cowboy bar. I said that he needed to dress appropriately and that what he'd worn at the museum would be fine. I also let him know that while it was not a requirement that he have boots and a cowboy hat, if he did, he could wear them. He ended the conversation with his standard "Great."

Naturally, on Saturday I had trouble concentrating on anything other than him up until he arrived that evening at nine fifteen. From past experience I had expected him to be early, so I was already dressed. My still ticked-off attitude aside, I thought he looked hot, especially with the boots and hat on. The museum T-shirt had been replaced with a standard cowboy dress shirt, the kind with the pearl snap buttons, and differed from my shirt only in color. Mine was black, while his was dark blue. I thought that if he threw a little dirt on those clothes, he could easily pass for a raunchy wrangler.

> Cowboys make this man hard,
> And just as stiff do bears.
> Both of these together—
> The answer to my prayers.

Jonathan commented on how good I looked, and I thanked him, returning the compliment. I suggested that we get going because I wanted to be at the bar before all the nearby parking was gone. When we got outside, he put on his hat and said that after our conversation the other day he had gone out and bought it. I smiled with some sincerity.

Before we got into the car, I warned him that once we parked if any guys in cars driving by should shout anything like "Faggots!" or even some real obscenities, he was to pretend that he didn't hear anything and just continue walking. I explained that if he should react hostilely and there was a bunch of them, they could stop and try to do more than shout at us, which was not the safest situation in which to decide you needed to defend either your masculine pride or heterosexuality.

He struck me as dangerously naive when he asked, "Does that really still happen?"

"Just because you are a tolerant person doesn't mean others are."

He started to lecture me on how terrible that was and how no one had the right to treat others that way. I said that he would get no argument from me about that but that homophobia was alive and well in this town like everywhere else.

Hatred does not cease because laws change
With tolerance as the trendy touch.
It stops only when people realize
That hatred is costing them too much.

"Remember the joke that first brought us together?"

"Yes, and I'm still ashamed that I laughed at it."

"You more than apologized, so leave it at that."

"More than" was only a half-truth. A full apology would have been him on his knees fellating this faggot's phallus.

"If you're too nervous about the possibility of such drive-by crap happening, we should cancel the whole evening, and you should simply go home."

"What will you do then?"

"I'll go to the bar either way."

"Then let's go."

I must admit that I was pleasantly surprised by his sudden unwillingness to be intimidated by the possibility of any homophobic encounter. However, I had by no means forgotten last Monday night. My wound was still open and hurting, and I still regarded tonight as but step one in my plan.

We got near to the bar, I found a reasonably close parking space, and we walked to the bar itself without incident, although Jonathan twitched at each passing car. It was ten thirty. The bar was two-thirds full and would reach capacity within a half hour. I let Jonathan stand at the door with this amazing look on his face as he reacted to the sight of several dozen men dancing together. About 50 to 60 percent were dressed in some degree of western wear. I bought two beers, giving one to Jonathan. I let him watch the dancing for about fifteen minutes before inviting him to dance. He made the excuse that he was not a very good dancer. I asked if he ever went dancing with Ruth, and he said that they used to but not recently and that when they did, it was waltz-like. I really wanted to say that if he could waltz, he could easily do what most of the guys here were doing, which was bouncing up and down and swinging hips, but I kept my mouth shut.

While swaying to the music in a manner that indicated I would be willing to dance, I caught the eye of a guy not too far away and nodded my head to signal willingness. He came over and asked me if I wanted to dance. Without a word, I handed my beer to Jonathan and went on the floor. I did the best I could to suggest that I was enjoying myself but made certain to periodically check on Jonathan, whose eyes, I could tell, never left me. When there was a break in the music, my dance partner and I introduced ourselves, and we walked back to Jonathan.

"Terry, this is Jonathan. He's visiting from out of town."

Jonathan smiled politely and said, "Good evening."

That I had company with me was enough to let the guy know that I was otherwise unavailable, should he have had further interest in me. He excused himself and went off to more-available pickings. I asked Jonathan if he had any questions about the scene. He said no but with what I could tell was either nervousness or annoyance.

I wondered if he was bothered by the sight of a pack of homos gyrating to the music, often in the fashion of a long-distance fucking. Sure, it was one thing to keep company with a single queer who for your own comfort you may have envisioned as sexless, but here was a crowd of queers flaunting their sexuality. Such suspicion, however, was quickly killed when he said, "If you don't mind a clumsy dance partner, I could try."

"Not at all."

Although he needed a lot of loosening up, he made a valiant attempt at doing what most others were doing. I was so pleased by this sudden change of events that I made sure that my body movements were conservative enough not to make his look amateurish. By midnight we had danced two more times, and he had gradually let himself go with the flow.

I was starting to have second thoughts about my plan, but I had committed so much emotional energy to it in the past week that I felt I couldn't just abandon it. Besides, I really wanted to see his reaction to the side room.

"Do you want to see the rest of this place?"

"There's more?"

"Yes, more."

I motioned him to follow, and we went through the doorway. It took a minute or so for our eyes to get accustomed to the much-dimmer lighting. Along the walls some couples were tasting the inside of each other's mouths with the intensity of those who hadn't eaten in a few days and were now being offered a feast. Other men were standing alone hoping for someone to come along and feed them. A few of the couples and singles had their hands on their own or each other's crotches. Jonathan's gaze quickly turned from the walls to the floor as though it had some significant scientific interest.

Coupling in the shadows,
They seek hormonal relief.
Introductions aren't needed,
Just sex now even if brief.

I figured he had gotten the point, which he could title "Anthropological Study No. 1: The Gay Male Meeting and Preliminary Mating Ritual." We left the Texas and drove back to my place. He told me that he had enjoyed himself with the dancing and complimented me on what a good dancer I was, saying that he was sorry he wasn't a better one. I said that even I couldn't do some of the more complex dance movement that he'd seen. He made no comment about the side room, and I didn't either. However, I figured if he was offended by seeing men with men in lascivious liaisons, that was his problem, and if it was a problem, I would soon know.

"Are you still up for next Saturday?"

Without any hesitation, he said, "Yes."

"In that case, I thought we would go to a leather bar called the Stag. It's quite different from the Texas. But you'll have to dress the part there too. At minimum you'll need a black leather jacket along with boots."

"I have a brown one."

"That'll have to do."

"Perhaps I could get a black one. Do you have any suggestions?"

"Dungeon Leather has a good selection at moderate prices. I could you take you there."

"That would be great." Again that word.

The possibilities were discussed, and we settled on Wednesday afternoon at three thirty. I dropped him off at his car, and since I made no attempt to get out for a possible hug, we ended the evening with a "Good night."

When I got home, I discovered I was really horny, and I somewhat reluctantly hand jobbed myself to what I imagined Jonathan would look like in leather. No sooner had I let loose my load to that image than I regretted having done so. After all, even if he looked like the hottest leather bear in the world, he was still vanilla and married. This was what I had to keep in mind to somehow neutralize any positive feelings I might have for him. He would never even understand the depth of my world, much less belong to it.

> Some call it just demented sex,
> But I, healthy release.
> Some think it is hatred repressed,
> But I, a love to share.
> No matter that some criticize;
> I know it otherwise.

From Sunday through Wednesday morning I was almost totally occupied by work on my book, which helped considerably to take my mind off both Jonathan and my plan.

When Jonathan arrived that afternoon, I took him to Dungeon Leather. He was captivated by every piece of wear and toy. True, the tit clamps caused him to suddenly cover his chest with his hand. The butt plugs only slightly embarrassed him, and the penis-enlarging pumps amused him. He could not believe that floggers were considered toys, but then he hadn't seen my closet with Brute Bliss and its relatives.

> Sir! This subject would have you as king,
> With lashes striking me with each swing.
> Let me hear and feel their thud and sting
> And believe that love is what they bring.

I had ambivalent feelings about Jonathan's lack of shock at some of what he was looking at. If he had been obviously grossed out, I would have canceled Saturday night, figuring that it would just be shooting an already dead horse, and I could justify being free of him once and for all. But the fact that he showed no sign of being deplored by anything made it more difficult to be angry at him, which only allowed for a continued attraction toward him. The first thing we needed to do was to pick out the right jacket and then get him to try on some chaps. As he was busy doing this, I was at the floggers feeling their different textures, and I began reminiscing about my first experience in being flogged.

It was one summer when I had gone back to New England to visit my mother. There was a new leather bar there called the Rack. There weren't many customers in it when I arrived, but to my surprise sitting at the bar was a former trick from the previous summer when I'd been in the city. We began talking, and before long we heard noises coming from the back room and went to investigate. There were only two men there, one of whom was shirtless and standing with the palms of his hands raised up against the wall and feet spread apart. The other man, who I judged was about 6'2" and 180 pounds, was flogging the back of the first one. The scene went on for about ten minutes, and then the two of them returned to the front room, leaving my ex-trick and I alone. He asked if I had ever been flogged, and I said no, that the most I had so far gotten into was ass belting, both as a top and bottom. He apparently remembered enough about my bar behavior to suggest that we do some of that right then and there, and I agreed. We both took our belts off and dropped our pants, and before I got a chance to become the bottom, he was already at the wall position waiting for my belting.

I had just started beating on his butt when the 6'2" guy returned. Apparently, the sound we were making attracted him. He watched for a minute or so, then approached us and handed me his flogger. I had never used one before and didn't know what my playmate could take. I asked him which he would rather have, my belt or the flogger.

"Flogger," he said.

I began to target his ass but not to the satisfaction of 6'2", who came back over, took the flogger from me, and started to use it on my companion, whom I was convinced was going to start screaming but didn't. This went on for perhaps five minutes until my playmate finally called out, pulled up his pants, and went back into the other room. This left 5'7" me standing in the room alone with 6'2" with my pants still down around my ankles. My head (the upper one) strongly advised me to pull up those pants and follow the example of my companion. However, my other (lower) head even more strongly encouraged me to stay, and that was the head I obeyed.

The guy gently pushed me toward the wall, but before he did anything more, I thought it wise to tell him the truth. I said, "Sir, I've never been flogged."

"That's all right; don't worry."

"I don't want to disappoint you, sir!"

Trying to be cautious while at the same time being aroused was not easy.

"You won't" were his assuring words as he nudged me to the wall.

Once I was facing the wall, he whispered to me in a very nonthreatening voice, "Take off the jacket."

"Sir! I have only been into ass play before."

He didn't press the point, which I was thankful for, and instead, he positioned me against the wall with my arms and legs spread. He gave a few hits to my ass, which I really enjoyed, and then pushed his body up against mine to whisper again, "Take off the jacket."

It so happened that this time, his beard stubble brushed against the back of my neck, which can send me into sexual overdrive. Off came not only my jacket but also the shirt under it. The guy proceeded to slowly and then more rapidly flog my back and ass. As he did, I began to experience an endorphin high, the likes of which I had never previously known. At the same time, I entered a kind of out-of-body experience in which I could see myself at a distance being flogged.

The flogging on my back I thought to fear,
But then I found it to be very dear.
It sent me to a world other than here,
Which made my painful ego disappear.

The guy, seeing that I was offering no resistance, soon stopped, introduced himself as Rex (he was really Richard), and suggested that we should continue playing at his place. I spent the next few nights with Rex, and, as a result of being trained to satisfy him, I discovered three new insights about myself.

First, in being flogged I felt an exhilaration in the temporary dissolution of an oppressive sense of adulthood replaced by the return of a child that had never had much of a chance to be. Coming from an alcoholic family too often meant that, even as a fairly young child, it was I that had to take on many of the responsibilities for keeping the family functional, responsibilities that parents are normally expected to perform.

There is a dungeon in my mind,
A torture-chamber paradise,
Where suffering transforms me,
A voyage of discovery.
Here I go to find the child
Who is an inmate deep within,
And through the power of the pain
The adult driven far away.
The child then is at last free,
And agony turns ecstasy.

The second discovery was that I like to be disciplined.

Leather as discipline,
My back his to beat.
Far from me to protest
And cheat us of this treat.

Third, I finally realized one of the reasons my relationship with my first two lovers had failed. Yes, the love had been there, but now I understood that we had been mismatched from the start, they as vanilla and I as an S-Mer. From then on I sought out my own kind.

Just this reverie about flogging made me ask myself, *How would Jonathan react not just to me being flogged or flogging someone else but to those I play such games with?*

Jonathan had finally found a pair of chaps he liked that would fit him. He put them on with the jacket and asked how I thought he looked. I said fantastic as my perverse prick went into overdrive.

> Leather-covered legs
> That frame the butt and crotch,
> They make both picturesque
> With or without pants.
> Few men are more sensual
> Than chaps wearing their chaps.

When Jonathan went up to pay for the leather, he saw the various hankies near the counter and picked a color he liked—kelly green. The clerk and I looked at each other and nearly burst out laughing. The clerk gave Jonathan a card that listed the meaning of the different handkerchief colors, and Jonathan read, "Kelly green: left side pocket—hustler; right side—john." Jonathan decided against the Irish.

On the way home we both laughed at what could become absurdities in the hankie code, although he also had a number of serious questions about it. I gave brief commentary on some and subtly skirted the issue on others. Oral (light blue) and anal (dark blue) sex were easy in that he knew that both hets and gays could be into it, and we agreed that condoms and general safe-sex practices (black and white checks) were essential, especially if one wanted to remain HIV negative, as I was. I didn't have to tell him that, but I wanted him to know, and he said that he was very glad to hear it.

> A condom on a cock
> Makes for a prudent prick
> With no bugs to beget,
> No reason to regret.

Next, there was rust, meaning cowboy when on the left and horse when on the right. I explained the obvious implications of that, and he showed just the slightest amount of embarrassment at that. Then he mentioned bear and cub (peach), and I could not help myself making a special comment on that.

"You can qualify as the former."

I was surprised by his very quick response. "And would you qualify as a cub?"

Without commenting more on that, I just smiled at him. That remark would call out to me in the very near future.

He saw leopard on the list and read aloud, "Tattoos."

"Yes. But I don't wear that as a code. I simply let people see them on me."

> Some said that one would lead to more,
> But I thought otherwise.
> Then two I said would be the end,
> But soon it was two score.

After reading that fuchsia was for spanking (right side for bottom and left side for top) and gray for bondage, he said, "I can understand the appeal of spanking and maybe even bondage for some people, but I don't think it would work for me." That didn't stop me from hoping he only meant that spanking was not for him as a bottom because I sure would like to get spanked by him.

Then there was yellow.

> A yellow bandana says just one thing,
> But along with that, what else might there be
> Just before or after the privileged pee?

Some of the hankie codes that Jonathan had the most problems with were whipping (black), branding (black lace), shit (brown), anilingus/rimming (beige), and cutting/blood sports (gold lamé). I tried to explain the appeal of each of these for some people while also acknowledging that they were potentially dangerous healthwise.

Momentarily I was concerned that he might ask if I were into any of them, but he seemed to shy away from the whole subject, perhaps to avoid asking. When I told Jonathan that fisting (red) meant a person's whole hand up someone's rectum, he was sure I was kidding. He figured the anus and rectum could not be stretched that much. I assured him that they could. I was glad that he didn't ask me if I knew that from personal experience. If he had, I would have told the truth—that while fisting was not particularly a turn-on for me, I had done it to guys who wanted it. If he had asked if I had ever been fisted, I would have explained that someone had made an initial attempt once but that I'd had to put a quick stop to it.

> Here was a bottom sodomite
> Who wanted anal play one night.
> But to his rear-end stud
> He gave just a handful of blood
> From a butthole far too tight.

The mention of cutting or blood sports (gold lamé) brought back another memory—the only blood scene in which I have ever been involved. There was this extreme masochistic guy I met at a punishment-club event. Hearing of my talents with a flogger, he wanted me to service him. I didn't know the extremes he was into at the time. In fact, I didn't even know what he looked like, since he was wearing a full leather hood that masked his face. But others at the event vouched for him, so we made an arrangement for me to top him. I went to his place—even then he was hooded—and was given a choice between two brutal toys, a very narrow lashed flogger or a cat, a braided whip.

106

While chaining him up, I noticed numerous scars on his back and chest, even in the forbidden zone, the small of the back, and I realized what I had gotten myself into. This hooded masochist was an edge player, someone who takes serious risks with his health and safety. I chose the cat and began to whip with medium power, but that clearly was not to his taste. So I upped to maximum force, and despite my arm getting tired, I continued until I gave him the minimum he wanted.

The cat cut several fairly long wounds into his back, and blood splattered out. There was a certain erotic excitement in this, partially because I had often fantasized what it would be like to be flogged until blood was drawn. But this guy seemed to have no limits and clearly was one who relished the hellish.

> Blood is so erotic
> And yet so dangerous.
> To taste the source of life,
> Also disease and death.

I knew without the slightest doubt that this guy expected me to continue, which was out of my league. Explaining that to him, I unchained him, wiped off as much of the blood as I could from the cat, made my apology, and left. Lesson learned: hands off someone with a hazardous blood fetish, especially when I suspect he has a possible death wish.

> The blood, the pain, and the scars
> Are simply extreme pleasures
> Or masochistic treasures.

While further exploring the code, Jonathan noticed that the list was not exclusively oriented toward gay males since it included breast fondling (pink) and menstruating women (maroon). I pointed out that these categories could appeal to either lesbians or straight men. I could not help being slightly irreligious at that point.

"I assume that an Orthodox Jewish rabbi might have real trouble with maroon."

"If I showed this list to an Orthodox rabbi, he would probably drop dead of a horror-induced heart attack there and then." This was followed by a good laugh.

As for the vampire-scene listing (red and black stripes), I told him that I was not familiar enough with the scene to comment on it. I partially lied.

> I fear I am a vampire,
> But not into red flesh.
> Yet for a victim, I still thirst,
> To drink from him his lust.

When we got back to my place, Jonathan said that he would not feel comfortable leaving his place in his newly acquired duds and asked if it would be okay if he left them at my place, which I readily agreed to.

Jonathan gave me a big bear hug and said, "So I'll see you Saturday."

"Yes."

"Great." And with that tedious word he left.

While waffling on my plan, I still felt I couldn't give it up, and it took me until the next day to figure out why. Holding on to the plan seemed the only justification for seeing Jonathan again. Yes, the whole thing was hopeless. I hated him; I loved him. I wasn't interested in the plan to hurt him anymore; I now saw it as a possible way of freeing myself from an impossible situation with regard to him.

The Stag would destroy whatever admirable image of me he had built up, and he would be so repelled that he would want to get as far away from me as he could. Then I would be free of the maddening incompatibility between the S-M me and the vanilla him.

His sex is just vanilla,
While mine is more gorilla
Spiced with a slight Godzilla.
At best mine would mystify
And at worst would horrify—
Anything but justify.

Chapter 8

Saturday morning, August 6, I awoke feeling confident that very soon I would be finished with the Jonathan issue once and for all, and I felt both relief and yet sadness. When he arrived that evening, I was already dressed—black chaps with a red stripe down the legs and a matching black vest also with a red stripe on the sides. These were the colors of my leather-club uniform. I usually only wore them to a leather bar for a club activity, but tonight I wanted to look especially sharp. Proper slave protocol is clear on this—red, like certain other colors, stands out and so is a color a dom/master can wear but not a slave, especially if he is with his master. The one exception is if it is part of a uniform.

Since Jonathan had arrived in plenty of time to dress, he spent a good five minutes staring at himself in the full-length mirror admiring how good he looked, which made it clear that he wanted my confirmation. I said, "You have the right look."

> Wearing black leather,
> Sexual warrior in
> Organic armor.

While driving to the Stag, Jonathan asked about possible homophobic incidents in that neighborhood. I told him that they did happen but less often than in the Texas neighborhood. We got to the bar but had to park two and a half blocks away, which implied the

Stag was busy. We had to push our way through to reach the main area, and this time Jonathan took the lead in ordering and paying for our two beers. I greeted a few people I knew, mostly former bedmates, but purposely didn't introduce Jonathan to them. That might have made Jonathan more comfortable in this atmosphere than I wanted him to be.

Fun and games started earlier in the Stag than in the Texas and with much less inhibition. Within a half hour or less of our arrival, Jonathan noticed one guy going down on another guy.

"Do they allow that in here?" he asked in surprise.

"They're not supposed to, and if the ABC came in and saw it, the bar would have their license suspended or even revoked, but such activities are what brings most guys into this place. That's also why the lighting is so minimal."

After a moment of silence the question I had been expecting materialized. "Would it be too personal to ask something?"

"Probably not."

"Have you ever done that in here?"

We were at the critical moment I had been waiting two weeks for, and in the most callous way I could, I replied, "I've been both the giver and receiver." Just so I could really rub it in how much of a slut I was, I added, "Over the years I've lost count of the number of men."

"I see."

While that was all he said, his voice clearly expressed disappointment. Was it because I was for the first time pushing into his face what a real slut I was? Was it because of the indifferent way I admitted to it? I think it was some of both.

Yes, this was the voice I had planned for, but now I felt guilty about it. I had made myself sound like sexual trash. I had started this whole damn scenario to wound him as I thought he had wounded me, but now it was boomeranging back on me. The truth was I didn't want him to feel this way about me. I wanted him to love me. I tried to counter some of the damage.

"I'm a gay man who right now has no one to go home to like you do, no one to make love to or cuddle up with on cold nights, to hold on to in the thick and thin. Some people have those treasures and take them for granted. I don't have that luxury, so I take what is offered me and make the best of it. Is that so wrong?"

I painfully realized that I wasn't just making up these words for him; they were my reality.

> I haunt the bars on weekends
> Unsure of what I'll find.
> I hate the smoke and don't drink,
> So no fun places these.
> Granted I enjoy the hunt,
> But only to a point.
> All of this to lead I hope
> To more than just a grope.

"Of course it's not. You deserve to have what others have. Everyone does."

Feeling miserable with myself and alienated from him, I decided that those words were nothing more than his feeling guilty for all the riches he had, compared to my poverty.

I could barely hold back the tears that I felt coming. I didn't want to be in the bar anymore and was thankful when Jonathan asked if we could leave, making the excuse that he was more tired than he thought. I knew he had heard my pain because we drove home in the kind of silence necessitated by the fear that if words were spoken, the pain would only be made worse.

We got back to my apartment, and while we were both taking off our chaps, I broke the silence. "I'm sorry the night didn't work out as expected, but maybe we were both too tired. We should probably have made it for another night. I'm just going to go to bed."

"That's probably a good idea." He then added, "Can I give you a hug first?"

"Sure."

He did, but this was not the usual bear hug but a far gentler and longer-lasting one. It was a hug that seemed more painful to me than comforting, and part of the reason was because of what I was going to tell him next.

"You should take your leather with you, Jonathan."

He broke off the hug. "Why?"

"Because I can't help you anymore with your article, and I will not be able to get together with you again." I wanted to say, *your damn article*, but I had no more revenge in me. It was over. Not only had I done more harm to myself than to him, but I was so in love with him that I didn't care anymore if he had just wanted to use me. I had never felt in such a self-debasing morbid mood in my entire life. I hated it, but I couldn't free myself from it. I didn't want to talk anymore, so I didn't appreciate his next question.

"Why not?"

"Because I don't have the time."

I thought a lie was safer, or, at least for me, less painful than the truth.

"Not even just on a Saturday evening?"

"You don't understand."

"Understand what?"

That question was the most taboo one he could have asked at that moment. But maybe only the truth, out there in the open, could relieve my pain. Relieve it by scaring him away.

"Jonathan, I've fallen in love with you."

I waited for a response, but he just seemed confused by my statement.

"Now as a straight man, you're supposed to run like hell."

"Why?"

Was this what his vocabulary had been reduced to? "Maybe you still don't understand, so let me be more explicit. I've been having sex with you for the past three weeks. Every time I've jerked off, I've fantasized about what it would be like to kiss you, to suck your dick, and to get fucked by you. Are you too stupidly straight to realize what that means?"

Again he seemed confused by my words, so I went to the door and opened it. "Go home, Jonathan. Go home to your wife, and don't forget your leather."

"I'd rather leave it here if that is still okay with you."

"If that's what you want, fine. Good-bye."

Jonathan, even at this point, seemed confused, but he walked out. I shut the door on him as if he were the most unwelcome of men, and I sank to the floor trying to hold back tears as I listened to the sound of his footsteps fade. The flood came. I had cried over the loss of past lovers, but this crying was totally different. It wasn't just crying because I was losing someone I was in love with; it was also because I had done the totally unacceptable. I had confessed my love to a straight man. It's obvious why straight society judges that as a serious sin, but gay society does so as well because confessing such love is ridiculously hopeless and opens you up to the straight man's contempt for showing your true colors as a homosexual predator toward normal men. The crying stopped only as I realized that at least the Jonathan issue was over and I could now go on with my life.

> Love enters life only to leave.
> It brings with it joy and pain.
> Is love in what we should believe
> Or think it always will deceive?

I wiped away the tears with my arm and removed my shirt. Before removing my boots and pants, I wondered if I should try beating off. The problem was whether or not it would be with Jonathan in mind. I turned off the main bathroom light, leaving only the dim shine of the night-light. Beating off in this semidarkness with boots on and my pants down around my ankles serves to constrain my walking ability, making things highly erotic. I tried to think of something supersexual, one vile vice after another.

When I feel really depressed,
I need a pick-me-up.
So I muse on joyous things,
Which bring me great relief.
I think of being handcuffed,
Of feeling a sharp whip.
I concentrate on hot wax
Dripping over me.
I meditate on spanking
And embalming too.
I fantasize some urine
On chest and crotch and feet.
Let's not forget boot licking,
Humiliation sweet.

I'm sure reminiscing about these things would have worked if Jonathan hadn't kept intruding into my mind. Rarely have I had much of a problem with one-handed self-stimulation accompanied by some fruitful fantasy, but despite the manual and mental effort I was putting into it, neither was working. No sooner would I rise to the occasion than I would lose the fantasy and then go frustratingly flaccid. I thought that perhaps I could use one of those little pills, those performance enhancers as they are euphemistically called. I rarely use them myself, but I've learned to keep them available for older leather tops—leather trumps age—who might at first have hardness problems. One lesson I have learned is not to underestimate gray gay.

Do not assume because of age
A penis will fail to perform.
The young may serve one's vanity,
But the point is for sperm to swarm.

Finding nothing in my past of any value to keep me aroused, I turned to the S-M magazines that had been piling up unread in the hope of help. The cover of the third from the top suggested itself as being the one to start with, and if whatever the others offered was better than this, I might not need the pill. This less-than-great literary reading was interrupted by the ringing of the doorbell. *Who the hell would be there at this time?* I went to the door and looked out through the peephole. *Damn! Jonathan.*

"What do you want?" I called through the door.

"Dan, I forgot something. Please let me in."

"What? What did you forget?"

"I can't tell you out here. Open the fucking door."

I had never heard him use a swear word in the whole time we had been together. I composed myself and opened it just enough for my face to fit through it.

"What did you forget?"

He pushed the door open, forcing me back. This kind of assertiveness was not part of the Jonathan I had known up to now. He shut the door behind him.

"I forgot to tell you that I love you."

"No! You're just saying that because you feel sorry for me."

"Dan, that's not it. I love you."

"You still don't understand, Jonathan. What I mean by love and what you mean by it are not the same."

"How are they different?"

"I've already explained it to you. Weren't you listening? Love for me means more than you can give me."

"What do you want? Tell me."

"I'm a gay man. I'm a fucking faggot, a queer. More to me means the bedroom, Jonathan—the goddamn, cock-sucking, fart-hole-fucking bedroom!"

I thought if I could be vulgar enough he would get the message.

There was a moment of killer silence. I figured I had given him a shock, at least with the word *bedroom*, and so I could hardly believe his next words.

"Then let's go to the bedroom."

"You don't know what you're saying, and you're torturing me by saying it. You feel pity for me because of what I said in the bar, so you want to give me a mercy fuck. You think that maybe that will make everything okay? It won't. It will only make things worse."

"No. Not a mercy fuck. I want to make love to you."

I was crying by now. Jonathan grabbed hold of me and held me tight against him, my face buried in his chest. I fought him to get free, but all I was able to do was to turn myself around with my back to him. Maybe it was because I was so emotionally weakened by now or because this was the way I had dreamed of being held by him. Yes, I wanted that teddy bear, in an overpowering way, to encompass this cub in his arms.

A toy teddy bear has no dick,
But real bears are complete.
And to play with that real-life prick
Is a great hard-on treat.

Then, as in the car that Monday night after dinner with Jonathan and Ruth, my emotional turbulence was replaced by an equally bizarre, but this time creepy, calmness that allowed once again for words, which would later just increase my pain.

"Jonathan, you belong to another, to Ruth. Don't you still love her?"

"Of course I do, but does that mean I can't love you also?"

My resolve to end this hopeless situation was dying. All the emotional armor I had so carefully built was dissolving there and then. Still worse, in that creepy calm state, I felt as though I, Dan, had suddenly disappeared and some other person—no, some other entity—from inside of me was speaking through my mouth. It or he took over.

"Jonathan."

The word itself, his name, didn't really say anything, but my desperate intonation spoke volumes. I suppressed saying anything else out of fear of whatever that voice inside me might further say. Nonetheless, I had used up all my strength to resist that which fantasy wanted but which I knew, in reality, could only be disastrous.

Jonathan could tell that I, or I and that other disembodied voice, was calm enough now, so when I pressed forward, he let me go. The voice, the entity, made me turn around and look right into his eyes. Then, in a tone that was at the same time an invitation and a threat, it said, "All right, the bedroom."

I walked toward the bedroom, half wanting him to follow and half hoping he'd take back his words and leave. I turned the bedcovers down all the way to the floor, sat on the side of the bed, and waited to see what Jonathan would do now that getting into bed was getting closer to being real. Jonathan sat down beside me, put his hand on the back of my neck, pulled my head toward his, and gave me a long kiss on the mouth. This was what I had been wanting since the day we'd met, but now it was a reality, and I didn't know if I could handle it. I didn't kiss back, but I also made no attempt to resist. Maybe I thought this passivity would turn him off, without having to lie about wanting him. It didn't work.

"Danny, get undressed." This was the first time he had called me Danny, and it made me feel like I was a child who couldn't resist his daddy's order. I looked down at my boots, knowing that as soon as I took them off, any sane resistance on my part would be over. They were my last wall of defense. I reached down and took hold of toe and heel. Then I closed my eyes and pulled off the first one. As stupid as it sounds, not watching myself remove them seemed to make me feel less guilty about whatever was to come. Out of sight, free of responsibility.

If I didn't want to face him while I was taking off my pants, I wanted to face him even less while he was undressing, for fear he might feel too uncomfortable, considering what we were about to do.

I stopped short of removing my briefs, for a moment telling myself this wasn't right, but then I heard from within that voice saying,

> *There is no sin found in the crotch*
> *But only within the mind.*
> *A life of lust is not a lie.*
> *Live it, and in peace, you die.*

I felt incapable of resisting the demands of that voice, and so in obedience I exposed my genitals and ass to the air and crawled up onto the bed, wondering whether to lie down on my belly or back. The first was safer in that I literally wouldn't have to face what I was allowing myself to do. However, I wanted more than anything else to face him. I wanted to see him as he came toward me. I wanted to see his daddy-bear stick and balls. I wanted to be able to put my arms around him and run my hands down and over his butt, and I wanted to feel his erection rubbing against mine. Besides, I thought I knew him well enough by now to know that he wasn't going to try to satisfy me just by climbing onto my back and fucking me. By my choice or his, unless he chickened out now, we were going to confront each other, face-to-face and meat-to-meat.

Confront is such an impersonal word, but it was for the moment the psychologically safer one. I got on my back and once again closed my eyes. I had exposed myself like this to other men more times than I could calculate with not the slightest sense of embarrassment or shame, and yet now that was what I was feeling. Or was it more like vulnerability? Perhaps it was to reduce that feeling of whatever it was that the ridiculous popped into my head.

> Is nudity a natural thing?
> Don't we begin this way?
> So why such shock and the dismay
> When natural we are seen?
> Perhaps it would be more decent,
> Propriety might say,
> That when each of us was born,
> Clothing we should have worn.

I was still flaccid, which I was actually thankful for. It was one thing for him to see me fully naked but down and a very different thing to see me there up and ready. Either way, I still wasn't convinced that he wouldn't have second thoughts, redress, and leave. But as I watched him pull down his underpants, exposing that tight butt of his, I just wanted to scream out, *Take me!*

> To depict the naked butt
> Could make of you a slut.
> But is it not just art
> Unless the cheeks you part,
> In which case it is smut.

Now, unashamedly undressed, he turned, revealing his amply furry chest and an even more so pubic pelt, which was, as yet, the background for a pendulous penis. Resting his hands on the bottom of the bed, he proceeded to crawl toward me as if it were the most natural thing, which didn't and yet did surprise me. I was sure he had done this with his wife thousands of times, but this time, it was with a man.

Oh my God! What if this wasn't his first time with a man? Had I been fooling myself all this time? Had I been putting myself through hell thinking that wanting a straight man was some violation of the world order? Was he really straight or maybe bi? Had he by simple silence been lying to me? Had he been torturing me by what had been unsaid? Was this why it seemed so easy for him?

He lay beside me on his side and pulled me onto my side so that we were facing each other with our bodies but inches apart. He crossed his leg over mine—the first tiny promise of him on top and me on the bottom.

I had to know. I had to ask him. "Have you ever done this with another man?"

"No."

I either had to believe him without further questioning or tell him to leave. What a contradiction. If he had said yes, I would have labeled him a matrimonial closet cock (the female equivalent, a lesbian with a husband, is rudely called a matrimonial closet cunt). For his deception, I would have told him to get the fuck out and never, ever, bother me again. However, his no left it open as to what he thought he was, and so he stayed.

He again pulled my head toward him, and this time, my lips actively pressed themselves against his. In no time our tongues were battling for room in each other's mouths. My gay gear grew, and I had to push his body back slightly so I could rest it flat between us. I still couldn't tell whether he was hard, but it almost didn't matter. As our oral exercises became even more intense, he reached down to position his dick next to mine. He, having touched me so, gave me permission to touch him, and touch I did.

He wasn't well hung, but he wasn't small either, and he seemed pleased enough by my attentions that he asked those magic words, "Do you have a condom?" I confess that at that point I would have broken my rules and allowed him to fuck me bareback, my justification being that having sex with a presumably, until now, monogamous man was quite safe. But he had asked for safety, and I wasn't going to risk his changing his mind about fucking me. I said, "Just under the bed. Hold on."

I leaned over the side of the bed to pull out the box that housed condoms, lube, dental dams, gloves, and a towel and said, "Turn on your back."

Given my choice, I usually want to remain underneath my partner, but tonight I wanted as much free access to Jonathan's body as I could get, and that meant being on top of him. Leaving the items on the pillow, I sat on top of him with my calves resting against his hips. I bent forward to kiss his mouth, then his neck, then each nipple. As I leaned back, his hands went from holding my head to holding my thighs. I delicately ran my fingers through the hair on his chest and followed the hairline down to his stomach. I could feel his hard-on pressing tight against the cleavage of my butt. While caressing him, I kept looking into his eyes, partly to make sure he was enjoying this as much as I was and partly to try, with my eyes, to tell him how much I really did love him. Yet I was aware that my face kept alternating back and forth between that of sweet love when I smiled at him and something hungrier when the smile was replaced by the clenching of my teeth. I leaned my head down again, this time forcing my tongue into his mouth to play. Then I heard the voice again.

His body is a canvas,
Upon which to work your art.
Your fingers, lips, tongue, and prick
Are the brushes with which
To paint your passion.

With such instructions my tongue went from his mouth back to his neck, to dwell on his Adam's apple. Then it meandered itself across his delicious chest, this time to taste his hair. Approaching his stomach, I steadily moved my body downward. My ankles reached the edge of the bed, allowing for a tonguing of the head of his elongated love. I could see his precum as I opened the condom and eased it over Jonathan Junior. If I had been having sex with any other man, I probably would not have put a condom on him before oral sex, but since Jonathan had used the word *condom*, I felt obligated to use it for both oral and anal purposes.

Once protection was on, I licked his shaft from top to bottom, bottom to top, and back down. I carefully lifted his balls as gently as I would touch the wings of a butterfly, and I permitted my lips and tongue to give adoration to them. I returned to his bear bone and slowly encased it with my mouth all the way to its base. I slightly, but wonderfully, gagged.

I was in no hurry to have him unload until I felt him not only with my lips, fingers, tongue, and throat but inside my holy of holies. I was determined to get as much out of this night as was humanly possible before I would release him back to another. I went down on him one more time.

> My tongue up, down, and around his flesh,
> Exciting it to stiffness.
> Then with a condom to dress it well
> And with lube to anoint it,
> It is ready to fulfill the prayer
> To penetrate my dark lair.

His chest had begun rising and falling heavily with pleasure, and I was finally ready for Jonathan Junior to work its magic on me. I put on a glove, squirted some lube on my fingers, and because I had judged that his manly pole was about three to four fingers thick, I inserted into my own hole first one, then a second, then three fingers, and just the top of a fourth. I massaged my rectal walls to forewarn them of what was to come, and before squatting on his pleasure pole, I once more rubbed mine against his.

I remounted Jonathan's thighs and slowly guided his rock-hard flesh into me. Junior was just a tiny bit thicker than I usually wish to take, but not only did I want to feel Jonathan deep inside me now, I wanted to feel him tomorrow, by having my hole just sore enough for me to imagine that he was still there—a good soreness.

It took a little while before my anus relaxed enough for me to ease myself down on his tool. Although I had to force myself to take all of him, I gritted my teeth while smiling so as to not show any sign of discomfort, much less pain. Once he was entirely within, I was able to relax most of the tension in my hole, and then ever so slowly I allowed my hips to rise and fall while tightening and loosening my rectal muscles.

I had returned to making eye contact and tried to hold it as long as I could. But what seemed like a warm animal energy inside of me gradually arose from my anus through my bowels, and I found it more and more difficult to keep any visual focus. What seemed like a kundalini kind of energy was soon moving faster through me, heading this time for my stomach, and the rise and fall of my hips accelerated with it. The energy reached its target, and the warmth that had been in my bowels now became major heat just below my diaphragm.

Soon the energy was on its way again, this time to become cardiac heat. But it didn't stop there. Instead, it continued on to my throat. I was losing all sense of self, and my body speed was near out of conscious control. My larynx was on fire, and I didn't care—far from it. I wanted to be consumed in this energy's flame. I was positive that when this murderous heat reached my face and then the top of my head, which now I knew was its goal, there would be an explosion, and there was! My head felt like a rocket on the Fourth of July that had just burst into a hundred particles of burning and glowing light. I cried out. At that same moment, I could feel from the intensity of his grip on my thighs and his own animallike groan that Jonathan was having his own convulsive orgasm.

A homo hole is holy;
It takes one right to God.
Few can say the same for church,
Which for guilt will search.

It took me a few seconds to realize that I had survived. Whatever creature had been aroused within me had all too suddenly returned to its resting place, apparently satisfied by the corrupting copulation of this virgin with another man's horny hole. Perhaps this was for the best, because I doubted if I could have taken any more of such exquisite elation. My brain was still reeling, and I could not yet think with any coherency, and so my only security was the feel of Jonathan's hands still on me.

Although my brain soon began to calm down, my heart was still racing. When was the last time I'd had an orgasm like that? I started to cry silently inside because I knew the answer was never before. Moreover, I was now back to a normal-enough reality to know that very shortly I would be sending my orgasmic knight away, forever. The jewel that was inside of me was losing its hardness, despite my rectal attempt to hold on to it, if for only a minute more. I wanted to at least keep him hard until I jerked off.

I soon regained my own hardness, which I had lost with Jonathan inside me. I lubed up and began to beat off, all the time determined to refocus on Jonathan's face as he watched me splatter my gay orgasmic gift over his stomach and chest. As I shot, I tried to muffle any too loud a cry, but some of that cry came out with my load.

Eternity is making love in time.
In each thrust, there is no past or future;
If in orgasm self you disavow,
Life and death become no more than the now.

I waited a moment to calm down and looked at Jonathan, who was smiling. It was with sadness akin to grief that I dismounted him and fell onto my back. He leaned over to me once more and pressed his lips against mine.

Pulling away, he removed the condom and was about to drop it on the towel, but I stopped him. I was not in the habit of being so attentive to my partner's rubbers, but this was the concrete proof of tonight, and as kinky as it sounded, I didn't want his sheath or its contents to be just tossed away. So I stretched out my hand and took it from him.

He was about to say something, but I put my other hand on his lips to signal silence. I didn't want the sacred time we had just spent together to be broken yet by mundane words. I toweled his still cum-covered cock, belly, and chest off with the hand that was not clutching his offering to me. Since I knew there was no way he was going to be able to spend the night with me, I figured it was best to get our parting over with as soon as possible.

I got off the bed, gathered up his clothes from the floor, and laid them on the bed. I picked my own clothes up and dumped them on a chair, went into the bathroom, and put on a robe. I went into the living room because I still didn't want to talk, and I couldn't watch him get dressed. While his body was naked, it belonged to me; clothed, it belonged to another, the wife whom I would now be returning him to. Dressed, he came into the living room. I already knew what had to be. What was right.

"You know, Jonathan, this has made it all the more impossible for us to see each other again. You have a wife and a life that has no place for me."

"But why can't we?"

"How? Lying to Ruth, you secretly come over here once a week to make love to me? I want more than that, Jonathan. I need more than that."

"Yes, I know, but ..."

"There are no buts. This should not have happened, and while we're both guilty of letting it come to this, I'm more to blame. I knew I had to find a way to end our relationship before it became too complicated. That's one of the reasons that I showed you the room at the Texas and why I took you to that sleazy bar tonight. I thought I could make you so disgusted with me that you'd want to get as far away as you could and would never call or see me again. Then I would be free to get on with my life. It didn't work, and while one part of me regrets that, the other part is glad of it. Making love to you was a dream come true. But we're awake now, and I must never try to dream that dream again. We can remember the few times we were together fondly, and with that alone each of us must be satisfied."

I could see his sadness, and it hurt me, but I was trying to do what was both sensible and even morally right, assuming it wasn't too late. I approached the door.

"It's very late now, and Ruth may be worried." At that moment I felt almost like I was saying to some trick, *Thanks for the fuck; here's the door*, and this caused my throat to constrict so much that I could barely say, "Good-bye."

I was thankful that he didn't give me any further argument. He just held his arms out. "Can I at least give you a hug?"

"I would love one."

We held each other as close as it was possible without squeezing each other to death. Since he didn't seem to want to be the first to let go, I did. I opened the door, and I remembered what started this, perhaps a foolish but not, at the moment, regrettable event.

"By the way, I'm sorry you won't get much of an article about the gay community from this, unless you plan to include tonight in it."

"It doesn't matter. I now realize that I didn't want to write an article so much as I wanted an excuse to continue to see you."

Of course, hearing that made all my previous doubts about his love for me seem as if they had been only a nightmare.

"Thank you. You can't know how much saying that means to me." I placed my hand on his arm, both to feel one last touch of him and also to gently push him out the door. "Good-bye, Jonathan."

I suppressed any tears, even though this particular good-bye left an emptiness deeper than I had ever experienced in saying my final good-byes to any of my other lovers.

"Good-bye."

He got a few feet away when once again I remembered his leather. "Oh! What about your leather?"

"I would still like to leave them here with you, if that's okay?"

"It's very okay. Anytime you need it, you know where to find it." I instantly knew I shouldn't have said that. It sounded too much like there was still the slightest of slight hope that we would see each other again, and that simply couldn't be.

I was about to say another good-bye, but the hollowness inside me would not let one out.

"I love you."

How could those three short words cut into me like they did now? I had to use every bit of my rapidly draining strength to suppress any crying that would only bring me back into his arms.

I gave him a smile, not one of happiness but of agonizing sadness, and I closed the door to his love.

> Let us not speak of tomorrow's love,
> For in this life, everything is flux.
> Passion of tonight only confess,
> And ask of each nothing more or less.

I went into the bathroom to pee and brush my teeth, only to realize that I still held the condom in my hand. I found an empty pill bottle just big enough for it to fit. I put it in and capped the bottle, and after finishing in the bathroom, I took the bottle into the bedroom and placed it on a shelf reserved for other small treasures.

> A too-short time of making love
> Yet not a common one-night stand.
> And so as its remembrance
> Only this as the evidence.

Chapter 9

The following morning I found his jacket and chaps on the couch where he had left them, and I carefully hung them in the closet next to mine. I was somewhat sad but not depressed, because every time I thought I might be heading that way, I focused on the soreness inside my ass and smiled to myself. He was still there, and that felt good. *I will get over my obscene obsession with Jonathan,* I told myself. It was merely a question of how long: weeks, months, longer?

I went over to the calendar on my desk and circled the dates we had been together, marking them with tiny annotations. July 11, met; 16, museum; 23, movie; 24, dinner; 29, Texas. I then realized that I hadn't turned the calendar page to August yet, and doing so, I noticed that I had Tuesday, August 16, circled with *Santa Fe* written down.

How could I have forgotten? That was the day I was to leave for the writers' conference in New Mexico. However, the Jonathan issue had become so overriding that it had made me forget something as important as that. I had been invited by the conference organizers to be part of two panel discussions and to lead a workshop.

I had felt so honored when asked to participate. Some of both my prose and poetry had been published and apparently had sufficiently impressed the organizers enough they'd assured me I would be an asset to the conference. They had even agreed to reimburse me for my plane ticket and hotel. It wasn't like me to forget anything such as this, but nothing before had come into my life to distract me like

Jonathan. Now I needed a distraction in the other direction. This could be just what I needed—to get away to a place totally free of anything to do with him.

The rest of Sunday was a blur of feelings—I had gotten what I wanted and yet hadn't. The problem was that I now wasn't sure of what it was that I thought I wanted. Revenge had disappeared before Saturday, and while having him make love to me was fine for the short time it lasted, now what?

> My love for him or lust
> Has been consummated.
> This should now be enough,
> Leaving me to move on,
> And yet it seems I burn
> For more of the same kind.
> I am irrational:
> In need of punishment.
> But what master have I
> To do the saving deed?
> Where to go, who to find
> To drive him from my mind?

By Monday morning I knew what I needed, and I knew who could give it to me. He was not a master, just an S-M sadist, but he was an expert with the whip. We had never played together, but we knew each other from the scene. I called him. I didn't give him all the details, just enough to make him understand what I needed, how badly I needed it, and how soon I needed it.

He reminded me of his reputation as a very heavy, even scary top and told me that I should take some time to think about what I was asking for, but I reminded him that I had been in the scene long enough to know what I need and that, as heavy as he may be, he also had a reputation of knowing what he was doing and never going further than a bottom could take. Finally, he said, "Okay."

We arranged for a 9:30 p.m. session. I got there, and since he wasn't into any master-slave protocol, I just stripped, went to the cross, and took far more than I had ever taken before or thought I could take. Besides being cathartic, it pleased me to know that I had crossed my previous boundary.

I breathe, and the pain goes in.
I breathe, and the pain goes out.
Every breath, a little death.
I am submissive to him
Who would take me from me.
I breathe, and the pain goes in.
I breathe, and the pain goes out.
Every breath, a little death.

He knew if he wanted to he could fuck me, but he was straight— not that some straight men, especially in the scene, will not miss the chance for a pole in a hole. But he had a reputation to keep up, especially with his female subs. I thanked him and left. Driving home, I could feel the soreness on my back, and I would periodically press into the back of the seat to increase the pain, keeping myself on an ever-so-mild S-M high.

The life of modern man
Is poorer, I believe,
Because he has lost touch
With what it used to be.
Pain as well as pleasure
Is what we fully are.
The aborigine
Freely uses pain
To alter consciousness
And find a deeper self.
Man today is trapped

In life ruled by machines.
His body is no more a friend
But an alien.
Yet some have recaptured
That ancient memory,
And in it, they indulge
The pain that sets them free.

Then the thought came to me, *What would it be like to have sex, as a top or bottom, in this state?* Every other time that I'd had sex after being flogged, it had been with the man who had flogged me, and I had more or less done whatever he'd wanted. Now I was free to do whatever I wanted, and I felt wicked about it. The Wolf Den was on my way home, so I decided to stop by. I got there a little before eleven, and not unexpectedly there were only a dozen or so patrons there. I ordered a beer and checked out the prey. I wasn't going to be choosy; if he was willing to suck me off, I would do the same for him.

While there were several younger guys whom I could have approached or for whom I could have waited to approach me, I saw an older man, maybe in his fifties, looking at me. He was good-looking, and I thought he might be more willing to do what I wanted without expecting more than I was willing to offer. I know that sounds ageist, but if he didn't work out, I could always try for one of the younger ones.

Since I wanted him to feel that I was really interested in him, I decided not to wait until he might approach me, even if I nodded, and I walked over to him.

"Good evening."

"Good evening."

"Name's Coy."

"I'm William."

"William, I like your looks, but I've got to get up early, so I'm in a hurry. I blow you, you blow me, my car or yours—that's it. Sorry, I can't offer more."

He looked around the room as if to check out the competition. Perhaps the fact that I had chosen him first, as well as the fact the others would see him leaving with me, influenced him to say, "Okay."

We got into my car, and I pulled a couple of condoms out of my back pocket and laid them on the dashboard. We did each other, but I must have been on automatic pilot, because all conscious thought was focused on pressing my back, which was already losing some of its sweet soreness, against the seat. My consciousness was only brought back to William when he said, "Thank you."

"You're welcome."

Pulling a card out of my wallet, I said, "But since I feel I owe you more than this, here is my number if you want to get together again, outside of a car. I'll be out of town for the next week and a half or so."

He seemed genuinely surprised, but, smiling, he took the card and asked, "Can I kiss you?"

I leaned forward, we kissed, he got out of the car and said thanks again, and I drove off.

I regretted that my back soreness was disappearing so quickly. Unlike those who are not into being flogged, the soreness or pain for those of us who are into it does not last as long. It is as if our bodies or brains are saying, *That was good, and so it is not to be interpreted as harmful, hence no need to be concerned with it for very long.*

Nothing is more relative
Than our pleasure and our pain.
What one thinks is just torture
To another is relief.
Something that will leave its mark
For a day or even more
May for another vanish
As if stolen by a thief.

133

The punishment and sex of Monday night forced all significant thought of Jonathan out of my mind for all of Tuesday. I hoped the same for Wednesday, but that was not to be. Instead, Wednesday brought with it guilt over what shouldn't have happened between Jonathan and me, and that guilt actually made me start to question my feelings about him and his supposed feelings about me.

Maybe what I had been caught up in was nothing more than an elaborate bicurious game on Jonathan's part. Guilt and doubt can have weird effects on the mind, and the only thing that helped was continually telling myself that I only had a week until I left for the conference. This reminder worked until that afternoon when the phone rang. It was Jonathan.

"Why are you calling? I thought that we had agreed that we could have no further contact with each other?"

"I only called to hear your voice and to tell you how much I love you."

"Jonathan, I told you that this would only be torturing both of us."

"I couldn't help myself. I can't get the other night out of my mind."

"Saturday night was a mistake. We should never have gotten into that. I'm sorry—it was my fault. I should never have said what I did, and then none of that would have happened."

"Does that mean you're sorry you said you loved me?"

"Please don't ask me that, Jonathan. Please."

"To never hear from me again, all you have to say is that you don't love me."

"That's trying to manipulate me, and it's not fair. If saying I don't love you is what it's going to take to free both of us from this torturous situation, then I will say those words."

"Can you say them in front of me, not just over the phone?"

I wanted so badly to say yes, but I knew I couldn't. "You'll just have to accept my words over the phone. Going to the Stag the other night put me in a very self-pitying mood. I desperately needed someone to make love to me, and you were there. That's all it was."

"I don't believe you. You said you had been jerking off to the fantasy of me for three weeks."

I wanted to end this call as painlessly as I could. "I'm going to a writers' conference in Santa Fe, and I'll be gone for about two weeks. I need time to think things over and get my life back on track. You need to remember that this whole thing isn't just between you and me. We both have to think of Ruth. She's there for you, and that's what you need to focus on."

"You never said anything about a conference."

"I know. I almost forgot about it."

"When are you leaving?"

I didn't want to tell him that it wouldn't be until next week in case he pushed to see me again on Saturday, so I lied. "I'm leaving early Saturday morning, and I have a lot to do to get ready."

I don't know whether he believed me or not, but if he didn't, he at least didn't accuse me of lying.

"Can I see you when you get back?"

I wasn't willing to give him false hope. I figured that only brutal honesty was what was needed at this point. "You have to return to the life you had before we met, and so do I. Now I have things to do, so please just say good-bye. Please."

There was silence before I heard the saddest good-bye I ever wanted to hear. "Good-bye."

I hung up the phone.

Once I had collected myself, I called the airline to see if I could change my ticket to Albuquerque for Saturday, but they informed me that on such short notice it could not be done without a heavy penalty fee. So what was I to do? I couldn't take the chance that Jonathan would call and find out I was still in town. There was only one thing to do. I decided to waste the plane ticket and drive to the conference. If I left on Saturday, that would give me enough unhurried time to drive there, and rather than fly back, I could give myself even more time to return some normality to my life.

The rest of the day I did everything I could to try to convince myself that it was unreasonable to feel so deeply in love with someone I had known for only a month. Certainly a separation of a few weeks should be enough to bring me to my senses. I still couldn't decide if Jonathan was a closet case, but even if he was, I had too much self-respect to feel that I had the right to threaten his marriage any more than I may already have done.

Self-respect. The thought of that concept suddenly hit me. It was as if a three-hundred-pound sumo wrestler had picked me up, thrown me down, and was now sitting on my chest. For a moment I felt that I could not breathe from the weight. I began to hyperventilate. A few minutes went by, and things calmed down, and then what had been going on inside of me since Saturday night became a dreadful epiphany. For the first time since coming out as a gay man, I now hated being gay. All these years my identity had been wrapped up in that three-letter word, and here I was feeling only self-contempt. If I weren't gay, there would be no Jonathan problem, and I would not be in such pain.

> There is a weight upon me
> Pressing out my self-worth.
> That which once I held up high
> Now just seems to want to die.
> What a monster love can be
> That it should wish to kill me.

To make matters worse, the very idea that Jonathan's marriage had lasted as long as it had only caused my failed relationships to assault me. Yes, there had been good reasons for ending them, but at this moment those reasons seemed insignificant. I could only think of those relationships as gay failures. I wanted to distance myself from my gayness, but I couldn't. I couldn't remember any time in my adult life that I hadn't been gay. In fact, the more I thought back, the more I kept coming up with that word. Even back into childhood, I had been turned on by men. As a four-year-old I'd had crushes on movie Tarzans, who, except for small breechcloths, had been naked men.

When was it that I'd first consciously known I was gay? It certainly wasn't when I'd had my first homosexual experiences. When I was fifteen, my mother asked her on-and-off boyfriend, Gerard, to explain the birds and the bees to me in private. One night while my mother was on the night shift at work, he came over and started to describe the physiology of sexual intercourse. I wasn't interested in his explanation, so I played dumb.

He suggested that we drop our pants, which we did. He saw I had a hard-on, and he told me to get some lubricant, which I did. With my being a virgin, he must have figured it was safe to bareback, so he got on the bed belly down, pulled his cheeks apart, and told me to put some lube on my dick and enter him. After that, about once a week, when he knew my mother was working late, he would come over to the apartment for repeat performances. All he wanted was to get fucked. That was it. No foreplay, no kissing, no romance—just ride his ass. That went on for two years until his final breakup with my mother. She never knew that both of us had lost out on our shared paramour.

I thought of those sessions as just something a teenager did to get his rocks off. I didn't consciously decide I was gay until my first year of college. I was at the library on a Saturday with a handful of books to check out, but before doing so, I needed to pee. The second-floor men's room had only two urinals, and when I went in, there was a guy at one of them. I put my stack of books down on the floor, unzipped, pulled out Dan Junior, and began to pee. I noticed the guy trying to look down toward my piss pipe without being too obvious.

He could tell that I was aware of his interest, and so he pulled ever so slightly back from the urinal, just enough for me to see his treasure tool. He moved forward again and began knocking himself up and down. It was definitely not the kind of shaking that we all do to get the last little bit of pee out. A chill went down my spine.

Then someone else came in, and we both resumed standard men's-room poses—close to the wall, eyes directly forward. I finished, zipped up, picked up my books, and left. I walked down the hall very slowly and looked back to see if he was following. He was. As I checked out my books, he waited near the door, and when I went out, he followed. Without introducing himself or asking me my name, he commented on the number of books I was carrying and asked what I was studying.

"English and writing."

"You must be a very good student."

I was just sophisticated enough to know that he didn't give a damn about my academic performance. But I thought I'd play along.

"Pretty good."

"Do you live here on campus?"

That was a fairly stupid question since most guys my age wouldn't be living elsewhere.

"Yes."

That gave me the opportunity to ask him where he lived.

"It's a short drive from campus. Would you like to come over to my place?"

I carefully looked around to make sure no one was in earshot. "Can you bring me back here?"

"Of course."

He got out of his parking space and was driving down the street when he commented that I might be more comfortable if the books were on the floor at my feet and not on my lap.

In my rush to put them down, they went all over the floor, and I had to neatly position them in two sections on either side of my calves. We stopped at a light, and he put his hand on my thigh. At first, I just tried to keep my left arm out of his way, but then I realized that the best thing to do was to rest my hand on his thigh. By the time we got to his place, about fifteen minutes away, we were rubbing each other's crotches.

As we got out of the car, I, like an idiot, started to pick up my books, only to be told that it was safe for them to stay there. We got into his apartment, and he offered to get me a Coke or beer. I opted for a Coke. I noticed a prominent display of small classical-style statues, naturally all male and all nude, on a nearby shelf. He returned with two Cokes.

"Nice, aren't they?" he said as he handed me a can.

"Yes, very nice."

He motioned me to the couch, and he sat beside me thigh to thigh. He took a few swigs of soda, put the can down on the coffee table, unzipped me carefully, pulled out Junior, and began to suck it. I tried to lean back as far as I could to give his head as much access to Junior as possible. This was more than a new experience; it was an *experience*!

After a little of that, he unzipped himself, pulled out his manhood, put his hand on the back of my neck, and firmly brought my head down to his own ground zero. At first, I gagged on it, and he told me to go only as far down as I could and to be careful of my teeth. He would have had to have been near brain dead not to have known that up to then I had been an oral virgin.

All this time I had been holding on to the damn Coke, and I suddenly spilled it on his carpet. I stopped sucking to profoundly apologize, but he said not to worry about it.

I guess he thought that my skills might be in another direction, as he said, "Let's go into the bedroom."

Taking the can from me, he placed his hand on my upper back and guided me into the bedroom. He threw off the bedcovers and told me to get out of my clothes as he removed his. We got on the bed, and he motioned me to lie beside him. He took hold of my arousal, and I took hold of his. I assumed we were just going to dick dock, but after a few minutes he asked, "Have you ever fucked a guy before?"

"Yes."

"You want to fuck me?"

"If that's what you want."

"Yes."

He reached over to the nightstand, picked up a condom, and handed it to me. While I had never used a condom to fuck Gerard, I had tried them a few times while masturbating, so it didn't take much for me to know what I was supposed to do. As I rolled the rubber on, he raised his legs in the air and spread his cheeks with his hands. This was like with Gerard, only in this case, with the guy facing me.

I got on top of him, inserted, and started to drive. It never even occurred to me that he might at some point have wanted to be the driver. I was still canned candy, and I was sure his can opener would have been too big for me. Little did I suspect that someday my chocolate chimney would open to a lot larger.

After a few minutes, I shot. I pulled out as soon as I went soft, and I was about to get off the bed when the guy grabbed me and pushed me on my back. Oh! How I loved that push! He straddled my thigh and quickly shot jack-off juice over my belly. He got a cloth, wiped me off, and thanked me, and we got dressed.

We went back to the car, and in silence he drove me back to campus. He then thanked me again and drove off. Evaluation: Sex—B. Romance—F. That was a part of my college education that was not in any catalog. Sucking, while being careful of the teeth, was the art I learned from him that afternoon. I soon joined the gay-and-lesbian student union.

<blockquote>
I am a homosexual
And very proud of it.
I suck cock, and I get fucked,
And I get sucked and I fuck
Some folks may think to criticize,
But they see not men through my eyes.
</blockquote>

If I was able to rationalize Jonathan away during the day, the night was something different. I knew I had to get out of the house, but where? Our time at the Stag now seemed so self-defeating. I should never have taken him there. It was not his place. It was mine. But could I go back? I knew sooner or later I would have to, if only to reclaim it as mine, with nothing to do with him.

I had no doubt that it would be near empty on a Wednesday night, but it only takes one other desperate dick to escape from oneself, and from the look of the few of us there we were all in that category. There was one guy who was sort of my type, but he had dropped shoulders and spent more time looking at the floor than at the others there. Even in a semihot guy this always bothers me. It was pathetic body language that suggested he was not just timid but also lacked self-confidence. Who wants to pick up that?

He periodically glanced in my direction, and even though I was annoyed by his stance, his looks gave me a hard-on. I held a steady gaze on him, which clearly made him nervous but didn't stop him from furtively looking at me. This was too much temptation. I walked over and stood directly facing him.

"You've been looking at me. Do you like what you see?"

Without looking up, he sheepishly said, "Yes."

"Man, my face is up here, not on the floor."

He looked up with a nervous smile and said, "Sorry."

"What's your name?"

"Ralph," he meekly replied.

"Well, Ralph, can you say that louder while looking right at me?"

He looked to his left and right to see if there was anyone close enough to hear me. Probably the two men to his right would have heard, but they were too busy with their tongues in each other's mouths to care.

I was now going to leave no doubt in his mind that I had taken charge of him.

"You got shoulder or neck problems, boy?"

He gave a surprisingly strong "No!"

"Then lift up your head and pull back your shoulders."

He did so, but I think it was more out of surprise at the order than it was as a bottom obeying a top.

I felt I needed to keep reminding him that at least I thought he had more going for him than he obviously thought he had. I took a chance. I placed my hand on the wall, allowing my arm to rest on his shoulder, and with a gentle but still-commanding voice, I asked, "How do you expect to attract someone worthy of you if you stand around like a scared mouse?"

I was actually hoping he would fight back at this point. He could have told me to screw myself or pushed me away or walked out of the bar, but he didn't do any of that. Instead, he tightened his lips as if to hold back any verbal defense. It was now time to prove to him that I really did think he was worth my time and that I did care. Touching his chin, I leaned forward and put my mouth so close to his that it almost amounted to a kiss. "Is there something here you want?"

"Yes."

"What?"

He slowly raised his right hand, almost as if afraid to do so, and touched my chest with his fingertips. He ran those fingers down to my waist, and then, instead of continuing to my crotch, as I or any slut would have expected him to do, he moved them to the right to touch the handle of Brute Bliss.

Smiling, I said, "It's okay. It's to be touched."

With the first sign of excitement he had so far shown, he fondled the lashes, letting them fall through his fingers.

"Have you ever been flogged?"

Quietly he said, "Once."

"And you liked it?" That was a rhetorical question. Of course he liked it. He wasn't just trying to secretly look at me; although I hoped I was part of the package, it was the flogger that had captivated him.

A toy, a toy, to wonder at
That holds in it a double truth.
It can touch you with gentleness
Or with something far more intense.
It is not for the many folks
Who only think of it with fear.
And yet from the selective few
Great praising for it you will hear.

I had given him enough of my time to let him know that I had an interest. But if he wasn't prepared to make a full commitment then and there to me as his top for the night, I was going to just walk away.

"I don't know how intense it was for you, but I do intense, as in heavy. I will make your ass and shoulders red, especially those drooping shoulders to remind you from now on to keep them up and show that you are proud, not ashamed to be a bottom. This toy is on my right, which actually signals that I myself am ready to be a flogged bottom, and I want everyone in this bar to know I consider myself in no way inferior to any man who would top me. Do you understand?"

His face brightened up, but I wasn't sure if it was from my offer to flog him or from my self-worth speech. I hoped it was for both.

I got back, "Yes."

I pushed my knuckles into his chest and said, "It's a 'Yes, sir!'"

"Yes, sir!"

"Where do you live, boy?"

"It's not close. I took a cab to get here."

"Boy, do you have a problem with ending your sentences with *sir*?"

"No, sir! Sorry, sir!"

"Forget that again, boy, and I'll conclude you're a slow learner, and I don't tolerate slow learners."

"Yes, sir! Sorry, sir!"

"Okay, you listen up well. If I accept you, we'll go to my place. But if you think for a moment that all I am is an arm to flog you and nothing more, you're dead wrong. After the flogging, I expect something in return, which means fucking your sore red ass. And if you're not willing to give me that, tell me now, because if so, I need to dump you and go on to someone who really wants what I have to offer."

"Please. I mean please, sir! I want what you have to offer. I really do."

"Prove it, boy."

"How, sir?"

"Since it's up to you to prove it, it's up to you to figure a way."

I thought that Ralph might fall to his knees or show some such submissive behavior, but he surprised me. He grabbed the sides of my face and pressed his mouth against mine with such vigor that I thought he was going to crush my front teeth.

Finally, he pulled back and stared at me as if to say, *Is that proof enough?*

Still not fully believing how animated he had suddenly become, I just said rather dispassionately, "That'll do." He smiled. "I'm going take a pee. I assume you'll be here when I get back."

That was half statement and half question. No matter how much someone seems to want to go home with you while the two of you are facing each other, there is always the chance that one or both will have second thoughts. Even though I was pretty sure he wouldn't cop out, by leaving him alone for a few minutes I was giving him the opportunity.

"I'll be here, sir!"

I headed for the restroom but had to wait in line for a free urinal. As I left the restroom, he was standing outside of it. I asked, "Need to pee?"

"No, sir!"

Maybe he was there to make sure I didn't cop out.

"By the way, I'm Coy. But you will always refer to me as sir. Got that, boy?"

"Yes, sir!"

I drove us to my place, and upon entering, I told him to stand up straight, with his hands behind his back and feet slightly apart.

"Move from that position and you're out of here, with no drive to anywhere."

Doing as he was told, I grabbed him by the back of the head and forced my mouth into his. I could tell he was about to bring his hands forward, and I pulled back and shouted, "I said don't move!"

"Sorry, sir!"

"Since you can't obey standing up, get on your knees without moving your hands."

He did so instantly.

> To be in charge is a sweet game
> When you know the other wants it.
> So you say kneel and he obeys
> You are like him to whom one prays.

"Now strip without getting up."

I stood there and watched him struggle to get his shoes and pants off in that awkward position, and while I found it very funny, I showed not the slightest sign of being amused. I checked out his body, which wasn't muscular but wasn't flabby either.

"Now fold those clothes neatly and hand them to me with both hands, shoes on top."

I took his clothes with me and left them in the bedroom while I grabbed my chaps. Returning to him I pushed them into his face to see if he liked the smell of leather. His inhaling showed he did. Throwing the chaps over my shoulder, I said, "Lick my boots, toes to tops."

Licking boots or watching someone else licking them is really erotic, but when the licker is totally naked, it is almost enough to

145

make one shoot. Five minutes of this was enough, so I said, "Now take them off."

I balanced myself on his head as he obeyed and then said, "Now the pants." He undid my belt and then unbuttoned and unzipped my pants. I could sense his excitement as he stared at my jockstrap holding in my maximized member. "Now fold those neatly and lay them aside. Then put the boots back on, and let's see if you know how to put chaps on a man." He had a little trouble with the chaps, which suggested that he was a novice at this, but he succeeded. "Good boy."

I now took off my jacket and shirt and said, "Why don't you show me what you can do with your tongue and mouth?"

He didn't bother with a verbal response, going right for my crotch and pulling the jockstrap down. He was surprisingly tongue talented. As an initial reward, I stroked his back with Brute Bliss, and that only intensified his efforts. He seemed ready for what he wanted more than anything else.

"You now ready for some pain, boy?"

"Yes, sir!"

"Remember what I said back in the bar. I give what I can take—nothing more, nothing less—and I can take a lot. I will only stop once my arm wears out or you start begging for mercy, and I do mean begging. So if you think you're going to wimp out before you really start hurting, say so now. As long as I can get some damn dick up an ass, I won't be too disappointed."

"Please, sir! I'm ready."

"Then get up."

My living room has a pair of closets that face each other. Each closet contains a set of chains, with one end of each chain attached to just inside the door frames. The free ends can be pulled out, and a person standing in the center between the closets can be chained by both his wrists and ankles into a spread-eagle position. When I opened the closet doors and revealed the chains, the boy showed no sense of fear or anxiety at the obvious prospect of being restrained in such a way, suggesting that I could do anything I pleased with him. This implied that he had either really come to trust me, perhaps because of our talk in the bar, or was a very foolish guy.

After chaining him, I started slow and gradually worked toward maximum intensity, stopping only occasionally to check up on him. His shoulders and ass were certainly getting red, but he neither whimpered nor begged for mercy before my arm gave out. To rest my arm, I took to playing with his pecker, and as much as he seemed to like that, what he wanted still more was the flogger.

> The lashes fell upon his back
> That was as if a barren field,
> But soon that surface was alive,
> A garden, the color of pain,
> And he who sadly was in need
> Was taking this with joyful greed.

I went back to that, but soon my arm had had enough. I insisted on unchaining him with the perfectly valid excuse that his hands and arms being in such an above-the-heart position could negatively affect his circulation. Once he was unchained, I had him lie on the floor on his belly, and I massaged his reddened shoulders and ass to stimulate the circulation there.

Unlike most vanilla sexual activities, after any intense B-D (bondage and discipline), S-M (sadism and masochism), D-S (dominance and submission), or M-S (master and slave) sexual scene, the players should do more than just going to bed or getting dressed and leaving. An aftercare of some kind should occur. This can be as simple as the dominant cuddling or talking to the submissive to show that he cares about the boy.

Kinky sex, especially if it involves pain, is more than what happens to the body; it is what is going on in the deepest parts of the minds of both players. Thus, after any intense scene, the players must make sure the invisible minds, as well as the visible bodies, of the players have come through safely.

The body of a player
Is always vulnerable,
But far more are the two minds,
Where damage may not be seen.
Avoid despair; be aware
Through sufficient aftercare.

After a few minutes of this I asked, "Are you okay?"

"I'm fine, sir! Thank you, sir!"

"You've had enough?"

"Yes, sir!"

"Enough to remind you not to slouch those shoulders?"

"Yes, sir! No more slouching. I promise, sir!"

"And when someone talks to you, what do you do?"

"I look him in the face, sir!"

"You ready to reward me for my kindness, boy?"

"Yes, sir!"

"Then get that red butt of yours into the bedroom. Front up."

"Yes, sir!"

I pushed him toward the bedroom and threw off the covers. He immediately got on the bed. I pulled off my boots, handed them to him, and told him to hold them against his chest. Since I still had the jockstrap on, I had to unzip the chaps, remove the jockstrap, and zip the chaps back up. I was about to take the boots from him when I realized I had lost all top mind space. Grabbing a condom and lube, I dropped down on the bed next to him and said, "Fuck me."

"Fuck you, sir?"

"Yes. You do know how to fuck, don't you?"

"Yes, sir!"

"Well, the sir who just mastered you is now ordering you to fuck him, and a good bottom boy always does what he is ordered to do. Have you a problem with that, boy?"

"No, sir!"

There are, thankfully, only a very few bottoms that so identify the act of fucking as something only a top should do that they are literally incapable of fucking someone they have identified as a top. Ralph quickly proved he was not one of those. In fact, like many a good fucker he tried to remain in as long as possible while I beat off.

We dressed, and as I drove him home, I hoped that I had helped him with his shyness problem, because I really thought he was a good kid.

> Shy need not be a fault
> Unless you make it so.
> Let it not interfere
> With living a whole life.
> Stand up straight; show your pride.
> Let courage be your guide.

Thursday and Friday I managed to push Jonathan out of my mind by working on preparing for the conference talks and the workshop. The first panel was to be on teaching college-level writing to students whose first language was not English. The second panel was on writing across language barriers. The third workshop dealt with the ins and outs of writing poetry.

I love teaching writing and poetry. I especially love to show students that each of them has a story worth writing and being read by others. As for poetry, students who are too afraid to be blatant in prose can safely disguise themselves in metaphors and similes and can put the richness of their potential in some uncensored rhyme or free verse. In fact, sometimes even the teacher's feelings can only safely be expressed in poetry.

> Love is the colors of a rainbow,
> The eyes to serenade.
> I should revel in their beauty
> But weep not when they fade.

The conference now took on a secondary meaning for me—time to try to regain my gay pride that had suddenly disappeared. It was one thing for something like that to disappear, but what if there was nothing—absolutely nothing—to replace it? In that being nongay automatically meant wanting to have sex with women, nongay was something totally foreign to my nature. Even as a teenager when I would go to high school social events with girls, they were always female friends, never girlfriends.

> No woman have I embraced,
> Nor with kisses have I graced.
> I've only had men in my bed,
> And none but them will I wed.

Wed brought me back to the present and to the painful dilemma that I was gay and nothing was going to change that, no matter how much I might murderously hate being gay at that time. I didn't know how, but I was determined to find some way of regaining my sense of self-esteem. I knew that if I could not love myself for who I was, I would never be able to authentically love someone else. *What have you done to me, Jonathan? What have you left me with but emptiness and loss?* By Friday night I was feeling so depressed that I wanted at least the limited validation that sex could give. But to merely dishonorably discharge was too depressing a choice, so I did something I had only done once before.

> He was a young top for rent
> With a cock that was extent.
> As I spread my cheeks wide,
> He got manly inside,
> And I cried once he was spent.

I drove down what was sometimes called Buying Boys Boulevard, where I saw what I was after. He looked slightly older than most of the guys that sell themselves there and that seemed to give me some added justification for my actions. I wanted his sellable sucking, and he presumably wanted the easy hundred, so to hell with principles. I stopped and flashed five twenties, and he got in. I drove to a dark side street and parked in the only available spot—a red zone. I unzipped and offered him a condom. He seemed surprised by it, which I assumed meant that most of his customers were not so considerate about safe sex. He took it, opened it, and slipped it on me, and with that, I pushed his head down on Dan Junior. Once satisfied, I gave my financed fellator his reward, dropped him back on the Boulevard, and drove home.

Sunset to near sunrise,
On either side of a dim street,
They stand and posture:
Embodiments of desire.
For a small gratuity
One of them will give
The love of Ganymede.

Chapter 10

I started out for New Mexico Saturday morning, August 13, with the expected very light traffic. As the crow flies, Santa Fe is about 700 miles from LA but is about 860 miles driving. I decided to do it in four leisurely parts: day one to Needles, two to Flagstaff, three to Gallup, and four to Santa Fe. On the way to Needles I had to pass by Barstow, which reminded me of Master Odin. Odin was never my master, just a former flogging trick who had his own slave.

He was a handsome, hunky slave bear

Who at home was allowed nothing to wear.
This upon my honor I will swear
Gave his master a huge reason to stare.

Odin was well known in the leather community for the formal dom-and-sub orgies he would host in LA. I had participated in a number of orgies before attending one of his with Master Peter, but with the exception of two, these orgies had not been preplanned but spontaneous orgies. In the preplanned orgies five to seven doms or masters, each with a sub, would be invited to a private LA dungeon where the rule was that each master would give his sub the freedom to play with any other participant, master or sub, except himself. The event was called the Saturnalia in honor of the seven-day Roman festival in which masters and slaves reversed roles.

The only preplanned orgy I had been in before had been when I was technically still a slave of Master Abe. The start of the sixth week with Master Abe had brought an unexpected situation. Master Abe's mother, who lived in Northern California and knew nothing about Master Abe's sexuality, was having problems that required him to travel up there and stay for at least eight if not ten days (it turned out to be nine). Abe decided that he was not going to give me, his slut slave, the freedom to do as I pleased for more than a week, so he convinced, rather easily, one of his party buddies to act as a guardian master. This is another master who is given charge of a slave while the slave's own master is away. Since I knew that the guardian was bound by the same contractual rules established between Master Abe and me, I had no real reason to protest.

> A substitute master
> For a week or so.
> While the games were the same,
> The players were not.
> Spicy variety
> To suck and to fuck.

Actually, to say the games were the same is only true in the sense that I had several partners. Not only did my guardian have a mostly separate set of friends from that of Master Abe, but he also had his own slave, which was good because he was more into real, or classic, orgies than was Master Abe. Only one bottom getting fucked by two or more tops, one after the other, is not a classic orgy. On the contrary, a classic one requires at least four participants (a fourgy) all interacting with one another. I hadn't been in any kind of orgy for over a year, so when my guardian asked if I would be willing to participate, even though it was outside of my contract, with hidden enthusiasm, I agreed.

> There is a play that some deplore,
> Of making love to four or more.
> Not quite a dozen times before
> So it is yet far from a bore.

The first of the two group-sex parties was with the guardian, his slave, one other (guest) top, and me. It started out as a wet-weather event. First, we the two slaves were required to piss on each other. Then the masters pissed on us, which was followed by an unusual flogging arrangement. A Saint Andrew's cross had been set up in the middle of the room, and I was secured to one side while the other submissive was on the other side. This meant that the two of us were facing each other and actually, with some difficulty, able to kiss or at least tongue each other. More importantly, we could see the expressions of pain and pleasure on each other's faces as we were simultaneously flogged.

> The sharing of face-to-face pain
> Builds a bond of brotherhood.
> So they share with each the secrets
> That their masters never would.

This scene then ended rather uniquely. We slaves were ordered to be on all fours (doggy position) but crisscrossing each other, with me over the other slave. With that, the two masters on their knees fucked us.

The second party was more standard orgy, to such an extent that it was difficult to tell who the tops and who the bottoms were. A hole was a hole, and in short, most played a flexible role.

The guardian and I decided not to tell Master Abe about this contractually unauthorized activity, especially because I had served as both a bottom and a top to the guardian, which according to Master Abe's rules required a penalty (punishment).

The drive to and night in Needles was uneventful, but on the way to Flagstaff I saw a sign for Sedona and remembered the one time I had gone there. I'd first visited Sedona several years ago because of its spiritual or at least New Age reputation. I had left the service of Master Peter only a couple of weeks prior. This meant that not only was I still in a slave mode of consciousness but that I had been experiencing a near-continuous case of slave-identity drift (SID). This may occur when a slave is not with his master for a certain period of time. It is not that he starts to feel like a free person but that his sense of submissiveness weakens, and this can be depressing for him.

SID can happen after only a few hours, such as when being away from one's master while he is at work, but usually it requires a day or two for such depression to kick in. SID can be especially bad if one is in between masters. I had experienced some of this drift after leaving Masters Hal and Abe but nothing like it was now. I knew what I was supposed to do to reduce the feeling, but that was not helping much.

A slave suffering from SID should try to wear his collar as much as possible and touch it often. He should try to avoid nonslave clothing as much as possible. He should seek slave friends or a slave rap group. Although hooking up with a one-night stand or a weekend dom will not relieve SID entirely, it may help significantly, especially if you have a sympathetic dom who will play master for you.

> A slave is more than a role
> To enter and to leave.
> It is his identity
> Once he has tasted it.
> To submit is in his brain;
> To not do so becomes pain.

The first night I was in Sedona, I stopped to get gas. While in the minimart next door, I spotted this guy who in turn spotted me. It was instant interest. I asked the attendant for the restroom key, and as I left, the guy followed me right into it. Before either of us said anything to the other, he put his hand on my shoulder and pressed down. This had been my first time on my knees since my last discipline at the hands of Master Peter, and I didn't even bother suggesting the need for a condom, instead going right to work. He clearly didn't want a stand-up quickie, because he said, "We need to go to my van."

I knew the guy felt comfortable ordering me around because my car keys were on the right and I was wearing the dog chain and lock around my neck. I returned the restroom key to the attendant, and the guy more or less pushed me toward his van. My passive willingness told him all he needed to know, and he had barely closed the van door when he made it absolutely clear who was in charge.

"Pull those damn pants down and be quick about it, boy."

The well-worn mattress and the immediate access to condoms and lube told me that I was not the first to visit this playroom on wheels. From the restroom activity, I knew my ass could take him, so I obeyed.

"Legs up and over."

He lubed me up and, without another word, plugged in. The speed caused some initial pain, but this guy's crude, even animallike forcefulness was such a turn-on that I took it without complaint. Once he'd shot and had let me beat off, he actually got gentle. Until now, the only interest in something other than dick and asshole that he'd shown had been forcing his mouth onto mine in the restroom. Now he kissed me, and our tongues played with one other.

"So what's your name, boy?"

"Coy, sir."

"I'm Carl. So where you heading to?"

"I'm staying here in Sedona, sir."

"Where?"

"At the motel just down the street."

"How long you here for?"

"Three more days."

"You want to check out of the motel and stay with me?"

To have simply said yes would have implied I had freedom to say no, and a display of freedom in this situation would have cooled down the heat, for me at least. Besides, he was offering me some escape from my SID.

"If that's what you want, sir!"

"You're damn right, boy. Now put on your pants, and lose the underwear. My boys don't wear anything that gets in my way."

"Yes, sir."

"I'll meet you at the motel. Get your gear, and follow me. Any questions, boy?"

"No, sir."

"Good. I don't like boys that ask a lot of questions. It gives them the wrong ideas."

I interpreted that statement to mean it gave them the right to think for themselves. Well, I think for myself, but for three days of hot submissiveness, I could joyfully suppress that. I checked out of the motel and followed him home. Expecting crude living quarters, I was surprised at how well the place was decorated and how clean it was. There was even a shelf with books on it.

"Have you had dinner, boy?"

"Yes, sir! I ate just before the gas station."

"I haven't, so I'm going to fix myself something to eat. You can store your gear in the bedroom, and if you want to watch TV, the DVDs are over there."

I found the bedroom. Actually, there were two of them, but one had been converted into a computer room. Both were as well decorated as the living room. I set my suitcase and backpack down and returned to the living room. Since I had been more or less ordered to settle myself down there, I thought it would be unwise to go into the kitchen and bother him. I did take the opportunity to check out some of the book titles.

I shouted, "Sir! May I look at one of your books?"

He shouted back, "Sure."

I got caught up with what I was reading and lost track of time, but I finally heard, "Boy. You want some pie?"

I took this as an invitation to enter the kitchen and said, "Yes, sir!"

The kitchen was as clean as the rest of the house, certainly cleaner than mine. He had presumably finished his main meal and washed up any cooking utensils and the dishes. All that was visible was a pie in its pan and two small plates.

"With or without ice cream?"

"With, sir."

He pointed to a chair, but I just stood in back of it.

"Something wrong, boy?"

"No, sir. It's just that I've been trained not to sit down before sir."

"Trained?"

"Yes, sir, as a slave."

"A slave?"

"Yes, sir."

"So where is your master?"

"We have recently broken up, sir."

He ever so slightly smiled and said, "Well, I may not be your master, boy, but I'm telling you to sit down."

"Yes, sir! Thank you, sir."

I sat down while trying not to lean back against the back of the chair, which is how a slave should sit. In fact, when eating with my masters, I was required to sit at the table on a backless seat—in other words, a stool. Chairs with backs and even more so with armrests are for masters.

Carl Sir served me the pie à la mode, then sat down, and we proceeded to eat.

"What other rules are you supposed to follow, boy?"

I told him the relevant one I could think of at that moment. "Never continue eating after sir has finished, and never leave the table without permission."

He slowed down his ingestion of the pie as I finished mine.

"Where did you get this slave training from?"

"Mostly from my first master, sir."

He just looked at me with that same subtle smile and then said, "Not too many boys like you."

I didn't want to sound too prideful by saying, *You're right*, so once again acknowledging his superiority over me, I said, "If you say so, sir."

"I do, boy."

He finished eating and got up, and of course I immediately got to my feet.

"Don't tell me. When the sir gets up, the boy gets up?"

"Yes, sir. Sir, am I making you uncomfortable?"

He thought for a moment and said, "Actually, no. It's just new to me, but I like it. Why don't you go into the living room, and I'll clean up here."

Normally I would have expected to be assigned the job of washing the plates, but I didn't want to impose on him any more of my slave training than I already had, so with a "Yes, sir," I did as I was told. Although he hadn't specifically told me to sit down, I thought just standing there waiting for him would have been carrying the whole slave thing too far in this situation, so I sat.

He came in, and before I could move, he said, "Don't get up."

I didn't.

"So tell me more about these rules of yours."

"When I'm with a master, I am expected to know how I should stand, walk, sit, kneel, speak, greet another master, dress, etc., sir."

"How would you do some of that differently from anyone else?"

"I was always expected to be on the side of my master's dominant hand."

"What about speaking?"

159

"A slave is not to be too talkative. He speaks when necessary, and that is determined by his master, sir."

"And what would happen if you didn't do one of those the right way?"

"I'd get punishment, sir."

"And how would you get punished?"

"With all due respect, sir, a slave does not talk about that issue without permission of the master involved."

"Of course. Sorry about that."

"No problem, sir."

"I'd like to hear more about this tomorrow, but now I think it's time for bed."

"Can I pee first, sir?"

"Sure. Then turn out the light and get your ass in the bedroom."

"What if I need to pee later on? Do I have the right to do so without waking and asking you, sir?"

"There are guys that really make you ask to use the john?"

"Yes, sir."

He just stared at me for a moment in disbelief, then asked, "And what if they say no?"

"Only one master ever did so, and he was just testing me. A moment later I told him I really had to go, and he allowed it."

"Interesting."

"So, sir, what about peeing?"

"Do it whenever you need to."

"Thank you, sir! And the bed, sir, am I to assume that you want me to sleep in your bed?"

"Where else would you sleep?"

"Well, sir, the natural place for a slave to sleep is on the floor, so it is improper for him to automatically assume he has been given the privilege of sleeping in the master's bed."

"Would you rather sleep on the floor?"

"No, sir, absolutely not. I just don't want to offend sir by making the presumption that he is going to honor me by allowing me to sleep with him."

The floor is where a slave should sleep.
Where else would be his natural place?
Only due to the master's wish
Should he rise to a better space.

"Go take your pee and get into bed."

"Yes, sir!"

Upon returning to the bedroom, I said, "Sir, could I ask a favor of you?"

"Sure."

"According to my training, I am not allowed into sir's bed without a reminder that it is an earned privilege, not a right. As a reminder, my masters would usually spank, belt, paddle, or cane my ass a little beforehand, as the price to sleep with them, sir."

I didn't want to tell him that most of the time just getting on my knees and thanking the master for the privilege was enough. I wanted to feel Carl's hand on my butt.

"You want me to spank you, boy?"

"If that would not be too much trouble, sir."

"My pleasure, boy. Get over here."

He had me lie across his legs, and he began to swat my butt. It felt so good.

"It's getting red, boy."

"Yes, sir! Thank you, sir! I really appreciate your kindness."

"Kindness? You must really like getting spanked."

"I'm a slave, sir. I like being dominated."

"Well, boy, then we're going to have to find ways to take care of that. But for now I'm ordering you to get into this fucking bed so we can get some sleep."

"Yes, sir! Good night."

"Good night, boy."

The sun was barely up when I was awoken by the feel of his hand running over my body, and we were soon going at it heavily.

It was nothing really kinky, but he did play the dom, and it seemed he liked dirty talk.

> Dirty talk while in the bed
> Is not an uncommon treat.
> But between a dom and sub
> That talk may be power sweet.

He made breakfast, and while he went to work, I played tourist before returning to his place that evening. We had dinner together, talked more about being a slave, watched DVDs, had sex, and did the same the following evening. Those few days in Sedona helped relieve some of my SID, and I will always remember them for that.

> A town with a reputation
> For spiritual contemplation
> Yet with sexual temptation
> While on a needed vacation.

I had heard about one bar in Flagstaff, and as one would assume, it was filled with cowboys. There were only ten or so in the place, but it turned out that one was enough. His name was Pedro, and he had wonderfully beautiful youthful mestizo features. His poor English, the roughness of his hands, and his body being lighter than his face suggested that he was a field worker, but I didn't inquire. As for his sexual performance, well:

> He was a promising trick
> With a sizable uncut prick.
> He was into my ass
> With a thunderous flash,
> But, alas, he shot too quick.

The rest of the route to Santa Fe was uneventful. My arrival there early Tuesday evening on August 16 didn't leave me any time to explore the city, and besides, the drive from Gallup to Santa Fe had been far more tiring than that between the other cities. So I ate dinner in the hotel restaurant and went to bed early. At first I had trouble getting to sleep because I kept thinking that it was five weeks to the day since I had met Jonathan, but finally I dozed off.

Wednesday I spent exploring Santa Fe itself. Considering the large number of residents of Mexican descent, an abundance of Catholic churches was to be expected. Although I was at best indifferent to Christianity, I investigated some of the churches for their religious art. In the last of which church there was a huge crucifix with an image of the asphyxiating Christ that particularly impressed me.

> He is there hanging high in front of me
> Above an altar set for bread and wine,
> A naked man except around his loins.
> His countenance is one of agony,
> Arms spread wide and nailed upon a cross.
> His feet are also brutally secured.
> Blood pouring forth from this pitiful man,
> Who legend says was innocent of sin.
> A crown of thorns impaled into his scalp.
> Gasping for air, he prolongs life and pain.
> Repulsion I should feel, but instead,
> I am fascinated by every wound.
> The unity of beauty, sex, and death—
> Magnificent, this masochistic man.

Without any question, this was the Christology of a non-Christian, gay leather queen looking at his tragic Tarzan on a cross. As I left the church, however, I was reminded of the Christian clergy—flip-collar fairies—I had played with.

163

First, there was Father Albert. He had been Catholic but turned Protestant.

> There was a priestly man
> Of the penis to penis clan.
> Without a doubt that God loved him
> Despite what might be called a sin,
> He changed from being Franciscan
> To a more flexible Anglican.

We met at a private and very heavily hedonistic Halloween party. Albert was there without a costume, while I was in a leopard breechcloth and nothing else. I was Tarzan. I especially remember Albert because he helped me learn how to ride a motorcycle, and ride on it in more than one way we did. Sex with Albert was the only time I've ever gotten fucked with chain grease. The first time I lay on my belly across the seat while he drove. The next couple of times he straddled the bike holding on to my hips while I sat on his rigid rider and, holding on to the handlebars, made like I was riding a bumpy road.

Then there was the second former man of the cloth, Bryan. I picked him up at Themes, one of the more interesting S-M bars.

> A dance bar below,
> But what is above?
> Sunday through Thursday,
> A stand-up sex hall;
> While on the weekends,
> An upstairs dungeon.
> The obvious sign reads,
> "Serious players,
> Others unwelcome.
> No shoes/boots removed,
> Nor pants off ankles.

Condoms plentiful,
So no barebacking,
And no drugs allowed.
A damnable den
To enter with risks
And your ten dollars."
The only real light
Was on the crosses
For doms to please subs,
While in the shadows
There were still more games
Of pleasure and pain.
Just two monitors
To police against
Unprotected sex.
Some violations
Are not caught in time,
Which can only mean
An unpunished crime.

It was my first visit to Themes, and I started out with the dance floor below before going upstairs.

Clothed in primitive black animal hide,
I entered the lair of the pleasure of pain
Of an urban aboriginal theme:
Another name for a discipline dream.

Standing in an obvious slave-mode position, I sighted Bryan in full leather, and he sighted me. He came up to me and asked, "Who owns the key to the locked chain?"

"Is that a polite inquiry or a demand to know?"

He thought a moment before saying, "Demand."

"Whatever master who can force me to one of those crosses and use my flogger on my bare butt and back until I cry and beg him to stop and who will then manhandle me until I agree to suck him off or get fucked."

It may seem difficult to believe, but despite the really rough action going on in an environment like that, I have often found to my regret that a bluntly violent answer like that scares off even some of the roughest-looking doms or pseudo doms. Not this one, not this time.

"So I assume you are looking for someone to put you on that cross?"

Letting the lashes of my flogger pass erotically through my fingers, I replied, "Only if that someone knows how to handle this toy."

"I do."

"Then yes."

We had to wait until one of the crosses was available, and in the meantime, there was mouth-to-mouth and hand-to-groin activity, soon halted by the groan of one of the men on a cross, which signaled that he had had enough.

"It looks like your turn, boy."

"Yes, sir!"

As I willingly stepped to the cross, I handed Bryan Sir the flogger and asked him to avoid the small of my back—the forbidden zone—and to target only my shoulders and ass. I pulled off my shirt and pulled down my pants only far enough to expose my butt. Bryan flogged me until I cried and begged for no more. Once off the cross, I was rewarded with his tongue in my mouth, followed by him pressing me against the wall and fucking me.

> It is not malevolence,
> Nor is it benevolence—
> Somewhere in between these is
> Awesome phallic violence.

I liked Bryan but also felt sorry for him. In marked contrast to Father Albert, Bryan was clearly still holding on to his biblical literalist hang-up that God could not love a horny homo.

> He was a pulpit preacher
> Of the Baptist Church.
> One day there came the shock
> He loved to suck on cock.
> "You should at least defrock,"
> Called out all of his flock.

My last experience with ecclesiastics was ex-reverend Phillip. He was very vanilla, to the point that he wasn't into anything more exciting than giving and receiving blow jobs. I nicknamed him Phil Fellatio. The one thing I admired him for was that he didn't wait until his sexual interests were uncovered and he was driven out of his church, as in Bryan's case. Phillip got to the point where he felt he had to admit the truth to himself and to his wife. Resigning his ministry, he got divorced, forgot about religion, and ended up working at Dungeon Leather, which was where I met him.

> In former service to his dear Lord God
> He found Leviticus a heavy cross.
> But adding Romans 1 to this weight
> For this queer clergyman was just too great.
> So abandoning the big boy above,
> He chose to do for the sin of love.

Chapter 11

On the way back to the hotel the thought occurred to me that religion is the kind of thing that is easy to either love or hate but difficult to treat with indifference. On the other hand, there was Rasputin's creed:

> Sin leads to salvation
> By a tortured path.
> You must know the former
> Before the latter gained.
> When your sins are complete,
> Their hollowness to see,
> Then your heart will open,
> And heaven's grace will be.

I had planned for an early-evening bedtime again so the next day I could drive up to Taos to see the pueblo and do some shopping. But between the end of dinner and thinking about bed, I got so horny I decided to try my luck at one of the cowboy bars. Naturally, since it was a Wednesday night, there were not going to be as many patrons as on a weekend, but after about twenty minutes I spotted a guy I liked wearing cowboy boots, well-soiled jeans, a rodeo belt buckle, a tight T-shirt that showed hard pecs, and of course a cowboy hat. Nothing was unusual in his appearance except for the long braid of hair running down his back. Now I've had men with all sorts of hairstyles from very short to very long. Ponytails, mohawks, scalp locks, dreadlocks, braided, and shaved heads, depending on the man beneath them, can each be a turn on.

> Hair has never been less than erotic
> Throughout the centuries and continents.
> Whether on the scalp, the face, or body,
> Folks have tried to turn it into an art,
> Even by removing it from one's view.
> A naked head may be right to pursue.

This guy's hair, however, reminded me of the last guy with a queue whom I'd bedded.

> One of the prettiest men I knew
> Had his hair braided into a queue.
> He loved to lie down on his belly,
> At which point he would become nelly
> And pull his queue to tell me to screw.

But that was just one man, and I had no right to judge this one by that experience. This queue guy kept circling around the bar, giving me a glance each time he passed. Although I had given a nod of interest the first time, he'd ignored it. He still kept looking at me but without any indication that he wanted any attention from me in return.

After the third pass of his seeming indifference, I stopped returning his glance. Since there was nothing else that suited my taste, I put my beer bottle on the bar and headed for the door, figuring the night would have to end with making love to myself like some lonely loser.

"Going somewhere?"

I turned to see the questioner. It was Mr. Indifference. "There doesn't seem to be anyone in here interested in me."

Although he was taller and heavier than I and his question had a certain commanding quality to it, I didn't really need to use *sir*, since this wasn't a leather bar.

"Let me buy you another beer."

"If you wish."

"I do."

I wasn't sure what kind of game he was playing, but the prospect of not playing solo tonight made me accept.

As he handed me the beer, I noticed that his hands spoke of hard, probably outdoor work—rough and cracked. Avocado oil and glycerin rubbed into them would have helped.

"Thank you."

"You're not from around here?"

"No, from LA. Here for a conference."

"What's your name?"

"Coy."

"I'm Joe. What's the conference about?"

"A writers' conference."

"I assume you're staying at a hotel."

"Yes."

"You want to come over to my place?" I actually liked this limited bar talk and the *let's get down to what we are both here for.*

"I have to get up early—heading for Taos for the day. But if that's okay with you, it's okay with me."

"Why don't you finish up, and we'll go."

Once we were outside, he said, "My truck is over there. You got a car?"

"Yes. It's that one across the street. By the way, can you tell me how far we're going?"

"Not far, about eight, nine miles. Too far for you?"

"Not at all."

"Good. I'll try to drive slowly so you don't lose me, but not much traffic at this hour, so it should be easy."

He headed for his truck, and I headed for my car. He waited near the parking lot entrance until I was able to get right behind him, and we were soon at his place—a small house, with a fair amount of space between it and the ones on either side, typical of those outside of the city limits. Once he turned the lights on, I could see that the interior was basic man, which meant it could never be mistaken for ever having a woman's touch, much less that of any faggot interior designer.

"What anything to drink? Beer?"

"No thanks, I'm fine."

"Bedroom's that way. Bathroom to the left if you need it."

He got himself a beer and headed for the bedroom. I followed. Maybe it was the fact that I had said I had to get up early that suggested that we should get right down to business, and we did. We did some mutual sucking before he made it clear that, like a good cowboy, he wanted to ride me, although he did ask if I had a preference.

> On all fours like a cub or pup
> Ready to take it from the rear.
> Needing no more than a hard dick
> That likes a dude more than a chick.

I think if I had had more free time, there would have been foreplay and afterplay, but that wasn't possible. I did stay the night though.

We both got up early the next morning, and as I left, he said, "I'm really glad I went to the bar last night. I almost didn't. Too bad you're only here for the conference. I suppose you won't have much time for anything else."

Having just escaped from the Jonathan issue, I wasn't emotionally ready to get into more than a one-night stand, so I said, "Unfortunately not."

"Yeah, well, I got a construction job I'm working on, so my day is pretty filled too."

A hunk, even vanilla,
Is not to be turned down.
But life has a clock that ticks
That will frustrate our dicks.

I had never been to Taos before and found it delightful enough to think I would have liked to spend more than a day there, but I had obligations, so it was back to Santa Fe. When I got back to the hotel, it was clear that most of the other conference attendees had chosen Thursday to arrive. I greeted several of those I knew, but it was too late to have dinner with them, so I ate by myself in the hotel dining room.

Friday morning there was a breakfast get-together for all the panelists and workshop leaders. I had been looking forward to this breakfast because the material guidelines sent to me months ago were little more than an outline. As I'd hoped, I received more details as to my participation.

My first panel was not until 3:00, so after breakfast I returned to my room and started on some of the reading I had brought to occupy me during conference downtime. At about ten the phone rang. I assumed it was one of the conference people, and when it wasn't, I froze.

"Hi, it's Jonathan."

"How did you get this number?"

"Simple—after you told me about the conference, I looked it up on the web."

"Of course."

"When you said that you wouldn't be back for two to three weeks, I couldn't stand it. I had to know if you could tell me you didn't love me if I was standing in front of you."

"Well, unless you have a magic transport device to instantly transport you from your place to here, you're not going to get that."

"I don't need one. I'm here in the hotel lobby. I asked for your room number, but the desk told me that I would have to call you on the in-house phone to get it. Please, let me come up."

I could barely believe he had actually followed me here and was downstairs.

"You're torturing both of us again."

He started to cry.

"Jonathan, you're probably embarrassing yourself."

"Please let me come up."

I could not leave him crying in the lobby like that.

"Okay, it's 417."

All that I could think was *What do I do now?* Before anything came to mind, there was a knock on the door. I let him in, and he just stood in the middle of the room like a little naughty boy waiting for his daddy to chastise him.

"Sit down, Jonathan. No! Not on the bed." I pointed to the chair.

He obeyed instantly. I sat on the edge of the bed in front of him just staring at him. He was still silent, waiting for whatever good or ill I might have in store for him. I began to quiz him.

"How did you get here?"

"I flew to Albuquerque and then took the airport shuttle to Santa Fe. I got in late last night but thought I should wait until this morning to see you."

"Does Ruth know you're here?"

"Of course. I explained that I had received an emergency request to attend this conference."

"And she believed you?"

"Yes. I get such requests a number of times a year, usually as a last-minute replacement for someone who couldn't make it for whatever reason."

"Does she know that I'm here?"

"No, she didn't ask anything like that. She doesn't know anything about you leaving town."

"I thought I made it clear, Jonathan, that we couldn't see each other again, that whatever happened between us wasn't meant to be."

"But I want to be with you so badly."

"But this can only lead to more pain for both of us. Is that what you want?"

"No. I only want to be with you."

"Jonathan, I just don't understand you. You have a lovely wife whom you've told me you dearly love. So why me?"

"I don't know. It's like there's something missing inside of me, and when I'm with you, that feeling disappears, and I feel whole."

"I don't like asking this, but I must. Do you know what a closet case is?"

"Yes, it means a man who is really gay living or pretending to live a straight life, and you're asking if that's me."

"Yes, I am."

"I don't know; I really don't know. I was never attracted to any man until I met you. And I never wanted to make love to anyone other than Ruth until you."

"Even if this means cheating on and lying to her?"

"It's not like I'd be doing this with another woman. I would never do that to Ruth."

"Jonathan, just because I'm a man, you think it's okay?"

"No. Yes. I don't know. I'm just so confused, so scared."

"Scared of what?"

"Scared of not being with you, scared of losing Ruth. Please. Help me to not be scared." Jonathan began to cry. This adorable bear I had in front of me loved me enough to follow me some seven hundred miles. I don't think any of my former lovers would have done that even at the highest point of our passion for each other.

Here he was to agitate
As to him to gravitate
And perhaps capitulate.
But I ought to hesitate
So as not to copulate,
Ending in ejaculate.

I couldn't just sit there and do nothing. I took hold of this desperately confused and frightened teddy bear and held him as closely and tightly as I possibly could, but now I was the one being torn apart. Then I thought, *Life is short, and no matter how responsible one tries to be, it only ends in the grave.* That was when the revolt against reason commenced.

I had been the strong one. I had made what I considered to be a Herculean effort to do the right thing, and it had been to no avail. It was just making me suffer. I knew in the back of my mind that I would have to make that effort again and find a way to make it stick, but not now. No, now I was entitled to take the reward for my previous efforts to try to drive him away.

The color and perfume
Of love's stolen flower
Promises great delights
For one who would seize it.
Yet everyone should know
Its thorns are dangerous.
So when you dare touch it,
Feel venom in its prick.
Wisdom and common sense
Warn you away from this.
Still, if you choose the risk,
Why not pain's pleasure pick?

Jonathan was here, and I didn't need to have some furtive sex and send him home tonight or any other of the next five nights. He was mine, and this time, the angel that said, "Do the right thing," was weakening, and my personal fiend was getting stronger and stronger. I could now turn this man that I had already turned into a bad boy into a full submissive and that submissive into a licentious lover.

"Jonathan, if you don't leave right away, we will both regret what will happen. Do you understand that? I mean really understand that?"

"Please. I just want to hold you."

"If you hold me, Jonathan, we're going to end up like Saturday night."

"Please."

I moved backward on the bed and turned my back on him. On the one hand, this was a way of symbolically saying that I was turning my back on this whole situation and that whatever happened after this was therefore not my fault. I was innocent—at least that was what I wanted to believe. Still, I also knew it was a way of letting him make the first move, which I really wanted him to do. I knew it would only encourage him to do so. I wanted the fiend to win, and to hell with the consequences!

There is an art that loves the night.
And hides itself by day.
With beauty great yet danger too,
So think before you trust.
It often blinds us to the right;
Our reason it corrupts.
Therefore, should you choose to indulge,
Life's muse you may abuse.
So please beware and dance with care,
Or yourself you could lose.
It is a magic black at times,
The sorcery of sex.

Jonathan came up behind me and put those big arms around me to give me his bear hug. His breath and beard on the back of my neck were too much to resist. I turned to face him. He leaned down and kissed me, but I remained uncommitted. I should have said no, but instead, I placed my arms around him, and that was all the excuse he seemed to need. We kissed, and what little resolve I had left disappeared.

I had done everything I thought right to end the corrupting craving between us. He was the one who was now guilty, and legalist logic told me I would be innocent of whatever came next. His hands moved down to pull my T-shirt out from my pants and up. The only cooperation I gave him was to raise my arms to allow the shirt to come off. It was as if I were telling myself that if I was going to have him, he was going to have to do all the work.

He gently pushed me into a sitting position on the bed as he squatted down to remove my shoes. I offered no resistance. Personally I find being undressed by another man, a handler, more erotic than being ordered to strip by a watcher. I was getting more and more aroused and stood to make his job easier. To balance myself, I placed my hand on his head, and a rush of energy went through me. He got my shoes off, unbuckled my belt, unbuttoned and slipped down my pants, and pulled them off.

For a moment he stopped at my underwear, but by this time I had an obviously visible bulge. He kissed it and pulled down and off the last piece of resistant clothing as I again balanced myself. Leaving me standing there semistiff, he sat down in the chair and removed his shoes, pants, shirt, and underwear. He stood up, and there we were, facing each other, two cocks in two pairs of socks. He moved toward me, and all passive resistance ended.

I moved up the bed as he climbed on it and on to me. Our mouths merged again to ravish each other, with tongues at such a speed to get inside that we hit each other's teeth. I knew now that over the next five days and nights, there would be no part of his or my body that would not be explored for pleasure and perhaps some delicious pain.

What good is pleasure without equal pain?
What good a sadist with no masochist?
To exist we need both light and darkness.
Either alone will mean nothingness.

If property was nine-tenths of the law, then the law of love said that he was my carnal captive and that I could do anything I wanted with him, and I intended to do just that. He had followed me here, and the price he was going to pay was to be trained to service and satisfy me in any manner I demanded. Although I had been physically on top that first night of love, it was I who had serviced him. Now I was on the bottom and wanted unconditional proof that he wasn't someone who thought he could be serviced by some homo hole without losing his sense of heterosexuality.

Yes, his presence here should have been more than sufficient proof that the night we'd made love had been in no way just a mercy fuck. But my loss of self-esteem as a gay man had been great enough to want extreme proof of his love if I were to get that esteem back. There was an additional factor—I was not vanilla, and he needed to prove he could love my dark side as much as he could my vanilla. It was no generic fiend that I was now giving myself up to. That person or thing whose voice had come out of me that Saturday night, and which was not quite Dan, was now manifesting itself in body as well as voice, and it silently offered me its name.

Behold your demon Debauchee.
I insert, and I receive.
In my horn and hole believe.
And I swear that both of these,
Jonathan, you'll learn to please.

I didn't really want to turn Jonathan into a bottom unless it became absolutely necessary, but at least one time he would submit to me as my top. Just one time, and I would be satisfied. Unless the suggestion came from him, it was not going to be this day though. I would be patient, but before Wednesday he would suffer my goy prick in his kosher hole as his had been so willingly and pleasurably suffered in mine. I wasn't planning on raping him, although the idea was rather exciting. It was just that his getting fucked by me would be my ultimate demand of proof of his love. If he should react to that demand with fear of emasculation, then that would make it all the easier to break from him. In the meantime, I thought,

> *As lips pressed against each other*
> *And noses rubbed one another,*
> *As my tongue inserted itself*
> *So readily into your mouth,*
> *This is to be a forewarning*
> *Of my bone blessing your butthole.*

For a moment the angel spoke: *If you must have him, be as gentle to his entire body as you were to his balls that first night.* But my fiery fiend demanded otherwise. It said, *Every part of this man's body is devilishly delicious, and as a bottom beast, take advantage of this besotted bear.* Perhaps I would listen to heaven tomorrow night, but now it was I as a haunter of hell that was in command.

I pushed him and forced him to roll over so I could be on top of my conquest and work my way down his body.

> My fingers playfully caressed his neck,
> Soon to move down to his slight cleavage.
> First going to the right and then the left,
> My lips and tongue desired to taste.
> Next, my hungry mouth needed to descend
> Slowly to his heaving sweet birth knot.
> Finally, only my forehead and nose
> Is all he could see if he so chose.

179

Again with a quick change of positions, I said, "Run your fingernails down the front of me." All that he did was use his fingers. "Nails, not just fingers. I want to feel nails," I snarled at him through gritted teeth.

This time, he obeyed, and I began to reciprocate, all the while watching for signs of pleasure and pain.

> Fingernails over chest and belly
> Leaving scratch marks as they dig in,
> Like strokes of a sadistic craving
> Of some creature clawing its kill:
> While I instruct, he simply obeys
> As he bends fully to my will.

"Now do the same with your teeth. Start by biting the sides of my neck."

"Are you sure? Won't that hurt?"

"If you don't want to make love to me the way I want, then just go."

"Okay."

I've always liked to be bitten and to bite, especially the neck and ass. It was obvious that, as a new experience for him, his enthusiasm for it needed a lot of cultivating, but that would come. I intended to make sure of that. In the meantime, we would start with the more vanilla—my hungry hard-on in his mouth.

Due to past experience, I had thought that there might be some other men at the conference that wanted some extracurricular activity over these five days, so I had earlier placed a bag of necessities strategically within reach of the bed. I told Jonathan to get up. I took the covers off the bed and grabbed the bag. I pulled out the lube, a glove, and a condom.

Once back on the bed, he put the rubber on his already aroused tool. Since he had once before seen me put on the glove, lube it up, and insert fingers into my own ass, he did what was expected of him as I lifted my legs and rested them on his shoulders.

With his fingers, he was very cautious, and for too long a time he had only one up me. I told him to try another; then, after a minute or two, a third; and finally a fourth. Once I was satisfied that I could take him, I made sure he knew it. He went into action with minimum discomfort on my part and began to thrust.

As he did, I verbally encouraged him. "Yes, fuck that ass. Fuck it."

There was none of the animallike power of that Saturday night arising in me this time, but then, I was clearly in a far-different head space from that night. Nonetheless, the ever-increasing speed of his thrusts made me cry not out of pain or sadness but out of sheer pleasure and joy. I could feel the power of his hands pulling my hips toward him while he simultaneously shoved himself forward into me. In a couple of minutes, I heard the sound in his throat that said he was ready to shoot. As he came, I told him not to pull out, and I began to beat off.

Unlike some men, I do not keep my erection while getting fucked, but once the action down there stops, I like to feel my hole squeezing what's still in me or at least have a few fingers in me to replace it. Taking care of myself didn't take long. Jonathan was still down below, and with the powerful feeling of him still there and his heavy body still resting against my thighs and butt, I shot with a fiendish force. I decided there and then that this would be only the first of several fucks I would demand from him. In fact, I planned to milk him dry over the next few days with my butthole and mouth. I would be like some sexual vampire.

Both drained—for the moment at least—we lay on the bed breathing heavily. He reached down to take hold of my hand, which I interpreted to mean *Don't let me go.* This moment of exhaustive silence, however, made me think. My indelicate indulgence and his indiscreet infidelity were both iniquitous, no matter how we tried to justify them.

Once my immediate sexual need was met by this smitten bedmate bear, I began to wonder whether it was love or vengeance that I was feeling toward him. I decided it was both. It was love to be sure, for I had never wanted a man more than I wanted this one. However, it was also vengeance for him having followed me here and forcing me to feel only more deeply my corrupt craving for him. It was like some sort of bewildering bewitchment, but who had bewitched whom? As both love and vengeance joined together, my being in possession of him now made my desire doubly ecstatic. Yes, a raging wildfire out of control, yet I wished no water to douse the flames in me.

> I want to love him
> With the gentleness
> Of a thirsty bee
> Sipping sweet nectar
> From a frail blossom
> Yet with the power
> Of an ocean squall
> that smashes itself
> Against a cliff wall.

More than libido had just transpired between us as far as I was concerned. First, Jonathan, by seducing me, had given me back what I had lost, positive acceptance of my gayness. What was now important to me was whether today's lovemaking was evidence of what we would have for the next few days. If so, then Santa Fe would be our erotic Eden of delightful debauchery or damnable depravity. Come Wednesday I would magnanimously manumit him back to the reality of the wife. In the meantime,

> Why worship a doubtful deity
> Of some passionless paradise?
> Far more certain is this blessed bed

On which together lovers lie,
Here to start with carnal caresses
Then on through to a throbbing thrust.
Such joy cannot come from a grave God
But from playful Lucifer's lust.

It was nearly lunchtime, and if Jonathan and I were going to eat before my panel, we had to start cleaning ourselves up pronto. I told Jonathan to run the shower for the two of us. Once we got in the shower, he once more wanted to know about my tattoos. On the upper part of the middle of my back I had *THE RACK* in good-size bold letters. I told him I would tell him about that one later, which only intrigued him more—part of my intention.

Among the other tattoos he wondered about was the *K9*, which I avoided going into detail about since it referenced the times I had worn a collar and been led by a leash. If I told Jonathan about that, I then would have to explain that I'm only an opportunistic dog, which is to say I only do it for those occasions I think I might get a fuck out of it. I have never been into the more extreme dog-fetish lifestyle that I know others are into.

While in the shower, I scrubbed Jonathan's back, including his butt. As I did, I slowly moved my soaping hand in between his cheeks until I could feel his anus. I gently rubbed its outer rim, deciding this was but a prelude to tomorrow, when my fingers would massage his rectum until they gently penetrated to feel the warmth within. Then his anus would be known by my tongue. I turned around to have my back, butt, and anus washed, and wash he did, though he did the last of the three reluctantly, barely touching it. I accepted this for now.

Getting out of the shower, I grabbed a towel, but Jonathan took it from my hands and began drying me. He said, "You have a really nice body. Do you work out at a gym?"

"No. Just at home." That answer reminded me why. Going to the gym and being a slut was not the best combination.

You go to the gym for your health,
But sometimes you find there more wealth.
First, you glance at his dick,
Then he looks at your prick,
And soon both of you forget stealth.

Jonathan and I got dressed and went down to the hotel restaurant for lunch. Jonathan knew from both the website and lobby sign that I was on a panel, and although I told him that he didn't need to attend, he said he wanted to. That became the pattern for the rest of the conference. Where I went, he went. It was kind of like having a puppy, only one you didn't have to walk twice a day. While I simply introduced him by his name, I have little doubt that people assumed he was my partner.

Actually, the only time Jonathan was not with me was when he called Ruth every day, as was his custom when away. He did this in his own room at my insistence, even though it was the only time in five days he was in that room. I somehow felt it was a little less like I was participating in his adultery or faithless fornication by making him do so. After each call, I would fulfill my polite responsibility and ask how Ruth was. The answer was always the same: "She's fine." Also, this was the only private time I had to put into writing the measure I knew would be needed to reluctantly end our romantic romp once and for all after Wednesday.

He loves me, yet he loves his wife,
But has he thought what this could mean?
Would she be able to compete
With "the other" who is a man?
A mistress she could tear apart
And with ease reclaim her husband.
But a cock is far from a cunt,
Which could mean much more to confront.

Chapter 12

On Saturday morning after breakfast, Jonathan and I went to the poetry workshop that I was to lead. I was pleasantly surprised that there was a full crowd. The workshop went very well because I tried to keep it as nontechnical as possible. After the poetry workshop, which turned out to be Jonathan's favorite part of the conference, he started writing love poems to me, and I to him. In fact, as the conference moved along, we made Erato—the muse of erotic and love poetry—work overtime.

Certainly by the end of the conference each of us would have a collection of scraps of paper with our feelings about the other's body and soul. I was quite amazed at how someone who had previously been so resistant to writing his own poems suddenly showed a flood of enthusiasm and talent for doing so. I wasn't sure whether it was my encouragement in the workshop, love, or both that had opened the floodgates. We became almost teenager-like. Poetry and sex—I came to realize that it was as much one as the other that made me desperately in love with Jonathan. My former lovers had treated my poetic interest as something sweet but nothing beyond that.

Saturday night Jonathan was to learn two new arts. The first was magenta.

> Irresistibly my nose and tongue
> Are without control drawn to the sweat
> Of his undeodorized armpits.

The second art was light blue. Before Jonathan had a chance to suspect anything, I handed him a condom and put one on myself.

"You're putting one on you?" Clearly he had assumed that like yesterday I was to get fucked.

"We need both to suck on each other."

"Oh!"

"Is that going to be a problem?" This was a serious question. The average heterosexual man regards sucking another man's member as a humiliating and even emasculating act. In contrast, being a top and fucking another man—as Jonathan had now done twice to me—does not necessarily have the same demeaning connotation. He was now being called upon to prove he was not a hung-up heterosexual.

He said, "No." However, there was a certain lack of enthusiasm in that reply.

I told him to lay his head on the pillow while I positioned myself in the opposite direction.

He looked at me and then looked at Dan Junior but waited until I commenced with Jonathan Junior. Then slowly, as if preparing to taste some food item that might be too hot, he put his mouth over the head but not the shaft. But as I put more and more of him in my mouth, he followed suit.

"It tastes funny," he said. Of course! He had never tasted a condom before and probably never a dental dam either.

"It takes some getting used to. Just don't use your teeth. It will break the condom." I thought that concern for the integrity of the condom sounded better than *Don't bite my penis.* He went down on me as I had gone down on him that first night, but as he was working, I couldn't tell whether he was really getting any enjoyment out of it.

> Cock sucking should not be a chore,
> Much less something to deplore.
> Instead, to give as well as get
> Makes a delightful duet.

As my enthusiasm increased and he got closer and closer to shooting, his willingness to reciprocate became more obvious. But when my expertise made him shoot first, his efforts became less than satisfying, so I stopped him and finished off with my hand.

"Didn't I do it right?"

"You did fine."

My last workshop was on Sunday morning, after which we explored some of Santa Fe. Passing a shop, Jonathan noticed a silver bracelet that he thought Ruth might like. Although I said nothing, I couldn't help but wonder how he could so innocently think of buying a gift for her while having his male paramour standing right next to him.

> He is like a child
> Oblivious to sin.
> His infidelity
> Is absent from his mind.
> Thus it will be my chore
> To be the saving whore.

Sunday night's erotic education involved my soaping up his shadow hole in the shower and rimming him. Although by this time he had gotten the message that whatever I was willing to do to him I more or less expected him to do to me, he still had not learned to reciprocate. I didn't press the point, since I knew how much of this was new to him and I wanted to be patient. We would wait and work on it.

> Assholes are erotic
> In many different ways,
> But none more than when they are
> Worshipped with the tongue.
> Yet to keep this rite holy

Precautions one must take,
So wash off before the fun,
Then no hepatitis won.

By that night I decided that I could get personal enough to ask him in a delicate way about his sex life with Ruth.

"Have you ever had anal intercourse with Ruth?"

"No. Why would I?"

"What about vaginal intercourse from the rear?"

"No. I don't think she'd like that."

"Have you ever asked her about it?"

"Not really. We just make love the regular way."

"How about oral lovemaking—you know, you licking her pussy and she sucking on your doggy?"

"No, not that either."

"Would you like to try any of these alternatives with her?"

"I never thought much about it until now, but I think I would. However, I'm not sure she would."

"Well, the only way to know is to ask her, isn't it?"

"I suppose so."

I was tempted to ask more licentious questions, but I decided he would be too uncomfortable with them, so I resisted.

Licentiousness is such a lovely word.
There's a quality of music to it,
As in pleasures that are thought to be forbidden
By all the moral missionaries,
Those who disdain the mouth that plays the flute
As well as the fingers that pluck the lute.

On Monday we drove out of town into the desert to be absolutely alone. We walked and talked, held hands, and embraced. We used our eyes, ears, and noses to experience the enchanted beauty all around us, and we recited absurd poetic creations to each other. That was when I realized another difference between Jonathan and my past two lovers. Both of those relationships had involved just serious love. But Jonathan and I could be unselfconsciously silly with each other. It was not only wonderful but liberating.

That night began wet. I had Jonathan stand in the shower while I pissed all over his crotch and then encouraged him to do the same to me. He tried, but no bear piss came out. I'd suspected this would be the case because we have been trained since infancy not to pee except in the socially assigned places. Telling him not to worry about this, I admitted that the first time a guy had wanted me to piss on him, I hadn't been able to. Nonetheless, the pissing thing had an impact on him, judging from his question afterward. He said, "I don't want to offend you, but I need to ask this. Have you ever wondered whether the kinky play you are into, and which I seem to be finding interesting, is psychologically healthy?"

I told him that I was not in the least offended by the question and that I was actually glad he brought it up. What I didn't tell him was just how kinky I could be. Maybe if I had, we wouldn't be here now. Whether that would have been better or not was now immaterial. I told him about the therapist I'd gone to and what he had advised.

I went to a therapist
Because of kinky needs.
I spoke about S and M,
Bondage and discipline.
I mentioned too water sports
And other pleasant deeds.
He asked me, "Do you mean to harm?"
And I replied, "No way.
I respect my partner's health
And never would do less."
So he said, "Go for them,
The floggers, handcuffs, chains,
Whether as top or bottom,
As long as no one complains."

My answer must have made Jonathan much more comfortable with my kinkiness, because, taking his cue from the previous night, he turned me around, washed my crap hole, and rimmed me, simply commenting that it tasted like soap. After that we found ourselves lying in bed composing senryus to each other. I would think up a poem, and then he would try his best to match it. Actually, Jonathan showed an intuitive grasp of that poetic form. I was surprised at how easily he could come up with rather risqué wording. Without any doubt, I was having a very indecent influence on him.

With the setting sun,	Sucking your pecker,
My shadow becomes longer,	The taste of adoration,
An erect pecker.	I'm sated by it.

Other than walking around town and finding places for lunch and dinner, most of Tuesday was uneventful. In fact, I wanted it that way. That night was to be the night of nights for me because the final proof that somehow Jonathan would be mine for the rest of my life, even if I never saw or spoke to him again, was required now. It was my turn to drive and his to be driven.

A virgin hole must be very carefully primed, and for the past three evenings, with a gloved hand, I had been gently getting his sphincter muscle used to relaxing as my finger entered his rectum. The first night I had used one finger; the second night, two; and the third night, three. I didn't tell him that the finger play was in preparation for fucking him. I told him that my fingers inside of him made me feel closer to and more a part of him.

He accepted that explanation with a smile and even allowed his rectal muscles to further relax. Also, that explanation made him want to finger fuck me, to which I readily agreed. Actually, my explanation was not a lie. Finger fucking, with or without subsequent cock fucking, did make me feel closer to my partner.

As truthful as this explanation was, the whole issue of being a predator came back. He still had a wife that he belonged to, and my intention to fuck him—to top him and to make him my bottom—could be considered as the final act that would turn me into a predator. On the other hand, I had to remember that he had followed me to Santa Fe, not the other way around. I certainly hadn't gone out of my way to seduce Jonathan away from his wife.

I had made more than enough effort to send him back to his wife. Besides, I suspected that in his relationship with Ruth, she was the one in charge of him, his top. So how could I be considered the predator, either as a top or bottom? The thought of Ruth as his top made me wonder if having been conditioned to being manipulated by her was making it easy for him to be manipulated by me. I suppose I should have been grateful to her for that.

> Manipulation is what we all do
> Despite its unseemly reputation.
> We learn to do it well before we walk,
> As every parent knows from midnight screams.
> But none have learned the art as well as those
> Who for millennia have handled husbands.

Although I had been priming Jonathan's hole for three days, I still fingered his anal muscles for a good twenty minutes before attempting to sordidly sodomize him with Dan Junior. To avoid any sense of future guilt over feeling that I raped him, I asked, "Are you ready?"

There was no enthusiasm in his "Yes, but please go slow," but there was permission, which was enough to relieve any guilt.

Nonetheless, as much as I wanted to be inside of him, I said, "We don't have to do this."

"But you want to."

"Yes, but not if you don't." That was only partially true. I had these past days been the bottom, and I now wanted to be the top, but to force him into it was not love.

"No. I want you to."

"Jonathan, you can please me in some other way."

191

"No. I've seen how much pleasure you get from me being inside you, and I want to try feeling what it is like for you to be inside of me."

"Okay. But we can stop at any time."

"Okay."

From the way his body relaxed ever so slightly, I sensed that my assurance reduced some of his anxiety. I put on the condom and pressed the head of my soon-to-be hole opener against its target and just rubbed. There was a sort of smile on his face, but it was not one of pleasure but disguised worry. I decided I would once again relax his muscles by a familiar finger fuck, and the way his ass moved to greet that fuck made me wonder if he thought it might actually be my macho already in there. Since his eyes were closed as if to help avoid a potentially unpleasant experience, he couldn't see what part of my anatomy was fucking him.

It was time. I inserted the head, let it sit there for a moment, and inserted deeper.

His body and anus tightened up, so I asked, "Are you okay?"

He didn't answer immediately, as if he needed time to judge the matter, but then said, "Yes."

I moved in more, moved out a little, moved in, and moved out, all the time watching both his breathing and facial expression. I moved in once more, deeper this time, and his body jerked a tiny bit.

"Still okay?"

"Yes, but please just hold it there, for a little while."

"Absolutely."

A few seconds passed, and he said, "Okay."

I slipped in halfway, stopped, waited, then pushed all the way in.

"I'm in. Completely in."

There was, this time, a genuine smile, but he said nothing.

I pulled out a little and pushed in, but I didn't begin really thrusting until I was certain he was relaxed enough to take it. Once more I was all the way in, but he tensed up, and I pulled back, asking him if he wanted me to withdraw entirely. If he had said yes, that would have greatly disappointed me, and I think he knew it. But for all my earlier sadistic bravado, I was still not ready to rape him.

The very fact that he had been willing to try being fucked would at this point have minimally satisfied me. But I didn't have to settle for the minimum, because after a minute or so he encouraged me to try again. This time, he was able to take all of me without any sign of distress, and I was fully fucking him.

The expression on his face was not that of pleasure nor of pain, and I speculated that all his attention was on the sensation in his anus and rectum. I suspected that he was evaluating this new experience and finding it was nowhere as negative as he might have originally thought it would be.

Normally, as one fucks, speed increases, but I was reluctant to go too fast for fear he might want me to withdraw prematurely. I consciously controlled my speed in a way I had never done before, and it was a new, although somewhat frustrating experience. It was only when I knew I couldn't hold back any longer that I finally drove into him with an obvious verbal acknowledgment that I was shooting.

I didn't withdraw immediately, as I wanted some feedback from him while I was still inside him.

"Are you okay?"

"Yes."

"I'm going to pull out, okay?"

I felt his sphincter tighten, and I wasn't sure whether it was because he thought that withdrawal might hurt or because he might really still want to feel me inside of him.

Withdrawing completely, I asked, "Do you want me to suck you off?"

"No. I'm fine just as I am."

Since I saw no evidence to the contrary, I suspected that he was fine and just needed some quiet time to process the whole experience. I got up, disposed of the condom, came back to the bed, lay beside him, and took hold of his hand as he had so often done with me.

He lay there for about an hour. Feeling he had had enough time to recuperate, I told him that for this last night I wanted just a little more of him—I wanted him to beat off while aiming for my mouth, no condom. Although I usually avoid swallowing a load, tonight I wanted to taste his man milk on my tongue and spread it all over the inside of my mouth and throat.

"Are you certain?"

"I've never been more certain of anything."

I got him hard with my mouth and positioned myself on my back. He straddled my chest and began his manly manipulation. With a loud "Now," his essence, his very genetic code, shot all over my chin, open lips, tongue, and nose. To me, it was a salty joy!

"Now kiss me."

Jonathan bent down close enough to my face to say, "That doesn't smell very good." I guess most straight men don't get their noses close enough, even to their own jock juice, to appreciate that under the right circumstances it can have its appeal.

I thought that I knew Jonathan enough now that if I had had more time, I could have turned him into a very versatile vanilla lover. But then I remembered that the next day would be a permanent good-bye, assuming what I had in mind worked out. I could tell that Jonathan was experiencing his own disheartening feelings about Wednesday, because after our sex, despite my suggestion we do so, he refused any attempt to engage in any poetics.

> Thoughts of a good-bye lead to sadness
> Which poetry cannot dispel.
> So try an unanswered question
> That was saved to near the farewell.

Although Jonathan had asked each previous night about *THE RACK* tattoo, I waited until this night to explain it. The delay had been partly to keep him curious but also because I was not sure how he would react to the idea that I liked being flogged. Until this night I had not really equated my kinkiness with S-M activities, and none of our activity had been more than what could still qualify as heavy vanilla.

Yes, he knew I was into kink, but the very closest we had come to S-M was him spanking me. However, being spanked is a common-enough fetish that it's not always considered an S-M activity. Flogging, on the other hand, is a major upping of the level of pain and is without question S-M.

> I have a serious toy
> Used by this mischievous boy.
> To flog or to be flogged,
> I hope you will agree
> Brute bliss is not to flee.

Pointing to the tattoo, I said, "You asked about this tattoo. It's the name of the leather bar where I was first flogged."

"Flogged, as in whipped?"

"Yes."

"Didn't that hurt?"

"Actually, it really turned me on."

"You like being flogged?"

Jonathan's initial reaction was to be expected and required giving him a careful explanation.

"Sure, it hurts, but it is a good hurt, especially in that it releases powerful endorphins that can give one an incredible high."

"But can't you get hurt, I mean like seriously?"

"Yes, if the person who is doing the flogging doesn't have the proper experience and doesn't respect the previously agreed-upon limits of the person being flogged. But only a very foolish bottom allows such a so-called top to flog him. Also, the body of a person who is into being flogged reacts very differently than that of a person not into that scene."

I wanted to say to him,

With a flogger make love to me,
For nothing can better be.
With the lash on my back and butt
Pray satisfy this leather slut.

But I knew that would be going too far, and his next words confirmed that. "I don't think I could ever do that to you or anyone else."

"That's okay. Unless you're into it as a top, you shouldn't feel like you need to do it with anyone. Flogging isn't like trying to piss on someone. It's a skill that someone who does not enjoy it will never master, so he has a responsibility to himself and others not to do it."

This last explanation seemed to put Jonathan's mind at ease. "So you would never want me to do that to you?"

"Not unless you really wanted to."

"I don't think I ever would."

"That's fine."

What I didn't tell him was that given time, which we would never have, I could probably get him to at least experiment with flogging to show him how safe it could be under the proper circumstances. But time was not on our side. Throughout the past five days, we had gotten to know each other in many ways, but I was still bothered by a few nagging questions, so I directed our conversation to them.

"Jonathan, when do you think you fell in love with me?"

"I'm not sure. Maybe it was that Sunday after leaving the café when you asked if you could hug me. It certainly must have been no later than the next day, since that morning I deliberately made up the story about wanting to do an article on the gay community so that Ruth would not wonder why I wanted to see you again."

"You're in love with a gay man who you've been having sex with for the past five days. Do you think that you're gay or maybe bisexual?"

"I don't know. Since you are the only man I want to have sex with, does that make me gay?"

"Do you still want to have sex with Ruth?"

"Of course. I love her as much as I love you. So does that make me bisexual? Is it possible to be heterosexual and still want you? Why do we need to have labels?"

"We shouldn't have to, but society forces them upon us."

One thing I was certain about was that this man was still in a deep, almost childlike love with his wife. He clearly put Ruth and me in two separate, nonconflicting categories. Of course, my feelings about her were not so simple. The Ruth that he knew and loved was the Ruth that was denying me him, and so while I was happy for what she meant to Jonathan, I hated her for what she meant for me. If being with Jonathan was like being in a private erotic Eden, then she was like the serpent whose presence would eventually contribute to our loss of this paradise.

The reality was that Jonathan belonged to a twenty-five-year relationship and not a five-day rogue romance. I told myself that I had been granted, by whatever power there was, the privilege to love and be loved in a very special way. To want, much less demand, more was to be totally ungrateful, and for me to be so would demean what I felt for him.

> Five days can seem so much more,
> If with the person you adore,
> For love is ignorant of time.
> Another view pray ignore.

"My turn. Why did you fall in love with me?"

"I've thought about that a lot, and I've come up with different answers. Naturally a big part of it is because you are physically my type, but you're also kind and intelligent, and you like poetry. I'm sure there are other reasons, but they seem to be hiding somewhere in the back of my gay mind."

"Have you ever had sex with a woman?"

"No. I have no doubt that I'm gay."

197

Not one drawn to women I.
They are quite safe from me.
Instead, it is their menfolk
To whom I a threat am.
From each dusk to each dawn
In this dark fantasy
I would ravish all of them,
Their worst nightmare to be.

We fell asleep as usual in each other's arms.

Wednesday morning we both awoke earlier than necessary and just held each other as close as we could. He cried, but there didn't seem to be any more tears in me to come forth. We had spent five delirious days of pure fantasy together, and that fiery cherub of reality had arrived. Since Jonathan's flight back to LA was not until eleven thirty, we had time for an early and quick breakfast before I drove him to Albuquerque.

When we got to the airport, I reminded him that he had a beautiful person at home waiting for him and he should never take her for granted. He said he knew that, but I had no one to go back to, and he could not stand that idea. Somehow I knew those words that I had spoken in the Stag would come back to haunt me through him. I also knew that it was Jonathan's way of saying he would not be able to resist calling and trying to see me again.

After day three in Santa Fe, I'd realized that things were not going as I'd been sure they would. I had assumed that in showing Jonathan just how kinky I could be there would be a point where he would realize that my S-M and his vanilla were not really compatible and that we should never have started this affair. He would then leave me without regret and return to Ruth, and I would be able to get on with my life, no worse for having loved him. To my surprise and disappointment, but at the same time delight, that point didn't seem forthcoming, which had forced me to an alternative measure. Before my last words to him, I handed him a letter that I had secretly written the day before, and I made him promise not to open it until he was home and totally alone.

In truth, it was not the first letter I'd written. That first one had said:

> Dearest Jonathan:
>
> I beg that you remember the rapture of our nights of love.
>
> There in my eyes the look of desire and how my lips pressed hungrily against yours.
>
> The way my arms eagerly embraced you and my hands caressed your skin.
>
> The ecstatic cry when you entered me and my tears when you withdrew.
>
> How after gentle presleep kisses our quiet breathing sent us off to dream.
>
> If you would know all that is in my soul, believe my life is full of love because of you.

However, I'd thought that would only make the break between us even more difficult, so I'd torn that one up.

There we stood, just looking at each other. The sadness in his eyes was near heartbreaking, but life is full of that, and we all need to be strong to deal with it. I had my doubts about how strong he was, so I had to be strong for both of us.

With a false smile, I said, "Good-bye, Jonathan."

"We'll see each other again when you get back to LA, won't we?"

"You need to get back to Ruth and decide what your relationship with her is. That takes priority. Nothing can be planned before that."

"Right."

"It takes a while to get through security, so you'd better not delay."

"Right."

I opened up my arms to give him one last hug and again said good-bye. The tightness of his hugging back made me feel as if my ribs might cave in. But he pulled back, and so did I.

I said, "Your plane."

He walked backward a little ways to keep me in his sight before turning around and heading for the terminal door. He turned once more to wave good-bye. Then he disappeared from sight. I turned and headed back to the car.

> You knew all along it was wrong.
> To you he never should belong.
> So will your guilt you now prolong?

For the first time in five days I felt depressed. What was peculiar was that the depression was mixed with a certain weird sense of satisfaction. This was an unfamiliar experience for me. Back in Los Angeles I had cried when I'd sent Jonathan away for the first time. Now there were no tears, no self-pity in which to drown. Jonathan and I may have had only a few days of bliss, but for those days he had made me feel like the most valuable person in the world. I would hold on to that for as long as I could.

> To fall in love with mortal man
> Will bring you grief at its death.
> Yet every day that this love lives,
> Inhale it with every breath.

Chapter 13

Before leaving LA, I had made a motel reservation for the next three nights in Albuquerque. One of the reasons was that I figured I might find some leather in a bar one of those nights. After checking in, I spent the rest of Wednesday and then Thursday exploring the town, and both nights I actually watched some idiot TV before going to bed. On Friday, I spent most of the day catching up on reading before the leather hunt. I wasn't in the bar for more than a few minutes when my eyes met another's, and it looked like I might be lucky.

At the crucial moment,
I see him, he sees me.
Eyes that speak of interest,
A smile that says much more.
One moves toward the other,
A greeting, then a touch.
A rising body heat,
No more to be discreet.

The guy was clearly a motorcycle type who I thought could be a rear-door roughrider to me. He had long hair tied into a ponytail. His beard was of the unkempt kind, and he had a beer belly, which, if not too protruding, can be sensual. I judged him a couple of inches taller than I and about twenty pounds heavier.

We started a bar conversation, which included his name—Jeff. When he went to get another beer, I noticed that he was signaling fisting top (red on the left). I immediately lost the hard-on I had gotten talking to him. I didn't want him to think he'd done anything wrong, so when he returned, I said, "You turn me on, sir, but the handkerchief suggests that we're not into the same thing."

"Okay. What are you into?"

"General sucking, fucking, and some discipline, sir."

Perhaps it was my honesty or the fact that there was no one else in the bar he thought as interesting as me or possibly the word *discipline*, but in any case, he responded, "That will work for me too."

"Yes, sir!"

"My place all right?"

"Of course, sir."

"Then if you're ready."

We left the bar, and he pointed to a pickup, not a bike, across the street. "That's mine."

"I'm down about a block, sir."

"I'll drive you down there."

He drove me to my car, and I followed him home, maybe a twenty-five-minute drive.

As soon as we got into his house, he headed for the bedroom and started to undress. Naturally, I did likewise. I had expected some mouth-to-mouth action to occur first, but no sooner did he have his last sock off than he turned to me, put a hand on my shoulder, and pressed down.

"You implied being a bugle boy, so let's find out how true that is."

Since words were not what he was interested in at that moment and I had forgotten to negotiate a condom for oral, I felt this was no time to be picky. My mouth opened, and his already full erection went in. While he was no horse, he was no hamster either, so a little of him went a long way.

He clearly must have remembered the bit about discipline, because as soon as he had had enough sucking (for now), he removed the belt from his pants, which were on the floor, turned it inside out (the outside was studded), pushed my head and torso down, and gave a single whack on each buttock. He waited a moment to see if I gave any negative response. Getting none, he continued until I showed a standard safe word. "Thank you, sir! Thank you, sir! Thank you, sir!"

Once again his dick, which by this time was oozing major precum, went into my mouth, but it was soon obvious that he didn't want merely to be sucked off. He withdrew and told me to stand up and turn around. When he started to play with my asshole with his fingers, I began to worry that this guy was going to be a deal breaker—someone who has negotiated not to do something but then wants to do it.

"I know you said no fisting, but how about a few fingers up there?"

I was not surprised by this request. I had been through situations like this before. The top always hopes that the reluctant bottom will either change his mind or at a minimum go for a compromising heavy finger fuck. I liked this Jeff and felt I could trust him, so I said, "Okay."

Without a moment's delay, he said, "Good. Follow me."

We entered a small spare bedroom or den that had obviously been turned into a playroom. There was no bed or other furniture, but hanging from the ceiling was a leather sling.

"Sir! I'm not able to take a fist."

"That isn't what I had in mind. Just get in it."

The sling was a little too high for me to maneuver into, so he lifted me up and into it. Although it had both wrist and ankle restraints, he made no move to restrain my wrists, only my ankles. This made me feel less anxious since I knew I could get out of something that was not going my way, but once his tongue went exploring my hole, it soon became clear that getting out was going to be the last thing I wanted.

"You like that, boy?"

"Yes, sir!"

This rimming lasted for a good ten minutes before he decided it was time for me to get fucked. I had been fucked before in a sling and had found it to be more erotic than in a bed because the motion of the sling added to the intensity of the man driving into me. It was somewhat like sex on a water bed, only with the addition of the intoxicating smell of leather.

Once Jeff Sir released me, he asked if I wanted to stay overnight, and I gratefully accepted since it was better than going back to an empty motel room. We went to sleep almost immediately.

That morning I awoke to the feel of a hand playing with my dick. As soon as it went up, he asked if he could sit on it.

"If that's your pleasure, sir."

The feel of his weight on my body was as good as the feel of my cock up his ass. He may have acted as a top on top last night, but he had no problem now bottoming on the top. He finished by beating off on me. After cleaning up, we went to breakfast together. By the time I returned to the motel and got on my way, it was about noon. This meant that I didn't get to my next destination—Gallup—until the early evening.

After checking into a motel I went looking for some place for dinner. That's when I remembered that, being Jewish, Jonathan and Ruth had probably gone to the temple that Saturday morning. I thought for a moment that I would have liked to have been with him there—without Ruth, of course. But then I remembered monotheism's morbid, minimally merry morality, which was just the opposite of my mania.

There is a power within me.
I just might call it God.
My life by night and day it rules.
It's I and yet it's not.
Both beautiful and ugly,
It's gentle and yet cruel.
As pleasure it is punishment;
As pain it is reward.
Transcending plain reality,
Raw sexuality.

I discovered a diner about a block away from the motel in Gallup and went there for a late dinner. Since I never miss the chance to look at male eye candy wherever I am, I was doing so there, and my eyes met the eyes of another guy who was clearly of Native American ancestry. We played the eye game as we both ate, and although he finished before I did, he made no effort to leave. He just sat there slowly drinking his coffee.

I hurried up with my meal, asked for the check, and got up to pay as he did. I waited outside just close enough from the door that he would see me but far enough away that others might not hear anything we said, assuming he was going to say anything.

He walked over and said, "Nice evening."

"Yes, it is."

"You're not from around here."

"No. Drove from Albuquerque and am on my way to LA."

"That where you're from?"

"Yes."

"What was in Albuquerque?"

"Writers' conference."

"You a writer?"

"Yes."

"What's the chain for?"

I figured this was the real opening question, and I was not going to miss it.

"Some men like to play with it."

He hesitated before he smiled and said, "Really?"

"Really."

"And how do they like to play with it?"

"Sometimes on the top, sometimes on the bottom."

"Really."

"Really."

He again hesitated, so I added, "I'm staying at the motel down the street."

"You want a lift to it?"

"That would be nice."

He showed me to his pickup, and we drove all of four minutes to the motel.

"You want to come in?"

"Okay, but I can't say long."

"Not a problem."

> When the two of us first got in bed,
> We gave each other real good head
> While waiting for this brave to say,
> "It's time for you to start to pray."
> And so I got upon my knees
> For on his hard-on down to ease.
> And let me tell you it's with awe
> I was able to play his squaw.

------------◆◆◆◆◆◆◆------------

On Sunday, driving through the vast open spaces of the desert on my way to Flagstaff helped me gain some perspective on my own existence. Compared to all that was going on in the world and the rest of the universe, my situation was pretty insignificant. If I had any sense of sorrow over having let go of Jonathan, I simply needed to get over it. As I had told myself several times before, it would not have really worked out, because vanilla cannot understand S-M. How could he possibly comprehend my obsession?

> Oh, Master, what will you do to me
> That I may know just how much you care?
> To feel the joy of a simple slap
> Such as one across my face or ass.
> Do not spend time on the best of words
> If not accompanied by the whip.
> Do not permit those who know not pain

To make you doubt that our path is true,
For our contract will create the bond
That will bring us to bliss and beyond.

I thought of going back to the bar in Flagstaff that I had visited on the way here, but my dick and ass needed a break, and I wanted to get an early start for Needles.

My dreams that night didn't lead to much rest, especially one that involved Jonathan in a dungeon. As a result I was up even earlier than I had planned to be and so headed out shortly after sunrise. The motel I found in Needles happened to be right across from a church and I thought,

Unfriendly are most religions
To out ordinary wants and needs.
They make so much of life a sin
With afterdeath a prize to win.

This town was not the most exciting one, but it had a bar that I had been told about. While it wasn't gay, one could make out there if one were discreet. It was a warm evening, and the crowd was either in shorts or Levi's, some with and some without boots. I was in Levi's, boots, and a T-shirt, with keys on the right. After about fifteen minutes, a bear type with keys on the left passed me, but I had no way of knowing if he just liked the keys there or was signaling top. I followed him with my eyes until he got a beer and found a free place to stand in the crowd. I walked by him, but he showed no interest, so I found my own spot near the opposite wall. About five minutes later a guy approached and found a spot right next to mine.

Without looking at me he asked, "That chain around your neck have a meaning?"

He was obviously trying to ask that question without others thinking he was actually talking to me, which suggested that his interest was more than simple curiosity. While the guy was nothing to write home about, he was worth a suck or a fuck. Besides, this was my last stop before going home and returning to a life far less sexually compulsive than the life I had been indulging in ever since meeting Jonathan. In that prelife, if I'd gotten laid once a week, I'd thought I was lucky.

Since I wasn't in a gay environment, I didn't want to do anything that might suggest that I was a faggot trying to pick up on a straight man, which could end up in violence. I just said, "Yes, the chain has a meaning."

"And that would be?"

I took a chance of being slightly bolder. "It means I like to please certain people."

"What kind of people?"

To keep from fully revealing myself, I said, "The kind that likes a man pleasing them."

"And how do you like to please them?"

"Usually with my mouth, dick, and whatever else might be agreed upon."

"What about an asshole?"

A straight man asking another man about pleasing an asshole is so rare that I almost said, *That too.* But I decided to still remain on the side of caution with "I understand that some women and some men like to take it up the ass."

"What about you?"

"If I answer that and it turns out that you're one of those guys who likes to prick-tease gay men and then yell out faggot, I would remind you that you are the one who approached me, not the other way around."

"You don't have to worry about that."

"Then you have your answer."

The negotiations began, but they were short and unsuccessful, and he walked away.

Caution should be a virtue
Regardless of time or place,
And should you not it observe
You will get what you deserve.

The not-interested bear across the room must have seen what had just happened, because he came over and said, "Good evening."

"Good evening."

He said nothing else for a moment, perhaps trying to figure out words to counter his earlier disinterest. Then the obvious came to him. "Name's Sam."

"I'm Coy."

"I couldn't help noticing the thing between you and that other guy."

At first no interest,
Then he sees the right scene,
Hard-on to intervene.

There was no way to be absolutely sure, but I suspected that he recognized that it had been a gay encounter and was comfortable implying so. Therefore, I took the chance of being honest with him.

"He was opposed to condoms. He said he was negative and we wouldn't need them."

"Yes. I've heard about him, and you were right to not give in."

"Thank you. It's not that I'm implying that he wasn't telling the truth. It's just that none of us can be totally sure of our status at any one time."

"True. Very true."

I said nothing more, waiting for him to continue.

"So besides safe, what are you into?"

It was time to show my true colors.

"Besides sucking and fucking, a hand and/or belt could warm up this boy's bottom, sir."

"Sounds like we could have a good time tonight."

"If you say so, sir."

"You ready to get out of here, boy?"

"If sir is ready, I am."

"I'll leave first, and a minute later you follow."

"Will do, sir!"

> You will find us everywhere
> If you should chance to look,
> Even in a crowded bar
> Full of the straightest guys.
> Be discreet, and you may meet
> Just the right pair of eyes.

We went to his place, where I was hoping for more than a vanilla scene, but while it was certainly worth going home with him, this was hardly a town where one might expect more than that. Once he'd withdrawn, he asked how I wanted to be taken care of. I told him I would prefer to jack off standing up while he beat my butt with his belt. He took off the condom and left the room. I got up, and he returned with his belt, which had been left in the living room.

"If we don't put a towel down, you're going to have jerk-off juice on the bed, sir."

"That's all right. I need to change the sheets anyway."

"Please give me a moment to get my hard-on, sir. And when I'm ready, if you would be kind enough, you can start beating my butt, sir."

"Take your time. I'm not going anywhere."

I got aroused in no time just seeing him standing there with the belt in hand. I turned to the bed and began to beat my meat and then yelled, "Go!"

The sting of the belt felt so fantastic I was aroused into a frenzy and, in no time, shot with a pleasurably painful force.

As I stood staring at the bed
With lust from my feet to my head,
I was anything but discreet
As I shot all over the sheet.

Despite the late hour, I returned to the motel because I wanted to get an early start on the road. After about four hours of sleep, I got dressed, checked out, found a doughnut shop for some high-calorie, poor-nutrition breakfast, and hit the freeway to LA.

The Tuesday traffic wasn't bad, but on the last part of the route, the uncomfortable heat of the Sonoran Desert seemed to encourage a return to self-pity, or was it guilt? Whatever misery I might be momentarily experiencing must have been a decidedly deserved penalty for pilfering another's partner. But then I had the horrible thought that in the future any potential lover I might meet would be measured against my poetry-bear Jonathan and would perhaps be found wanting.

I tried countering this depressing thought by telling myself that my feelings for Jonathan had more to do with simple libido than real love, especially since I really wasn't made for monogamy but born to be promiscuous, as the last few weeks had proven. Moreover, as soon as I found the next man of my dreams, a master, the memory of Jonathan would fade rapidly.

How I miss the feel of slavery
Where body and mind surrender.
Even if not for an always state
Then at least for a few days each week.
So absurd it is to want this man
When it is a master that I seek.

Then it came to me.

I am a slave but failed to say.
Why did I not tell him so?
A subject most think forbidden,
Why should it have been hidden?

Considering all the other kinky things I'd revealed to Jonathan, why had I never told him that I had been a slave? Was I ashamed of it? No! That wasn't it. In fact, it had nothing to do with Jonathan. After my failures in a couple of vanilla relationships and with three very different masters, I had thrice gone through the miserable slave-identity drift. I was afraid of trying to find a new master, and maybe that was one of the reasons I had allowed myself to fall in love with Jonathan. That relationship, as hopeless as it was, could not hurt my identity as the other failures had. But where did that leave me? Was I to spend the rest of my life being afraid to try again?

To be without love, to be without pain,
To be without an owner these would mean.
So seek for the one who will dominate
With his kindness and cruelty to mate.

By the time I approached LA, my mood had once again shifted. Instead of dwelling on my loss, I began for the first time to think of all that I had gained from Jonathan. I knew then that because of the letter I had given him at the airport, I would never see him again. Despite this, I now felt that I would be able to go on with a joy in my soul for having loved and been loved by him.

Life is a road from birth to death
With little that's redeeming.
But if by chance you find real love,
The pain at least has meaning.

Chapter 14

After the emotionally grueling drive through Southern California, I got home late Tuesday afternoon. There were lots of phone messages on my landline, but only one stood out as likely bad news: "Dan, this is Ruth Miller. Would you please call me as soon as you get back? It's very important."

Upon hearing those words, every negative possibility went through my mind. If it was so important, why hadn't she called my cell phone? Then I realized that Jonathan only had my landline number, and she must have gotten my number from him. While she was one of the last people in the world I wanted to talk to, I made the call. Jonathan answered.

"I had a message on my machine from Ruth."

I could hear him tell Ruth, "It's Dan."

He came back on the phone sounding nervous. "Ruth wants to speak to you."

She took the phone. "Hello, Dan. I'm glad you got my message. We need to get together and talk."

"What about?"

"About Santa Fe and your letter to Jonathan."

I froze. *My God! She knows, and she's read the letter. Jonathan, what have you done?*

"I'll never contact Jonathan again. So there is nothing to talk about."

She now brought out the ultimate persuasion. "If it were that simple, Jonathan would not have been in the hospital because of everything."

The word *hospital* went into me like a megabullet, as I suspected she knew it would. My anxious voice only proved it to her. "Hospital? What's wrong with him?"

"Calm down. He's all right now, but we still need to talk about it, and we can't do it over the phone. Could you please come over tonight or tomorrow to just talk?"

Having read the letter, she knew I would have to know more about the hospital.

"All right, I can be over there tonight after dinner."

"Okay, I'll see you then."

She hung up, and all I could think was *What woeful web we weave when willfully wanton.* I had given myself a couple of hours leeway to try to think up some way of helping Jonathan. The worst she could do to me was rant and rave, but her calmness bothered me.

I drove over there thinking that I should never have uttered those disastrous words, "Jonathan, I love you," that very first night. Or I should have been pitiless enough in Santa Fe to have sent him away. If I had murdered their marriage, I would never forgive myself.

I reached the apartment house and rang the bell. Again Jonathan answered, buzzed me in, and said he would be there. I waited. Jonathan arrived looking miserable.

"Are you okay? Ruth mentioned the hospital."

"I'm okay."

"What was wrong?"

"It was just an anxiety attack."

Upon hearing the word *anxiety*, I was afraid to question him anymore, and he didn't seem to want to talk about it. I just followed him in silence through that labyrinth toward the She-Minotaur, who was waiting with the door open. I went in, and I could hear the trap shut.

"Thank you for coming," she said and motioned for me to sit down on the couch. She was still calm and to my mind suspiciously

214

gracious. With a smile, she turned to Jonathan. "Jonathan, I wish to talk to Dan alone. Please go upstairs and close the door."

I suspected that she didn't want him to witness my being torn apart by her claws. Jonathan protested, which I felt was only prolonging my presence there, and I wanted out as soon as possible. So I turned and shouted at him in a testy voice, "Jonathan, do it, please."

He looked at me as though I had wounded him. But he obeyed, and the she-creature dared to thank me, which only made me dislike her even more. She waited in silence until she heard the bedroom door shut, and in the meantime all I could think of was that she was his dominatrix. My mind went to Mistress Cynthia, a comely cougar.

She was a hell of a dominatrix
Who owned this pair of twin slave-boy pricks.
When she wanted play with her moist cunt,
She would shout to one, "Up with your front."
Yet more than this were her other tricks,
Like when she would play with other chicks.
She was a bi-dame bewitching bitch.

My attention was brought back to Ruth as she broke the silence. "Why don't we go into the dining area where we will have more privacy? Would you like a cup of coffee?"

"No, thanks."

She got herself a cup and sat down at the table, but in such a way that I noticed the calm confidence that she had greeted me with had faded into something less. Before she could say anything, I spoke up.

"I told you on the phone I'd never see Jonathan again. I can't do anything more than that. You may not believe it, but I am not trying to mess up your marriage."

"I understood that from your letter."

"Then what more do you want from me. Why am I here?"

"Because it's not as simple as you never seeing Jonathan again."

"Why not?"

"Before I start, I would like your promise not to relate anything I tell you to Jonathan."

I stared at her for a moment. *What could she possibly tell me that she doesn't want him to know?*

"You have my promise, but only as long as what you tell me will not hurt him."

"It won't if you don't tell him."

Despite her assurances, I was suspicious. It sounded like she was going to divulge information to me—a man she barely knew—that I could possibly use against her. *Why would she be so accommodating to her husband's* ... My thought paused for a moment. ... *lover?* In all the time Jonathan and I had been together, I had never until now thought of myself as that—something between a trick and lover, yes, but not the real thing. Her words brought me back to her.

"When Jonathan came back from Santa Fe, I immediately noticed there was something wrong. First, he was clearly depressed, although he just claimed he was tired from the flight. Second, in the past when Jonathan came back home after an assignment of several days, he would always want to make love to me that night, but after three days he still had not gotten out of the depression or been intimate with me. Also, he barely touched his food, and in all the years we have been together, he has never been disinterested in food. I kept asking him what was wrong, but he would only say he was tired. I wanted him to see a doctor, but he refused. When Saturday came, I asked him if he was not still working with you on the gay-community article, and he said no. He then started to cry. I knew then that whatever was wrong had something to do with you. I demanded to know what had happened. That's when he showed me your letter. He said that he could not stand deceiving me and would rather take the chance of losing me than be untruthful after all the years we had spent together and that if I wanted to leave him, he would understand. I read the letter."

My dearest Jonathan:

You have given to me a gift that no other man has ever given: the feeling of being loved unconditionally. For this, I will be grateful for the rest of my life. So do not feel sorry for me.

Unfortunately, our affair was madness from the very start, and so it was doomed beforehand. Yet every time you put your arms around me, it was such magical madness that I felt bewitched. I suspect that you will try again to call and see me once I am back to LA, just as you did by following me to Santa Fe. But I cannot allow this for either of our sakes.

First of all, as I told you before, I need more than to have a lover who secretly comes to me maybe once a week for a few hours and then goes back to another. I need a pair of warm feet on cold nights. Second, I have lived my whole gay life out in the sunlight and will not live part of it in a shadow of deceit. Third, such a clandestine affair would eventually be discovered by Ruth, and that would destroy what you and she have together.

I know that you love Ruth, for you have said so often how she has always been the love of your life and always will be. In fact, she has always been more to you than just a wife; she has been what her name means in Hebrew—beautiful friend. As long as you belong to Ruth, you cannot give me what I need, and I cannot even ask you for it, and since Ruth is not about to let me share you with her, you cannot have both of us. So you must refrain from contacting me again. To make sure that this time you understand that I mean it, I must warn you that if you try, I will have no choice but to go to Ruth and tell her about Santa Fe. If I do this, you will lose her and hate me for the loss, so you will have neither of us.

Jonathan, above all, accept that I will be happy in just knowing that you are loved by Ruth and that you love her. I will rejoice at being a voyeur through your lips as you remember there is no part of her body that does not deserve your attention. Place your kisses on her mouth, her neck, each nipple, her navel, and down to her most intimate part. Do not forget to make love to the back of her neck, her shoulders, the length of her spine, and down to the richness of her buttocks. Nor must you forget her feet. If it pleases her, you must massage and kiss them also, not missing a single toe. She is your Venus, so you must worship her properly.

Finally, I hope you will continue to write poetry now that I have shown you that you have the very soul of a poet.

Love, Dan

Those words were meant only for Jonathan to read, and the fact that someone else had read them made me feel furiously betrayed.

Black ink, white paper,
Words of good-bye forever.
A pen into my heart.

I wanted just to grab the letter and run, but I suppose it was the seeming lack of hostility on her part that kept me sitting there.

"After reading your letter, I was furious. Every possible threatening scenario went through my mind. Was Jonathan really gay? Had he had unsafe sex with you? He said that he didn't think he was gay, because he was not interested in men in general but had for some reason fallen in love with one particular man. He told me that you were just as concerned about the possibility of getting AIDS and that all your sex was with a condom.

"He was crying and suddenly started to hyperventilate. He grabbed his chest and fell to the floor. I was sure he was having a heart attack. I called 911, and they took him to the hospital. They did some tests and asked me what he had been doing just before the attack. I explained that he had been depressed for several days and we had gotten into an argument. I didn't tell them what it was about. They said it was probably a severe anxiety attack, but they kept him in the hospital overnight just to make sure. After I left Jonathan in the hospital, I came home, and I found the letter where I had dropped it and read it again. By the time I brought him back from the hospital, I must have read it five or six times, trying to make sense of Jonathan's relationship with you and what that now meant to our years of marriage. Despite my anger about the affair, I found it more and more difficult to hate you considering what you said in the letter about not wanting to harm what Jonathan and I had together.

"Then, of course, there was the way you wanted him to make love to me. I found it a little unsettling to have another man instructing my husband in such personal things, but I also found it charming, especially the part about him worshipping me as a goddess."

Yes, I had written that, but this woman had no idea of what I really thought about deities, male or female.

> I do not believe in some lustless love
> Who dwells in some so-called holy heaven.
> More real the moon and stars that lovers see,
> The music and perfumes they hear and smell,
> The moistened lips together pressed to taste,
> The forceful power of his mad embrace,
> The pleasure and the pain of his command.
> Here alone is the face of divine grace.

Nonetheless, I had written what I had written, so I said, "I meant every word of it. As much as I care for Jonathan, I'm not about to even try to tear him from someone he loves as much as he does you. There is little enough happiness in this world, and I'm not interested in destroying yours. You may not believe it, but I did everything I could to resist falling in love with him. I am still at a loss as to why Jonathan, who I'm almost certain is not gay, fell in love with me when he already has you."

"I think I can answer that."

"You can? If you have some insight into it, please."

"Once I had gotten over my anger, everything started to come together. When Jonathan got home from the workshop at which he met you, he could not stop talking about you—not only about your standing up for yourself but also your interest in writing and poetry. And after he got home from the museum, he continued to talk about you. Then that evening he asked me, right out of the blue, if I ever wondered what our lives would have been like if our son, Daniel, had lived. Jonathan had not mentioned our son in nearly eighteen or nineteen years. And then I remembered that he had grieved more for Daniel than I, who had carried his life in my womb, only to give birth to death."

With the words "only to give birth to death" I detected a change in Ruth's voice, as though there were tears inside that she was determined not to let me see. Also, up to then, she had been looking directly at me, but now she was gazing downward toward her coffee cup, which she was nervously playing with. I was getting very uncomfortable because I sensed that "only to give birth to death" was the prelude to a still more personal confession that I was still far too much of a stranger to have any right to hear.

Even if she had learned something about me from my letter, that should not be enough for her to open her soul to me. I wanted something to stop her, but what? Maybe a spider suddenly running across the table? No, unless she was arachnophobic, that would not do. A cockroach? Yes. A woman who kept a home this immaculate would be horrified at the presence of a cockroach, especially if a guest should also see it.

When needing one around,
Not one cockroach is found,
But when the need is not,
They visit you a lot.

I was a stranger to her but not to her husband, and she certainly could not regard that as anything other than a threat. Once again, I was becoming suspicious of her true motivations for these confessions, wondering how she was going to use this against me. But what was I to do, tell her to stop? I just continued to listen.

"I guess it was the fact that I had a daughter to console me. I don't know if it's true for all men, but it is for many men that having a son gives them a sense of wholeness, of completion, that having a daughter does not always do. I'm sure that this would have been true for Jonathan. There must have been something about meeting you that revived his grief. Perhaps, at first, it was just your name."

"But my name isn't short for Daniel. It's just Dan, as in one of the twelve Hebrew tribes." I knew that in Hebrew the names meant different things. *Daniel* was Hebrew for "God is my judge," and *Dan* was Hebrew for "judge."

"I doubt if Jonathan cared whether it was the shorter form or the longer. Either way, when he told me he was planning on asking you to the movie on Sunday, I suggested to him that he invite you to dinner. I think even then I had in the back of my mind the idea that he was looking at you as what he would have wanted his son to be like. What made me absolutely certain of this was when I brought him home from the hospital, I asked if he knew exactly when he was aware of falling in love with you. He wasn't sure but said it might have been when the two of you went to the café after the movie and he told you about Daniel."

I then remembered what I had been thinking after I'd left Jonathan that afternoon, and I automatically blurted out, "I was right."

This brought her back to directly looking at me. "What do you mean, right? Right about what?"

"That afternoon on my way home, I couldn't help wondering if Jonathan saw me as some kind of substitute for his son. But I'm a gay man. How could he identify me with his son? I put the whole idea out of my mind, but now you're telling me I was right."

"Well, first of all, neither Jonathan nor I have ever been prejudiced against gay people, and if Daniel had lived and had turned out to be gay, we would not have loved him any the less for it. Moreover, Jonathan has always been sympathetic to the underdog, and he may have seen the gay thing as part of that. But more importantly, he didn't see you just as a gay man. You're a writer like Jonathan, you have a common interest in poetry, and there's your beard. It makes you look a little Jewish."

Despite the otherwise seriousness of this conversation, while listening to these compliments, I had the mischievous thought that she had no clue about what putting the words *gay* and *underdog* in the same sentence implied to me.

> There is a certain position
> Which, believe me, is quite gay.
> In it he's the underdog
> During erotic play.
> What this means is a bitch boy
> Will gladly bark and bay.
> All you really have to do
> Is fuck the canine way.

It wasn't so much that I was trying to take this woman's words frivolously, as it was that I was trying to lessen my own discomfort at what they might imply. Still, there was the issue of my age.

"But I'm a thirty-three-year-old, not a twenty-year-old."

"Your age doesn't matter. You are close enough for his need for Daniel to be transferred to you. And the fact that your father died when you were an infant only made it easier for him to see himself as a replacement."

Those words hit me like a club. She was right and not just about Jonathan. What I had been trying to ignore or suppress was finally out. Despite knowing he could never fit into my S-M lifestyle, he was my ideal for the father I had never known. Should I admit this to her? I thought not.

"But what I have become to Jonathan is not what a son is. You don't normally screw around with your son figure."

Based on her reply, the graphic use of the word *screw* was a little much for her. Clearly, she would have preferred a more sanitized and generic word for what we had been doing.

"If that's the way you wish to phrase it, although I would have preferred *making love*."

> Making love is so much more polite
> When you compare it to a screw around.
> Yet no matter which of these you choose,
> The same orifice you will abuse.

"Fine, making love. But where does that leave us?"

"I can't completely explain how Jonathan's grief for Daniel eventually led to an affair with you, but that is what I'm sure has happened."

"That being the case, I don't understand how you can be so calm in this matter."

"If he had fallen in love with another woman, I would probably be ripping out her eyes right now, to make sure all he ended up with was damaged goods."

Just then I was extremely thankful that I had a cock, not a cunt.

> At times there are advantages
> To one's anatomy.
> But I never saw my pecker
> Ophthalmologically.

She continued, "No matter how much I love Jonathan, there was something you could give him that I couldn't, and don't even think to get cute on me and act like I'm just referring to human plumbing."

She might not be so concerned about plumbing, but I damn was. It was called Jonathan Junior. That was when I realized that I had not told Jonathan that every poet, or at least male poet, should compose at least one penis poem.

> That organ is so versatile,
> It overwhelms the mind.
> First, there's masturbation,
> Alone or mutual.
> Then there's oral and anal sex,
> Both penetrating themes.
> And water works don't forget
> For golden shower queens.
> What further praise to apply,
> They are all plumbing scenes.

"He's your husband. Regardless of any father-son substitution, I have no right to him, so what more is there than this?"

Ruth sat there silently, once more playing with the cup. She had a pained expression that told me she was trying to say something she didn't really want to say. When she finally did say it, I was sure I had heard her incorrectly.

"Yes, he's my husband, but that doesn't mean he shouldn't continue to see you."

"See me? You mean in some sort of platonic way?"

"Of course not! That wouldn't work anymore. I mean in the same way he has been seeing you."

Although surprised—no, shocked—by her words, at the same time I thought this was getting interesting, but I figured I would be delicate about it. "If I understand what you're saying, you're suggesting that I continue to have a physical relationship with your husband?"

She waited a moment before answering. "Yes. I couldn't give him a son, but maybe I can compensate by letting him have you."

"No! I made it perfectly clear to Jonathan before leaving Santa Fe that I was not going to be some guy he secretly—or, as you're suggesting, openly—comes to once a week for a romp in bed. That to me is not love, and I need more than that."

"Yes, from the reference in your letter about warm feet on a cold night and from what Jonathan explained to me, I understand that. Once I thought about it, I found it very endearing."

Endearing, she says. How discreet.

> *Endearing* is such a lovely word.
> It makes you feel cuddly and safe.
> Thus, you say the kitten is endearing,
> Until its claws begin appearing.

"If from my letter you understand that, then why even the suggestion that I continue to see him?"

"I thought you might be willing to compromise, especially if such an arrangement was out in the open."

I still could not fully believe what I was hearing from this woman. Wives, unless they're swingers, which I seriously doubted she was, simply do not condescend to loan their husbands out to another sexual partner, female or male.

> My morals are far from conventional,
> But now and then I can surprise myself,
> How prudish I can be regarding mates.
> As if I followed scriptural dictates.

Then I remembered what Jonathan had told me about how much she loved him, and this helped to override my surprised moralism. But there was more. I suddenly thought, *What a delightfully deviant idea!* If she was serious, she was suggesting something that religious bigots would probably regard as even more socially taboo than an exclusive homosexual relationship. The very wickedness of it was unusually exciting and certainly worth talking more about.

"You love your husband so much that you're willing to share him with a gay man?"

Again, she was silent for a moment, but then she answered with what I could tell was slight discomfort, if not embarrassment. "Yes."

"This has to be one of the crazier ideas I've ever heard. Your love must be greater than I can comprehend."

"Well, you could comprehend it if you were trying to atone for not giving him the son he so wanted. And if the idea is crazy, it's as much your craziness as mine, since I got the initial idea from your letter. You wrote, 'Since Ruth is not about to let me share you with her, you cannot have both of us.'"

Oh, when I'd written those words, if someone had told me she would read them, much less take them seriously, I would have accused that person of absurdity, if not insanity.

"Okay, I plead guilty to having made that statement. But you have nothing to atone for. It was not your fault that Daniel died. How could you think it was in any sense?"

"Intelligence sometimes never penetrates the heart, especially when it knows how much Jonathan wanted a son."

"But Jonathan could never blame you for that. Besides, if Jonathan wanted a son so badly, why didn't the two of you try to adopt one?"

"We could have adopted, but I think by the time Jonathan overcame enough of his grief, the bond between Esther and me had become so obvious that he felt that an adopted son could never be as much a part of him as she was a part of me."

I wondered if this was how Ruth was able to be so calm about the affair between Jonathan and me. Was her outer calmness a defense against the inner struggle with her guilt, which presumably had been brought to the surface after all these years by our affair? She was now offering me the opportunity to take advantage of that guilt. I thought what she was suggesting was a little like offering someone a reward for having stolen something that rightfully was yours.

> For a long-dead child, there is grief,
> And it is natural to want some relief,
> But to share your husband with a thief
> Leads to considerable disbelief.

Ruth's proposal that I might continue to be Jonathan's lover made me wonder if she really believed in my willingness to end our affair.

"You can have your husband back entirely to yourself if I just drop out of the picture, which I have already committed myself to do."

"Maybe!"

Both the word and the intonation in which Ruth said it made me certain that there was going to be a new and intriguing shift in this conversation.

"What do you mean by maybe?"

"I know I'm right on the reason Jonathan has fallen in love with you. What if you drop out and Jonathan's need has not been fulfilled? What then?"

"Are you suggesting that he might turn to some other man?"

"If he had not met you in the first place, that may never have happened. But he did, so yes."

For the first time this evening, I felt that the issue was neither guilt on my part as a thief nor guilt on her part as a barren womb. Was the whole empty-womb guilt trip just one way for her to deny to herself and me that Jonathan was gay?

"You're saying that your husband, having been corrupted by me, might now turn to another man. And even though I corrupted him, you would now rather him see me, a known quantity, than take the chance of someone worse? In short, I might be the lesser of two evils."

"I didn't use the word *corrupted* or *evil*. Besides, love is more complicated than that."

Perhaps evil, perhaps not. Corrupting was another matter. Had I not once corrupted another man?

> He was a fundamentalist,
> A very faithful fellow.
> He talked a lot about his God
> And of being saved from sin.
> Then he met Mephistopheles:
> This slut in mere nude skin.
> A moment's thought of suicide
> But then love entered his backside.

"I still believe that if I just refuse to see Jonathan again, it will end the matter. He'll have no reason to be interested in another man."

"Are you that sure that you are the only possible boy toy he could find interesting?"

"Boy toy? I don't know whether to be flattered or insulted by that description."

"It wasn't meant as flattery."

She was suddenly showing a bitchy side. At the start of this conversion I was held up high as a poetic lover, then as a substitute son. Now I had been downgraded to one of a good number of boy toys.

> A boy toy can be more than one thing.
> It will all depend on what both need.
> A father-son or more carnal fling.

I could use this insult as a perfect excuse to become indignant and tell her what she could do with the offer of her husband, but I hit back with a pseudosympathetic concern.

"Even if the three of us could live with such an arrangement, there are others that might not be able to live with it or, more to the point, allow you to live with it. People can be incredibly merciless when faced with something they don't understand or don't want to understand. If people found out about such an arrangement, they might either condemn you for agreeing to it or think you had no real choice in the matter."

From the surprised, if not slightly shocked, look on her face I knew I had caught her off guard by mentioning such a delicate social issue that she had clearly overlooked. It was at least thirty seconds before she responded, clearly trying her best not to sound humiliated, "He's my husband, and I can do with him as I please. Besides, I wouldn't be putting a notice in the *LA Times* about it. Would you?"

Although I wouldn't, the idea did have a certain depraved delight to it. Sunday *LA Times*, the California section. Or would it be better in the calendar section as part of entertainment?

There is a Jewish wife
Whose husband has a right
To weekly spend a night
With his sodomite.

"Ruth, it's safe to say that most would never know, but what about your daughter? How would she react if she found out that her father not only had a boyfriend but had so with your consent?"

"It's none of her business. I wasn't planning on consulting her about it either. She has her own husband to worry about. This arrangement would be between you, me, and Jonathan, no one else."

"To worry about"—an interesting choice of words on her part. Certainly that was a Freudian slip that really said, *I'm more anxious about my husband's interest in you than I am willing to consciously acknowledge to you or myself.* This thought only increased my belief that she was being rather naive, but I didn't say that. Instead, since I had gotten to the point of so enjoying the weirdness of this conversation, I couldn't help but bring the Bible into it. So I playfully offered up God.

"I don't know how religious you and Jonathan are, but what about Leviticus?"

"Leviticus?"

"Yes, you know, 'Thou shall not tolerate a man sleeping with another man.'"

Jonathan, her husband, is Jewish
Despite having a goy boy toy.
In practices oral and anal
J. Junior he should not employ.

"Oh yes. Well, my husband and I have already broken so many of those laws that one more couldn't hurt."

My dirty little mind started to imagine what at least one of those broken laws might be. Perhaps they already had violated Leviticus—Leviticus 20:18 perhaps. Maybe Jonathan should show Ruth the hankie code, maroon specifically.

If a man lies with a woman
During her illness,
Both of them shall be cut off
From among their people.

Leaving sordid imagination behind, I thought of an important question I had not yet asked. Considering the significance of the question, I was quite taken back by my absentmindedness.

"By the way, have you discussed with Jonathan the idea of us sharing him?"

"No, not yet. If you and I agree on it, he will too. He doesn't really have a choice."

It was clear who the top was in this family, and I delighted in the thought that maybe after twenty-five years Jonathan had developed just enough of his own castration complex to need my cock to counter it. And speaking of castration, I thought of still another argument against this arrangement.

"As much as I might want to consider such an arrangement, there's still one major problem. Every time Jonathan would come over to me, I would think about how you must resent it, and I would feel very guilty about that."

"How sweet."

If she thought that was sweet, I wondered what she would think sour.

"But I can assure you, knowing that he was with someone like you would not make me resentful."

"Be that as it may, there is still the problem of guilt."

"Guilt?"

"Being a woman, you wouldn't understand."

"Try me. I've been around."

I now found myself caught in my own embarrassment. "You don't know what guilt can do to a man's"—I didn't want to say erection—"performance."

"Oh! That."

She was smiling, but I couldn't tell whether it was because she was embarrassed or thought it was funny. Maybe she thought my not getting a hard-on was sweet.

"Dan, the more I talk to you, the more I find you charming. As for performance, considering how romantic your letter was and knowing Jonathan's 'performance' ability, I don't think you would have anything to worry about."

"Thank you, but the bottom line is that I want the same thing that you and Jonathan have had all these years, and an arrangement would not even come close to it."

"Of course it won't, and I'm sure you will find that ... someday. But in the meantime there's Jonathan."

The word *someday* penetrated me like an arrow and left me momentarily silent. I didn't appreciate her pause before that word, and I wanted to come back with *How about tomorrow with your husband?* But I kept my cool. After all, she did have a valid point. A guaranteed getting laid once a week, which I suspected was the arrangement she was thinking about, was better than any prospect I had now. True, my chances for that on the weekends were good, but this was a better than good offer, and it was certainly better than the only other option I could be guaranteed of—one-handed love.

> We all know that for a mate
> We need to negotiate.
> But who thinks it's his wife
> That one must accommodate?

I had to admit that it was not the most ideal situation, but I had done everything I could to dissuade her from the arrangement. And I certainly didn't want to hurt her more by refusing it. Besides, without question, she was right in that she could trust Jonathan with me more than with another man, and I would need to keep this thought in mind when he was with me. But still, in agreeing to this would I be selling myself short? Someday might be far off, but it could also be tomorrow. On the other hand, there was that licentious compensation of being a boy toy to a married man with his wife's approval.

> Sartre said life was ridiculous,
> And this would prove his point.
> What could be more ludicrous
> Than this ménage à trois?

I'd sent him away once, and in less than an hour he'd returned. I'd sent him away again, and days later he had been back. I'd sent him away a third time, and now I could have him partially back.

> I never thought to get a man
> Would require this kind of plan.
> Worse, it means we would need to share,
> Which is for both of us unfair.

Her share was the ultimate issue here. She was concerned that Jonathan might find some other man that would not be as willing to share him. Yet for me, the issue was not the share but the unfair, and this was what determined my decision.

"Maybe you are right to think that Jonathan might turn to another man, but maybe you're wrong.

"So as much as I'm in love with Jonathan and as tempted as I am by your offer, I still cannot accept that he belongs to anyone other than you. Perhaps I am egotistical to believe that I am all he will ever need as a 'boy toy.' And so I have to say no. However, with your permission, I would like very much to remain a part of Jonathan's life, and yours, but as a loving friend to both of you, not his lover."

She looked at me for a long moment, and for the first time since the start of this conversation her body seemed to actually relax. "Are you sure that would work for you?"

"If you're right and what Jonathan really wants is a son, I can be that to him and be so without the sex. I've come to love Jonathan enough for that."

She said nothing for a moment, then, smiling, said, "That might work."

"If Jonathan wants me in his life, it will have to work."

"I think you will be one of the best friends Jonathan and I have ever had. May I give you a hug?"

"Sure."

We got up and embraced. I suggested that we call Jonathan down before he had another anxiety attack, and she asked me to do it. As he slowly came down the stairs, I knew I had done the right thing for all of us.

As a hunk he did excel,
And a top he was as well,
But for this boy toy slave
There was still more to crave:
A master more drawn from hell.

233

Jonathan saw the two of us standing in the living room next to each other and was obviously puzzled by our apparent amiability. I figured it was up to Ruth to tell him in private what she deemed appropriate about our conversation. So I said to both of them that it was getting late and that I should be heading home. I thought she would not mind if I gave Jonathan a friendly hug, so I did so and said good night.

Naturally, the hug in front of his wife made Jonathan nervous, but there was no way I could simply leave with something as impersonal as a handshake, and I was sure she understood that. The fact that at the door she embraced me again and whispered "Thank you" told me I was right.

Rather than have either of them guide me out of the building's maze, I took the chance of finding my own way out, and I succeeded. Driving home, I felt an acute sense of being the master of myself and felt prouder of myself in both my manifestations.

Angel and animal,
I travel different trails.
One that flies high to heaven,
There to breathe in its bliss;
The other to descend the depths
Of hellish jungle jaws.
As pleasure and as pain
Each is enrapturing.
And though heavenly wisdom hopes
That I select it solely,
My soul in sin I may waste,
That life's erotic I may taste.

Epilogue

Several days later, I called Jonathan to find out how things were going. He told me that Ruth and he had had a long talk after I'd left and that over the next few days they had shared with each other long-unspoken feelings, bringing them closer together. A week later, the three of us had dinner together, and while Ruth was away from the table, Jonathan proudly confessed that their sex life, which had earlier been good, was starting to be "great."

> Having learned to tongue cock,
> Expanding on that talent:
> Cunnilingus.

As for me, I returned to my search for a master, and to try to maximize interest in me as a potential slave I published *The Slave-Training Protocol*, by slave Coydog. In it I pointed out that my book was different from most slave-training manuals in that it was written by a slave, not a master. Even some of the best manuals written by masters, as might be expected, have only a limited understanding of what goes on in the mind of a slave, which is very different from what any master may imagine.

> The mind of a master
> Is not that of a slave.
> What the first does not know
> Could not fit in hell's cave.

My book did attract the interest of quite a number of people, but in the end only one of those mattered.

Whisper, my sir, of all you'll do to me,
My heart to beat in expectation of.
Drive me to madness with your voice and touch,
And tantalize with blissful agony.
Make me a raging fire of your lust,
Which cries in suffering to be put out.
Toy with my soul till I no more can bear,
Just as the cat plays cruelly with the mouse.
Take hold of me like a taloned eagle,
And as that beast I beg my life consume.
Plunge me into a tortured ecstasy,
That is a death of self while yet alive.

Author's Note

Terms and concepts the reader may need some insight into are top, daddy, dominant (dom), master, bottom, boy, submissive (sub), erotic voluntary slave or v slave, servant, S-M (sadomasochist), owner/owned, the power exchange or the leather community,[1] and master-slave (M-S) rituals and contracts.[2]

Please note that most of my experiences have been with male masters, doms, slaves, and subs. I have had occasional interactions with female slaves of male masters, female slaves of female masters (mistresses), and female masters (mistresses) with male slaves, but I do not know enough about the inner dynamics of those relationships to legitimately judge how much my experiences can be thought to match theirs, although I suspect quite a lot in that the will to obey is genderless. In any case, I will focus my explanations on the male experience of all these terms since that is where I am most knowledgeable.

A top is the individual who receives oral intercourse (a blow job) or is the giver during anal intercourse (fucker). A bottom is

---

1 This is a catchall term that includes those who not only find it erotic to wear leather but also rubber, latex, and military-/police-style uniforms.

2 I need to point out here that there is a strong movement in the leather community to always write words referring to dominants with a capital (Daddies, Doms, Masters, Owners, Tops), while words for submissives are not capitalized (bottoms, boys, owned, slaves, subs). I actually prefer that, but on my editor's advice I settled for the more conventional approach.

generally the individual who gives the blow job to (fellates) the top or is the receiver in anal intercourse (gets fucked). Some men regard themselves as exclusively tops or bottoms and cannot or will not take on the other role. Most tops and bottoms will, however, under the right circumstances, go the other way. For example, two horny tops may compete (playfully fight) with each other to determine who is going to do what to whom, and with two horny bottoms whichever one can switch the easiest will be the top.

That the designation of top is not too rigid is further shown by the top who will bottom for a specific activity, such as getting flogged by his bottom, unless he prefers to use another top. This lack of rigidity is likewise found in the bottom who, although more rare, will only top in a specific activity, such as pissing on another bottom or even more rarely, on a top.

Something that must be made immediately clear is that the term *bottom* should not be equated with the term *submissive* nor vice versa, any more than a top is automatically a dominant or master. This is because one man topping another man does not automatically mean that the bottom considers the man behind the dick in his mouth or up his asshole to be an authority figure of any kind.

As a top has the complement of a bottom, a daddy has the complement of a boy, but before going further, it needs to be made absolutely clear that this second complementary pair (D-B) may have nothing to do with the age of either of the individuals. While in the majority of cases a daddy is older than his boy, in a minority of cases the younger male (or female)[3] takes on the more parental role. Even less so does the age issue usually enter into the dom-sub (D-S) or master-slave (M-S) pairing. It is true that a minority of masters feel comfortable only with slaves younger than themselves; however, since slaves are difficult to come by, most masters will gladly take on

---

3 There are women in the kink community who assume daddy-boy (typically spelled boi in this context) relationships.

slaves older than themselves. In fact, as a teenager, and well before becoming a slave, I was a dominant to a much-older submissive.

Of all the above pairings the daddy-boy seems to be the most common. There are several main reasons for this: (a) a D-B concept is a more familiar one for most people, (b) it requires far less extreme (radical) psychological adjustment than an M-S one, (c) it is more socially acceptable to both the general gay and straight communities, (d) it is easily open to the love and romance that most people are looking for, and (e) it does not imply any S-M in the relationship. Even if D-B spanking scenes might be part of the relationship, that scene is so widespread in the nonkinky community to hardly qualify as S-M.

Another clarification that needs to be made is that the terms *submissive* and *slave* in their respective D-S and M-S pairings are not identical. While all slaves are automatically submissives, all submissives are not automatically slaves. In fact, most submissives are not slaves and never will be. Slaves are actually a rather tiny minority of submissives. The slave submissive is sometimes called a natural submissive who, unlike the psychological submissive or sexual submissive, craves the submissive role even outside of any scene-specific event.

Also, one should understand that the term *submissive* is not to be equated with passive. Few doms want subs who offer little or no response to the dom's sense of being in charge. Such passives are sometimes called do-me queens and are far more interested in what their doms can do to and for them than in what they can do for their doms. This is not to be confused with force-me queens, who are subs and slaves who try to force their doms or masters to do something to them.

The opposite of a passive sub is an active one, a sub who will actively do things to and for the dom, such as performing really good oral sex on him, rimming him, licking his boots, massaging his back and feet, or trying to satisfy any masochistic needs the dom may have.

We now need to return to the title of boy. While the title boy is always the complement to the title daddy, it is also used as a general synonym for any male (and sometimes female) sub or slave. However, in a true daddy-boy relationship, *boy* has no necessary submissive connotation; in fact, there are even daddy-boy relationships in which the boy is the more dominant of the two. In other words, in a daddy-boy relationship *boy* is a term of endearment. Calling a sub or slave a boy, on the other hand, does imply a full submissive or subordinate status or role with no necessary endearment involved.

Caution: The use of the term boy as a reference to a submissive or slave is to be confined to very specific situations. A man's dom or master may use the term as such, but others should typically not use the term in this way unless the master or the slave himself has either directly or indirectly given permission. A master other than the boy's own may use it in front of the boy's own master in such utterances as "And this must be your boy" but not otherwise without the boy's master's permission.

For example, I attended a master-slave gathering in which I arrived before my master. A master who knew me noticed I was standing alone, and although he was talking to another master I did not know, he signaled me to approach him. I got within arm's length of him and assumed the proper slave stance—that is, standing tall, chin in, feet slightly parted, and both hands behind my back—while waiting to be recognized, since a slave is never supposed to be the first to speak to a superior. The master I knew asked rhetorically, "The boy's master isn't here yet?" He had every right to assume that, since I would not have been standing alone away from my master, and he had the right to refer to me as boy since he was a master known to my master and me.

"Right, sir!" I replied.

He then turned to the master he had been speaking to and said, "This is Master Hal's boy."

The second master acknowledged me by nodding his head and saying, "Boy."

Without having received any permission to respond except minimally for the purpose of politeness, I returned the nod and said, "Sir!"

In this case, everything was properly done. The known master had the right to use *boy* as long as he linked it to my master. The second master had received the right to call me boy from the first master but only on the assumption that he was shortening the phrase "Master Hal's boy."

In situations other than this, the slave may indirectly give his permission for use of *boy* when he wishes to make his sub status clear to a dom/master—for example, "Sir, this boy is pleased to meet you." Also, slaves who know each other, especially if they are friends, can call each other boy. Thus, when a master introduces his slave (boy) to another master's slave, the slaves can acknowledge each other with *boy*. A nonalpha slave, however, does not refer to a training alpha slave as boy but as sir or as alpha (slave), unless the two slaves are on very friendly terms. In all of this, it needs to be emphasized that the use of *boy* in the above allowed-for contexts is regarded by the boy and the dom/master as a direct empowering of the dom/master and an indirect but equal empowering of the boy. Beyond this, the term *boy* will usually be regarded as a put-down, and the person inappropriately using it might find a boy's fist in his face.

To summarize the differences between a daddy-boy and a master-slave boy, a daddy's boy and any other nonslave boy does not follow the rigid slave protocol found here. For example, a nonslave boy does not follow the very specific standing-and-greeting protocol of slaves, is not required to kneel at his dom's feet, and is more or less free to speak and dress as he likes. Also, negotiated compromises are much easier in a nonslave-master relationship. For example, in my one attempt at being a boy to a daddy, the latter wanted me to shave off my beard. When I told him I was too attached to it to lose it, we found a compromise. He shaved off all my pubic hair, making me look absolutely prepubescent down there. Rarely would such a compromise be found in a master-slave relationship. Since I much prefer the master type over the daddy type, it was only a one-time shave.

A daddy is delicious
But not my standard fare.
A master with whip and chain
Is more like my chow mein.

What has been said above should not be taken to imply that a master and a daddy are totally separate categories. There are relationships in which a dom will be the master to a slave and a daddy to a boy. In these relationships the slave will usually not have any real need for a romantic relationship with the master, and if the master wants that without giving up his slave, he may also have a boy toy who will offer him that romantic element. This triple relationship (master/daddy, master's slave, and daddy's boy) works well if all involved respect each other's role and jealousy can be kept to a minimum.

My personal experience in such a triple relationship was that with Master Peter as mentioned in *Tuesday beyond Lust*, and the relationship was not positive, because the boy toy and I could not accept each other as equals. This was largely based on the fact that a slave's role implies punishment while a boy toy's role does not.

This leads into the issue of slavery and punishment, but first, it needs to be made clear that a dom and a sub that are into S-M are not necessarily into any kind of master-slave scene that involves what one would think of as punishment. Some individuals get off on receiving pain (masochists) and some on giving pain (sadist), but there is no real master-slave authority role here, and the administering of pain may have no disciplinary, punishment, or humiliation connotation. The dom and sub are into scene-specific role play. Once the pain-pleasure S-M scene is over, both players regard each other as equals in all ways. The fact is that most sadist doms have no interest in taking on any authoritarian role and the responsibilities that role entails. Likewise, most slaves are not simple masochists, because the role of a slave involves far more than most pure masochists are interested in assuming. In other words, in a strictly dom-sub S-M relationship, like that of the daddy-boy relationship, there is none of the elaborate slave discipline found in the more complex master-slave relationship. For example, a nonslave sub may not wear a collar or may do so only during play at home. But a slave wears a collar as much as is practically possible to signify he is owned. If possible, he will even wear it hidden under his regular clothes. Also, the light to heavy S-M component in most master-slave relationships is not independent of but completely bound up in the authority role that is at the core of that relationship. In other words, the strictly masochistic individual need not be a submissive. He seeks pain to please himself, not to be dominated. On the other hand, for a masochistic submissive, pain becomes more complex, but he still is not automatically a slave. It is only when you add obedience that such a person, whether masochistic or not masochistic, becomes a slave.

As far as I'm concerned, every genuine master-slave relationship has a punishment element, although this need not automatically involve pain (S-M), especially since there are an infinite number of painless punishments that a creative master should be able to come up with. This actually means that there does not need to be any significant sadomasochistic punishment element in a master-slave relationship. But while I will acknowledge that the punishment doesn't need to be pain oriented, I challenge those few individuals who say that there doesn't need to be any punishment element in a master-slave relationship.

A slave can perform any of four actions: (1) He can do what he wants to do that the master does not care about one way or another. (2) He can do what he wants to do that the master also wants him to do. (3) He can do what neither he nor the master wants to be done but nonetheless must be done. (4) He can do what the master wants him to do that he does not want to do. The one thing the slave cannot do is what he wants to do but that the master does not want him to do. This last action is at the heart of the M-S relationship in that to not obey the master's wishes will result in punishment. Numbers 1, 2, and 3 are neutral as far as an M-S relationship is concerned.

Furthermore, unlike in a non-M-S situation the submitter (slave) has agreed inwardly (within himself) and outwardly (with his master) that he will hold no resentment to doing what the master wants and not what he wants. Thus, in theory, a slave may never need any kind of punishment, but submission is rarely so ideal. This so-called always-compliant slave is the type most likely to be taken for granted, and no slave will tolerate this for long. This means that he will at some point make his displeasure known, which will be a challenge to the master's authority, and even though the master may acknowledge that the rebellion was justified, he will have to discipline the slave or leave his authority open to question.

Most masters, however, will probably not start out with such an ideally compliant slave but one with more self-assertion. In these situations the master will have to start out with the clear statement "You [the slave] will do as I [the master] want, not as you want, and if you do not do what I want, I will discipline you."

I have known of only one M-S relationship, if it can be called that, in which there was theoretically no punishment involved. One of the men was in his early twenties and the other in his late twenties. The younger had the label of slave and the older the label of master. The slave was always naked at home and never sat on the furniture (two common, but not universal, slave traditions).

I asked the master, "Do you ever have your slave do what he doesn't want to do?"

"I love my slave," he replied. "Why would I want to make him do something he doesn't want to do?"

"Never?" I asked.

"Well, sometimes, but we work it out."

"How?"

"We usually compromise."

"Does your slave ever want to do something you don't want to do?"

"Sometimes."

"What do you then?"

"The same. We compromise."

"Do you ever discipline your slave?"

"Of course. He likes to get spanked, and I like doing it."

"Is one of you more on top than the other?"

"He likes to bottom, so I always top. I'm the master."

I won't go on with this dialogue, because I think this short excerpt already makes several points. (1) *Compromise* is not a word one expects to hear from a master, because compromise is not submission to a master's will. (2) Discipline is not kinky sex that a slave likes. (3) Being on top because the slave prefers the bottom does not determine a master; giving the order as to who is on top or bottom does. (4) Also, someone wanting to be nude and not sit on furniture, simply because they have heard that this is how slaves are supposed to be, does not automatically make him a slave.

In my experience, the slave in these punishment-free relationships is mainly someone who does all the housework, and what sex may be involved may or may not be particularly kinky. I consider such relationships as more master-servant than master-slave in nature.

> A slave, a slave, what is a slave?
> Someone to serve the master's will.
> A slave must always keep in mind
> That discipline is due his kind.

It is true that what one person calls a servant or sub another may call a slave; however, in the dictionary sense a slave implies a person who is owned by and labors for another person (the master) under the threat of punishment. A servant, on the other hand, may, at worst, be verbally chastised for poor performance, and generally, the only real punishment would be a loss of pay or being fired. A master-slave relationship is one of power exchange while that of a master-servant is far less so, if at all.

Let me make this still clearer. In the power-exchange subculture, some slaves do not labor for their owners as domestic help but are slaves only in a sexually submissive way while sharing all domestic activities with the master.[4] In other cases, it is common practice to make the (voluntary) slave responsible for the maintenance of the master's erotic wear, especially his boots, and for any power-exchange toys or dungeon space. If the slave lives with the master, this responsibility could even be extended to making and unmaking the master-slave bed as an extended play space.[5] The slave may take care of the master's laundry, cook for and serve the master his meals, and keep his (erotic/play) social calendar. In other cases, a true household slave does far more. But whether the servant responsibilities are minimal or maximal, if they are not done properly, the slave will receive punishment.

When it comes to the issue of slave discipline and punishment, most people are likely to think of such punishment as abuse, but in the context of master-slave role play there should be no place for abuse. The reason for this should be obvious. Unlike in true slavery, where the slave has no rights, the voluntary slave allows himself to be disciplined or even punished mainly because it enhances the scene or the relationship between the master and slave.

Another reason punishment need not equal abuse is that punishment does not necessarily involve pain. In fact, if the slave is a true masochist, painful punishment is a contradiction, and real punishment would consist of depriving him of pain. The fact is that most of the discipline a slave will receive will consist of little more than requiring him to get down on his knees before his master, acknowledge his offense, beg for his master's understanding, beg to be pardoned,[6] and promise to be a better slave in the future. At the

---

4 In my present relationship both master (owner) and slave (owned) wash the kitchen floor, etc.

5 Unless the slave is not allowed to sleep in the bed but must sleep on the floor.

6 *Pardon* is a better word than *forgive* for a slave to use, as it has more of a dominance quality to it. Also, if at no other time, when asking for the mercy of the master, the slave should drop using the first-person pronoun ("*I* am sorry") and instead use the third person ("*This slave* is sorry") to show absolute deference to the master.

other end of the punishment spectrum, some version of temporary exile may be the deepest pain. The bottom line is the good master never uses punishment simply to inflict pain.

A further insurance against abuse in a healthy master-slave relationship can be achieved by the master asking the slave what he (the slave) feels would be the appropriate punishment. The true slave will never try to take advantage of this by choosing too little punishment but will always choose what he knows he deserves.

While in theory the master has the right to punish the slave at will—that is, even if the slave has done no wrong—if overdone, this would keep the slave in such a constant state of anxiety that he either would become too neurotic to be an efficient slave or would bolt the relationship. In most master-slave relationships there is a well-established middle way. Even a master with a perfect slave (a myth) who never does anything wrong nonetheless may once in a while feel the need to remind the slave of his (the master's) authority by a mild otherwise-undeserved punishment. The limits of such punishment should be specified in the M-S contract.

This undeserved punishment will rarely cause the sincere slave of a skillful master to bolt, especially when the slave knows that his skillful master will soon find some way to reward him for accepting this technically unfair punishment. The master who does not periodically reward his slave for acts of exceptional submissiveness will soon find himself without a slave. Again this is the opposite of abuse, as it clearly shows that the master respects the slave for his loyalty. A master who does not respect his slave's right to proper treatment is a master who will lose both the respect and loyalty of his slave and end up with a bad reputation in the M-S community.

When the issue of abuse within an M-S relationship does arise, there is an automatic tendency to focus almost exclusively on the master as the abuser, but the fact is that a slave, under the right circumstances, can become abusive of his master. This usually happens when the master has made a poor choice in the type of slave he has adopted, and by the time he admits that to himself, it may be more difficult to unadopt (dump) the slave than may be commonly thought.

Naturally, any association of an M-S relationship with the issue of abuse is reinforced by the close association of slavery and sadomasochism (S-M), so it is important to examine this association. But before that we need to take a step back, because the exact nature of S-M has not been made fully clear as yet.

Just because two or more people play with belts and paddles, whips and canes, and so on, does not always make them S-Mers in their own minds. Some of these players simply consider themselves as being into rough play, nothing more, and do not appreciate being included in the S-M label. So what is an S-Mer? The easy answer is someone into rough play who wants to call himself or herself an S-Mer. For me, however, I think it requires more than that. An S-Mer is one who, as a bottom or top, experiences a heightened sense of self-worth (power transfer) after a really fulfilling scene in which both parties experience a power exchange. This sense of power may continue on for hours or even days until a new scene is needed. Naturally, this positive definition of an S-Mer would exclude those who suffer afterward the *rebound syndrome*—a sense of remorse, fear, guilt, and self-loathing that some experience after really kinky sex.

To return to the issue of S-M and slavery, when it comes to the slave who is accepting of pain, there is generally (a) the one who is a true masochist and gets primary or direct pleasure from the pain inflicted upon him by the master, and (b) the slave who is not necessarily a true masochist but gets secondary or indirect pleasure out of knowing that his master (a true sadist) is being pleased. In other words, the slave's pleasure comes from his total submission to and obedience to his master, so the master's pleasure is the slave's pleasure. There is also (c) the slave who gets both primary and secondary pleasure out of any pain inflicted on him. It might be thought that what all three slave types have in common is their submissiveness, but that is only a superficial commonality.

The deeper commonality is that just as they must satisfy (pleasure) their masters, their masters must satisfy (pleasure) them and that in receiving satisfaction there is power.

As noted earlier, in none of the above slave types is the sadomasochist (power-exchange) element sufficient to make someone a slave. The slave-making element is the authority element. Whereas a simple power-exchange element is in force during a play scene between any dom and sub, it is not in force when the sub is functioning independently of the dom. In other words, that element of dominance does not cross over into the outside world. The authority element, on the other hand, is in force with or without the master being present, meaning it does cross over into the outside world. How far or how much it crosses over should always be clearly stated in the master-slave contract. The importance of this crossover must not be underestimated, because for the person for whom being a slave is not a part-time game but an authentic lifestyle, every reminder that he is a slave brings a sense of fulfillment and happiness.

That the authority element rather than any S-M or discipline/punishment element is what differentiates an M-S from a non-M-S relationship can be seen from the fact that slavery requires behavioral and communicative abilities that can only be described as a ritual art form, which is described here as slave protocol. In particular, the slave must be constantly aware of the need for differential speech and speechlessness; what he can and cannot wear; how he undresses or is undressed; how he stands, sits, and walks; with whom and how he can have physical contact; how he may have to relate to family members, non-M-S friends, and even his coworkers and boss; how he handles his finances; how he uses the restroom at home and outside; and how he otherwise behaves in private and public.

In other words, the slave role involves the slave altering his behavior to satisfy another person (his master) to a degree not found in a non-M-S relationship. This is because the master and slave roles make for a true authority as well as power-exchange relationship not normally associated with a simple top-bottom, daddy-boy, dom-sub, or S-M relationship. Also, there is generally no need for a formal master-slave contract in a non-master-slave relationship.

There is one more pair of terms that might be added to those that have so far been mentioned, namely the owner and the owned. Some in the master-slave community believe that an owner and owned can be distinguished from a master and slave in that whereas a master and slave have a contract by which they both must function, an owner and owned have no such contract but in all other ways have an M-S relationship. This lack of a contract technically gives an owner far more authority (power) over the owned than a master has over a slave. While this does not automatically mean an owner-owned relationship is going to be more open to abuse than an M-S relationship, the very fact that a master has signed a contract with a slave implies that the master recognizes certain limitations on his authority. The owner offers the owned no such limitations.

Contract-oriented slavery is also called conditional slavery, which says a slave is such only under the conditions of the contract. This would mean that slavery without a contract is unconditional. The master (owner) has unconditional authority over the slave (the owned). For me, a master is synonymous with an owner and a slave with an owned, so I would recommend that any M-S relationship without a contract find a different designation. From now on any mention of an M-S relationship implies one with a contract.

As I understand it, the primary argument for not having a contract is that the document has no legality and so is meaningless. I disagree. Yes, it has no legality; however, it is not meaningless. To the contrary, a contract serves four very important functions. First, it encourages the master and slave to communicate to each other exactly what they expect and do not expect out of the relationship. Second, the contract is a record of what those expectations are and are not. Masters and slaves may forget some specifics of what was originally negotiated, and the contract is there to remind them. Without this reminder, it seems that an owner or an owned can easily misremember, especially as the weeks and months go by. Third, the contract makes it very clear to both signers that their relationship is not that of a daddy and boy, a simple dom and sub, or a scene-specific role play (S-M); instead they are signing on for something of far greater commitment and intensity. The fourth reason for some of us is actually the most important one. No matter how many doms or masters I had unofficially submitted to, it was not until I actually lived as a slave under a contract that I could be certain that my sense of being a slave was more than something superficial that I could easily take hold of and let go of. In other words, being under a contract made me for the first time realize that my being a slave did not depend on whether or not I had a master; I simply was a slave.[7]

Regardless of the exact meaning of *owner* and *owned* above, the owned is synonymous with property, and if the term *slave* is a controversial one to the general public, referring to another human being as property is even more so. However, the reality of the human species is that we are very territorial, and property is a part of who we are. This is proven by the fact that in an M-S relationship of any duration the slave will come to think of his master as being as much his property as he is his master's property, and the master who fails to understand this is naive. I have found that the most intense bond between a master and slave develops when the master realizes and accepts mutual ownership.

A major misunderstanding about slaves is that they are trying to become nonpersons, and while that may be true for a tiny minority, the majority of slaves are trying to become even-fuller persons than they feel they are as nonslaves. This is actually the complement to the majority of masters who feel that they are completed only by having a slave. This mind-set makes slaves very valuable pieces of property, which is why very few masters are into any kind of abuse of their slaves.

---

7 Please also note that I do not recognize the concept of a slave for a one-night stand or a weekend affair unless there is such an absurdity as a one-night-stand or weekend contract. In something that short, the slave enters into a simple dom-sub get-together.

Of course, the problem with all the aforementioned terms is that they are not absolute. For example, there is the alpha dilemma where someone who takes the authoritarian role (i.e., top, dominant, master—the alpha) may like to get fucked or even flogged by his bottom, sub, or slave.[8] In fact, I had one master for a short while who, after flogging or otherwise disciplining me, would feign being very tired and, without any words, would lie down on the bed on his belly and pretend to be half-asleep. At that point, I was allowed (expected) to fuck him. The absolute rule here was that neither of us spoke during or afterward about it. It was understood by both of us that it never happened. Another dominant (not master) I played with a lot enjoyed getting fucked, but to make sure it was understood that he was always in control, he would either (a) have me on my back, hands restrained to the sides of the bed, while he sat on my dick doing all the necessary work or (b) put me in handcuffs while he lay on his belly and made me do all the work. In other words, a bottom can be a dominant. This is referred to as a case of the top ordering from the bottom. Finally, there are the cases when two tops find each other so hot that, after fighting or not fighting for dominance, one buck will ride the other.

> He and his mate first may fellate
> Until their pricks start to pulsate.
> When this is done, they fight to fuck
> Until one of them is the buck.
> Thus they fulfill their gay mandate.

Even if the most uncommon relationship is where the master bottoms and the slave tops, all that really matters is that both parties find their satisfaction in whatever arrangements they make. Sexual roles that are fluid are usually the most satisfying. Naturally, all this is a very touchy issue in the dom-sub and master-slave community

---

8 This is not to be confused with the alpha-slave issue in which a fully trained slave is assigned by his master to train new slaves (gammas).

and is never much publicized or admitted to. The alpha dom/master wishing to sometimes bottom must find the right sub or slave who is not only willing and able to act as the once-in-a-while top but who can also be trusted enough to keep the matter private.

To reiterate, no commanding or obeying may necessarily be involved in either the simple top-bottom or daddy-boy roles. One person may simply like to fuck more than get fucked and vice versa. Here there is no power exchange or authority element. Moreover, even in the simple S-M power exchange, there is no necessary authority or punishment element.

To even more blur the lines of all these roles is the situation of a dominant masochist (D-M) and a submissive sadist (S-S). In this seemingly contradictory case, while it is the sub who is the pain giver (sadist) and the dominant who is the pain receiver (masochist), the sub only gives the kind and degree of pain demanded by the dominant, which eliminates any commanding creativity on the part of the sadistic sub. This D-M and S-S situation is not the same thing as what is called *topping from the bottom.*[9] This phrase signifies a bottom, sub, or even slave who, while wanting to still identify with that role, tries to control a scene or even a whole relationship because he has a more dominant personality than the top, dom, or master. In most cases this will become debilitating for the master, and the relationship will not survive.

A milder case of this is that of the pushy slave bottom, which most masters also have problems with. However, there are masters who like pushy bottoms because it gives them more than enough right to periodically discipline such slaves, even though they have done nothing more than be pushy.[10]

---

9 The first retains the respect of the kinky community, while the second does not.

10 A pushy bottom should not be confused with a *brat*, or a submissive who likes to rebel in a childlike way to get the dom's attention. Brats are common among the subs in spanking scenes.

I am a bossy bottom
Who tries a wicked work
To control from underneath,
My master to enslave.
This is such a heinous wrong
That punishment is due.
Flogged until my sin expunged
And I to boss no more
Or until no longer sore.

Serious problems can arise if the pushy bottom is also a resister (fighting) bottom—one who gets his pleasure by fighting the attempts of the master to control him in sex scenes. If their game is carried too far, one or both players can easily get hurt, and unfortunately, one or more bad experiences with such a power-hungry bottom can end with a master brutalizing the slave and ruining himself as a master. Each player needs to know the safe and sane limits. This is what keeps the master-slave relationship loving and not pathological.

While bossiness or pushiness may not be in most tops', doms', or masters' list of requirements, there is one case where such bossiness or pushiness is at the very top of the list, namely when dealing with a shy master.

It may seem a contradiction that a top, dom, or master would be shy, but it is far more common than is thought. Once the top and bottom are together in privacy, the top's shyness usually disappears, but that is not of much use for initiating the processes, which is where a bossy bottom is useful. Of course, the Internet has made such encounters much easier for the top, as initial anonymity helps protect from possible rejection. Still, many shy tops prefer the old-fashioned bar scene over technology.

The reality is that everyone has to start somewhere, and unless a top, dom, or master has come up through the ranks (started out as a bottom, sub, or slave), he will probably be clueless on a lot of topping things and may need an experienced bottom, sub, or slave to guide him through scenes until he gains the confidence and knows how to be a true top, dom, or master. This is *guiding from the bottom*, and no honest bottom wants to do this on a regular basis; however, even after this guidance stage is finished, the active slave recognizes that there are always things a slave can teach his master, as there are always things that a master can teach his slave. This is called mutual growth. Naturally, such growth has its risks in that instead of the master and slave growing toward each other, they can grow away from each other.

The opposite of the active slave is the passive slave, who is not into teaching the master anything and just expects the master to know everything, which leads to no growth in the relationship. Unfortunately, some novice tops, rather than learning from experienced bottoms, allow their insecurities to lead them to abuse their bottoms, and if this becomes a set pattern, the tops will never learn how to be confident tops.

Of course, the growth one experiences as a top or bottom can actually lead to a reversal of roles in or outside of a relationship. The easiest of these reversals seems to be a bottom or sub becoming a top or dom or even a slave becoming a master. Going the other way seems harder for individuals because of a seeming loss of rank versus a gain of it. Nonetheless,

Beautiful it is
To watch the transformation
From a man who fears to kneel
To the one who will lick boots.
Beautiful it is
To watch a once top realize
Pride can be to surrender
To the will of another.
Beautiful it is
To watch how in the dungeon

> He who was a torturer
> Become one of the tortured.
> Where once he heard others yell
> For the pleasure found in pain,
> He is now one who will scream
> And in this will find his dream.

A further sign of the nonabsoluteness or relativity of all the aforementioned role terms is the fact that, while not too common, a slave can be the master to another slave or, even rarer, a master may have his own master.

Before leaving the subject of what makes a master and what makes a slave, I will say that it has been my experience that within every master, no matter how well hidden, there is a self-indulgent child that wants his desires satisfied at a moment's notice. If the master's desires are not satisfied or are frustrated for too long, the master will have an adult or not-so-adult temper tantrum. Therefore, it is the responsibility of the skilled slave to subtly act parent-like in dealing with this child element. The slave who cannot manage this will find himself in a less-than-satisfying relationship.

> It is not the way for he who fears
> To venture into the strange;
> It is not for he who just likes pain
> Or just wants some kinky sex.
> It is not for he who seeks escape
> From responsibilities.
> It is not for he who cannot kneel
> Before an authority.
> It takes an uncommon bravery
> To love life in slavery.

Lightning Source UK Ltd.
Milton Keynes UK
UKOW01f1425171017
311149UK00001B/21/P

9 781532 020407